I0548987

Cruel...and Unusual

By

D Michelle Gent

GINGERNUT BOOKS Ltd
www.gingernutbooks.co.uk

Copyright © 2010 D Michelle Gent

The right of D Michelle Gent to be identified as the Author of the Work has been asserted by her in accordance with the Copyright, Designs and Patents Act 1988.

First Published in 2011
By GINGERNUT BOOKS LTD

Cataloguing in Publication Data is available from the British Library

ISBN 978-1-907939-09-9

Back cover design © Paul Mudie
Front cover © Gingernut Books Ltd

Printed and bound in Great Britain

GINGERNUT BOOKS LTD
Head Office
27 Sotheby Ave
Sutton-in-Ashfield NG17 5JU

www.gingernutbooks.co.uk

Cruel...and Unusual is the second novel in Michelle's highly acclaimed Werewolf series.

Following...

'DEADLIER... than the male'

Which is set in and around Mansfield, in the heart of Sherwood Forest, England and takes the reader into a dark and dangerous world where Werewolves not only exist, but exist alongside humans – undetectable until just before the human becomes the victim.

Werewolves do exist and they exist alongside our society, they have their own rules and hierarchy, they hide in plain sight and have done for millennia.

Sometimes, the female of the species is
Deadlier... than the male.

What people say about Deadlier:

"Forget Twilight, Michelle has written a book that is not only incredibly well researched, but also highly entertaining - the next blockbuster in the making." ***Philip Gardiner, author and filmmaker.***

"Very well done. Lots of action and if the reader believes in werewolves, it is very scary indeed." ***Bill Newton Dunn MEP author.***

"One of the best reads I've had in a long time, each page left me waiting in anticipation for the next, didn't want to put it down until I'd savoured every word!" ***Donna Sanders***

"An adult book that leaves the reader anxious to keep turning the pages... holding the reader riveted, and not wanting to put it down!" ***Roma Walsh***

Available from all good bookshops
Hardback 978-1-907939-00-6
Paperback 978-1-907939-01-3
ebook 978-1-907939-04-4

Once again, thanks have to go to my supportive family.

Thanks to my parents-in-law for encouragement and help for every step of this long and winding road.

To my long-suffering husband Trev – again, where would I be without you?

To my son, Haydn – so photogenic!

To my daughter Danielle who has to share her birthday with Easter sometimes, now you have to share your birthday with a book launch date too!

To Julie for proofreading

To every single person that commented on Deadlier... Than The Male – Thank you too! Without the readers of books, where would writers and authors be?

A message from the author.

Whilst this novel is based on a well-known piece of English history, it is still a work of fiction and as such I have taken a few liberties with certain facts and figures.

I do realise that there are many students of the Jack the Ripper cases and I admire them, it is a harrowing subject to immerse oneself in. Having said that, most of those people will realise that some of the story prior to the 'Canonical Five' are documented cases. Some cases are of murder, some of mutilation and I could list them all but I think it would be more interesting if you, dear reader, were to figure out for yourselves which I made up and which I found during my many months of research on the subject of London's most infamous serial murderer.

Follow Michelle at
Blog http://deadlier-than-the-male.blogspot.com
Website www.gingernutbooks.co.uk/authors/dmichellegent
Facebook Michelle Gent
Twitter ShellGent

Also by D Michelle Gent

DEADLIER...THAN THE MALE

DREAM LOVER - A DUSTY THE DEMON SLAYER STORY

Today...

She arrived back at the house, feeling a wave of reminiscence wash over her, almost as though she had been gone only a few weeks rather than the decade that marked her absence. She recalled the last time she had been here, a routine visit which went exactly to plan and resulted in the expected findings.

She locked the car door using the key rather than the keyfob, not by force of habit but for her own comfort. Her hearing was far too sensitive to use the high pitched remote control and so she never used it.

She looked up at the house and saw that her arrival had been watched. She had no need to knock upon the door; it was opened for her before she reached the first step.

"Good evening madam, I assume you have no luggage?"

"Good evening Dixon, that's right, I travelled light again. I'll be staying for the night but I shall be leaving right after breakfast. Will you inform his Lordship please?" She carried her own bag, a small, light briefcase and Dixon did not make any move to take it for her.

Dixon did not need to reply, she saw the nod of acceptance as she crossed the threshold and he closed the door behind her,

1

almost without a sound. Dixon was one of the old fashioned butlers and though she had known him for a long time, longer than any of the other butlers before him, he kept his protocol and not once did he call her by her name, nor would he refer to her as anything other than 'Sentinel Exemplar' when making the announcement of her arrival.

Red was back.

She went up the stairs to the room which was kept just for her use and opened her briefcase. In it was a small case with toiletries and a change of underwear. She would not be changing clothes for her journey back tomorrow but she would dress for dinner. The wardrobe contained an evening dress – a new one. Anton had been shopping again. She smiled as she lifted it from the rail and looked it over. It was a very simple gown, midnight blue silk, with no fancy, frilly bits to detract from the beauty of the cut or the fabric. The matching shoes were in a box on the floor of the wardrobe.

She showered and dressed for dinner and as she expected, Dixon was waiting for her to come down and he opened the doors to the dining room and announced her with the formality deserving of royalty.

Red walked into the dining room and all eyes turned to watch her entrance. She was the last to arrive and she had spoken only to Dixon before now.

The conversation had dropped as Dixon had spoken and started again once he closed the door behind her. Everyone that was there knew her well and her entrance was not dramatic. She crossed the floor to kiss the host on his cheek, placing her hand on his shoulder as she did so. He glanced at her and smiled, but continued his conversation. He placed his hand over hers and squeezed it in greeting. Red smiled and wandered farther into the room to greet the other guests.

The evening, though formal dress, was light and cheerful,

friends that had not seen each other for a long time were greeting each other in fondness. There was no animosity, no ancient grudges or scores to be settled, it was a perfect mix of good friends and acquaintances and the night was set to be perfect.

Then Anton tapped his family ring on the side of his glass. The crystal gave a perfect and clear tone which cut through the conversations and caught everyone's attention.

"I have two more guests to introduce to you this evening. Please be upstanding for your Lycaeon and her Consort, Victoria and Oscar."

Silence reigned as the woman and her partner entered the room by the same doors that Red had used a few minutes earlier.

Red smiled, she had not known Victoria would be here and she was pleased – both in the fact that she had not spoken to Victoria in a few weeks and in the fact that her presence was important to the upcoming event. Something was going to happen – a change from the usual procedure upon these occasions.

They sat down to dinner and Red waited.

After they had eaten and the table had been cleared and moved out of the room, Anton placed himself in the most prominent position in the room. He stood in the large bay of the window, his form was framed by the dark velvet curtains, and his white tuxedo was shown off to perfection.

He lifted his champagne glass and made a toast:

"My Lycaeon, to her best health and prosperity, long may she reign."

Then he began his speech. "You have all been coming here on a regular basis since we were bonded in tragedy. Tonight, as I promised a long time ago, it is to be the end of my experiments. I have exhausted the subject and it has come

3

time to draw a line under the events and move forward. I have discovered everything I can and, as I promised, you shall all be a witness to this."

Anton took a sip from his glass and continued. "I have learned many things over the years and it has now come time to tell everything that I have found – not only scientific fact but confession and revelation. I know why the events happened and I choose to share them with you in the hope that you too shall understand why tonight is to be the ending, the culmination of my work and the final chapter to this sordid story. For the benefit of our Lycaeon and her Consort, I shall tell everything from beginning to end. Bear with me please; it will be a long night so make yourselves comfortable."

Then Anton began his tale.

The Zoo

Little Jack stood in the parlour, his mother fussing over him, wiping one last imaginary mark from his stern little mouth. She looked him over once more, his suit was immaculate, his dark-blonde hair neat and combed, shining and clean. He was a serious looking little boy, but not sulky, and very handsome nonetheless. And although his hair was growing darker year by year, he bore a striking resemblance to her father's side of the family, especially in the shape of his dark brown eyes, the colour of which was her own contribution to his visual heritage.

Just a few years before, they both had the exact same shade of hair - honey-blonde. Combined with the dark eyes, the light hair was striking, and her well-proportioned and petite figure made it no wonder that Amelia had had more than her fair share of would-be suitors.

"Uncle David will be here presently. He is taking you out for the day. You must promise mama that you will be a good little boy, won't you?" She fussed some more as she adjusted his hat.

"I promise, mama. Don't I always behave well for Uncle

David?"

"Yes darling you do, but it cannot hurt to remind you, can it?"

Then they heard the carriage arrive and both went to the door to greet Jack's favourite adult – next to mama of course.

Uncle David was a tall and well built man; he was fashionable and very handsome. As usual, he too was immaculate in his attire, wearing a new suit which was of course the height of fashion in London. He carried a shiny black cane in one hand and his top hat and gloves in the other. He had grey eyes which were sometimes a little scary and seemed to have the same patterns running through as marble does, but Jack was never afraid of him.

"Now Jack, young man, are you ready for your special birthday treat?"

"But Uncle David, it is not yet my birthday, not until next month, two whole weeks away." The boy, as any other, was counting down to his special day and there seemed to be an age to go.

David laughed at his agony. "I know my boy, but unfortunately, I shall be out of the country on your birthday and so, for this year at least, you shall have two celebrations. How splendid is that?"

Uncle David lifted his nephew into the carriage and turned back to the soon-to-be eight year old boy's mother.

"We should be back in time for supper, Amelia. I will stay too if that is convenient?"

"Of course it is convenient, David. I shall look forward to this evening then."

They embraced for a brief moment and then David kissed Amelia on the cheek. Jack watched his mother with fierce intensity and waved as they began to move away. Then she smiled her special smile, the one reserved just for him, and his

6

stern expression melted into a huge grin. "Goodbye mama. I promise to be good!" he called as he waved out of the carriage window. He watched until the blue of her dress was hidden from his view by the hedgerows. He knew that she was standing there watching as the carriage disappeared from her view.

Then Uncle David was talking to him, asking him if he had any idea where they were going to spend the day.

"No sir. Mama would not tell me where you were going to take me, only that you were coming to fetch me and that I must look my very best in a new suit and coat. Where are we going?"

"We are not going very far at all, Jack. We are going into London. We shall have an early lunch at a nice restaurant and then on to the surprise that I have arranged for you."

Jack nodded with solemnity but did not question further as to their destination. He was a patient boy, hardly spoiled at all by his mother. David was pleased that he was growing up so well. He was a handsome little lad, but a loner - not surprising under the circumstances, but David sometimes wished that he was a little more boisterous at times. Still, he was an absolute pleasure to escort out, always polite and well turned out. Indeed a credit to his mother.

It was close to lunch time when they stopped outside a small but fashionable restaurant at the northern end of Regent's Park; David's favourite, he assured Jack.

"I only come here on special occasions, with special people, or when I particularly wish to treat myself."

"It seems to be a fair establishment, uncle," Jack agreed as he copied the older gentleman's manner in eyeing up the frontage.

Both stood in front of the restaurant, hands folded in the small of their backs, for the entire world to see - the man and his miniature mimic. Then they went inside, both removing their headgear as they crossed the threshold. David held the door open and Jack thanked him most politely.

The pair were seated and then served by attentive waiters. Jack also noticed a serving girl dressed in a white starched bonnet and black dress, with a bright white apron over the top, and a plump woman in a light coloured dress and white mob-cap peeping from behind a door, smiling at him as he ate and listened to his uncle.

"Ah bless the little chap," the woman said.

"Yeah, don't he look like a proper little gentleman already?" the girl answered.

Then the head waiter ushered them back inside the kitchen, back to their duties.

Jack had heard the exchange, as had David, but neither mentioned it.

After Jack had finished his pudding - a wonderful concoction of strawberries, meringue and whipped cream, David called for the bill, which he signed. Jack watched carefully; he had never asked, but noticed that Uncle David's last name was not the same as his own. Jack resolved to ask his mother all about that when he returned home.

From the restaurant it was just a short stroll to their destination and the walk would be an excellent way of settling their lunch. The stench from the sewage which permeated the air was not as foul as it could be, for the day was not hot, but it bothered Jack more than a little, for living in the country meant that he was not used to it, and David handed him his scarf with which to mask his nose and try to keep the worst of the stink out.

The companions approached a large building and Uncle David paused in his walk. He turned to Jack and said: "Now then, these are the Zoological Gardens. Do you know of them?"

"Yes uncle. I have been told of them by one of my classmates at school. His family are friends with someone who gives them tickets from time to time; I think he is a kind fellow indeed. It is a wonderful place, filled with wild beasts and birds." The boy looked thoughtful for a moment and his uncle waited. "Are we going to visit too, Uncle David?"

"We are going to visit, yes, and you are correct in what you say; friends are allowed to visit on occasion and if your school pal has told you of the wonders that lie inside, you already know what a lucky young man you are."

"Oh yes sir, I do. Thank you Uncle David!" Jack looked up into his uncle's eyes and caught a smile there. It matched his own because he had not guessed that he would be coming here today and they had the whole of the afternoon in which to explore.

Jack took hold of his uncle's hand and squeezed it in appreciation and smiled again as his uncle squeezed back.

They approached the entrance and the man in the dark brown uniform taking the green tickets from the people looked at David and tipped his hat.

"How do sir, nice to see you back again. And who's this then? I'll bet he's an adventurer come to see we're keeping the lions and tigers nice and fierce for him."

Jack looked on in awe, nodding shyly. David laughed and replied:

"Yes, something along those lines, Stafford. This is my nephew, Jack. Jack, this is the head keeper for the carnivores. You are not usually on gate duty are you, Stafford?"

"I takes a turn on here every once in a while, sir, especially on Sunday lunch time, gives the lads a little break, you know. Oh, that reminds me, if you call at my lodge after five or so this evening, sir, I have something which might be of interest to young Jack here."

"I am sure I will be reminded. Stafford. Thank you." And David led Jack into the birthday adventure.

David and Jack strolled through the gardens and then up onto terraces above the lion's quarters to view the vista.

"We shall go and see as much as we can, Jack, for in a short while it will be feeding time for the lions and I would think that would interest you a great deal, and we shall need to be early to ensure a good vantage point."

They made their way down through the gardens for an hour or so. Jack took a ride upon the elephant's back and looked terrified but delighted at the same time. Uncle David said that he did not care to ride upon its back but walked alongside, watching Jack.

A little while before the scheduled feeding time, David and Jack went back to the lion's cages and chose a good place to watch from, for Uncle David knew the exact place where the lions were fed.

People were already amassing for the forthcoming spectacle, but David and Jack were fortunate enough to get the exact spot that they wanted. Even though this was Sunday and only open to Fellows of the Zoological Society and their guests, there was still a very large crowd. The sign warning to "Beware of Pickpockets" proved how popular the lions feeding time was.

They waited with as much patience as Jack could muster as the crowd swelled, their place at the front of the broad barrier - which separated the visitors from the cages and so prevented the lions being teased - was a sought-after vantage point and the space around them shrank. Jack was being pushed a little too much and so Uncle David pulled him in front of himself so as to protect him from the crush.

As they watched the massive lions pounce upon the raw,

10

bloody carcasses, Jack was half aware that his uncle's hand was no longer resting on his right shoulder, where it had been a reassuring connection to his guardian. He heard his uncle whisper "Keep the line" and felt him tense just a little, but did not wish to miss a second of the spectacle before him.

It was only after the lions had finished devouring the meat or had dragged off their prize, that Jack looked around and up into his protector's face. Uncle David wore a very different expression to any that Jack had ever seen. The boy was well aware that his uncle's eyes were very capable of being scary (but never to him) but now, Jack saw that they could be truly terrifying too. The marbled grey eyes were cold and very fierce, they were narrowed almost to slits and Jack was pleased that they were not directed towards him.

Jack's mouth and eyes opened wide in surprise and he was about to ask what was wrong, but Uncle David, only glancing sideways at Jack for the fleetest instant, put his left index finger to his lips and Jack was silent.

A strange man, dressed in similar fashion to David - although not quite as impeccable - stood next to Uncle David, his face was twisted in pain, but he too was quiet.

Ignoring the man next to him, Uncle David directed a stage whisper to Jack "Here's a lesson, Jack. Watch now." Then his accent changed and his voice became a little louder, and with more of a coarse quality "This 'ere *dinger* an' 'is *Adam* were *all set* an' *anointed* wi' me as a *plant*." Then he took his eyes off Jack's widened stare and snarled at the man next to him "Werncha?"

"I dunno what you mean sir."

"So when I let go of your hand here," he said, dropping back into his usual eloquence whilst lifting the squirming man's hand in an awkward and painful way - if the man's contorted face was anything to go by - "You'll not have been *drawing a*

11

thimble will you? So that won't be my watch in your *mawley*. Having a *nibble* at my expense are you? Well, as you've just heard. I'm no stranger to your *canting*. I tip the nod at more than one *arch rogue*. Now, here's the *grunt*, I'm what's known as a right *Tarter* and you've been *touting* me for the past hour or more, but if you'd rather be at the business end of my *Bilboa* here," he nodded to his cane and allowed the wooden shaft to slip forward and show the sharp steel concealed within. "You'll keep trying to *gammon* me. Otherwise, you'll keep your *flippers* to yourself, because next time you try it with me, if you're lucky, your *better half* will be a *hempen widow*." His voice dropped lower as he said: "If you're not so lucky and catch me when I've got my *monkey up*, I'll hand you to the *resurrection men* - afore you're ready!"

In the face of all the street slang emanating from what he had taken to be a *cove* ripe for the *bilk* and accompanied by the sinister threat, the thief decided to continue playing it calm.

"I must apologise to you and the young gentleman here sir. I'll take your leave and be off if you've a mind to let go me 'and. It wouldn't do for your son to be worried by any violence, would it? I'll be away now, with your kind permission an' I'll make sure 'Adam' knows too, but let go me *fishhooks*, you're breakin' 'em off!"

David let go and the pickpocket dropped the watch back into the pocket he was lifting it from, tipped his hat and walked away at a fast pace, clutching his hand. As he joined up with his accomplice, David could hear their conversation.

"'e was *flashing 'is gab*. I wouldn't 'ave took 'im for a *Spicer* 'imself, but 'e knew we'd been *toutin'* 'im."

"A *Dandy* like that 'ud probably be a *High Toby* not a *Spicer*."

"Whatever 'e is, 'e's broke two of me *fishhooks*, the bastard!"

As Uncle David walked Jack around the gardens, Jack's curiosity overcame his shyness.

12

"Uncle David?" he asked as he looked up at his uncle.

"Yes Jack." David met Jack's eyes and it was a great relief to see they were returned to their normal calm state.

"What did you say to that man? I understood your words and yet I did not. I cannot work out what you said to me or him."

"That was street slang, *flash patter* - criminal language, my boy."

"Can you understand criminals? Who taught you? Do they have a whole different language, such as French?" Jack babbled with excitement.

"It is of no consequence for now, Jack, but I will tell you what I said - as long as you promise not to tell your mother." he winked.

Jack looked stern once more. "I cannot promise that, Uncle David. I do not keep secrets from mama."

David was taken aback at the boy's forthright refusal and so responded in a more responsible manner.

"All right then, I will tell you on condition that you allow me to tell her when we return."

"Yes I can agree to that." Jack said after only short deliberation.

"Good lad." David beamed at the boy. "Well now, I saw the two thieves a while ago. I kept my eye on them and realised that they were behind us when we watched the lions. That is why I pulled you close to me. I did not wish to chance that they were also kidnappers." David saw that he had once again lost Jack with the slang. "Stealers of children," he whispered.

Jack's eyes grew wide once more. "They steal children as well as pocket watches?" he asked in awe.

"Yes lad. I told him to '*keep the line*' which meant for him to behave with decorum, which of course, he did. At the same time, I had hold of his '*mawley*' - his fist, which was in turn,

13

wrapped around my '*thimble*' or watch." For effect, David drew out his watch and dangled it in front of Jack's nose and he wrapped his own fist around it to show him. He put it away again and continued with the lesson. "If you recall, I used the term '*dinger*' which is a pickpocket. An '*adam*' is an accomplice and to be '*all set*' and '*anointed*' means they are ready for a spot of mischief." David paused and made sure that the boy was following and understanding.

"I was their '*plant*' or target for the theft. He had been trying to '*draw a thimble*'. Now, do you remember what a 'thimble' is?

"Yes sir. It is your pocket watch."

"And so '*drawing*' it would be to…"

"He was going to try to steal your pocket watch sir."

"Very good; '*having a nibble*' is another way of saying 'to steal'. Can you understand why they use the different terms, Jack?"

"I think so sir. It is so they may talk freely about crimes even in the company of others."

"That is exactly so, Jack. Well done."

They had arrived at another set of cages. While they had been talking, they had passed the monkey houses, which Jack found uninteresting due to the difficulty in seeing over or around the other boys crowding at the front. And at the hippopotamus enclosure, because the animal was not doing much at all, just bathing with only his nostrils visible, Jack showed almost no interest. Yet at the enclosure at which they had recently arrived, Jack's attention was captured right away. The sleek grey and beige creatures lurking in the shadows perked up their ears and moved forward as Jack and Uncle David approached.

"Do you know what these animals are?"

"They are just like big dogs, sir. Yet they have such wildness about them." Jack looked up at his uncle and their eyes met.

14

Uncle David looked away, back to the caged animals.

"These are wolves. Centuries ago, our country was home to these creatures, but Humes... I mean humans - men - hunted and killed them all."

"But why did they do that, Uncle David?"

"They gave many reasons, Jack, but what those reasons boil down to are greed, fear and superstition. A wolf will kill to eat, but soon man's livestock would become prey to them. After all, if you were hunting in order to live and you had to chase down your prey, would you choose a rabbit - fast and small - or would you choose a sheep or a cow - fat and fenced in?"

"I would choose the fat one which cannot run far of course."

"That is logical and so the farmer would be angry at the loss of a valuable animal. Not for this reason alone were these creatures eradicated, however. As I said, superstition played a great part too. Myths of man-wolves were rife and although a wolf in its natural environment would rather flee from human contact, the stories told to frighten youngsters grew and wolves were feared as supernatural and evil beings." He paused in order to watch for a while.

"Jack, do these creatures seem supernatural or evil to you?"

"No sir, not a bit." Jack studied the animals for a little longer, watching them pace their cave mouth, all the time, watching him - or so it seemed to Jack.

"Please tell me more about wolves, Uncle David."

"All right Jack."

They stayed by the cages of the wolves for longer than they had meant to. Jack missed the last ride on the elephant and they did not see many of the other animals at all. The public were beginning to desert the gardens as the light faded from the day.

"We must be going, Jack. Our carriage will be waiting."

15

"Already?" Jack began, then realised the lateness of the hour. "Oh, I almost forgot. Stafford asked that you should call on him, do we still have time?"

"A few minutes are all we have then, Jack, and we have missed tea by now. I doubt we shall eat until supper at home. Can you wait that long?"

"I think I will be able to manage, Uncle David."

They walked towards the entrance and Stafford's lodge. Jack knocked upon the door and Stafford opened it.

"By gum, lad, you've had a long day of it," he said, opening the door a little wider. "Come in and take a look."

Inside the small room was a wood-burning stove that had just been lit to stave off the evening chill. Beside the stove, in a sturdy wooden box were three small and fluffy grey shapes. Jack gasped in delight as they turned their heads towards him.

"Baby wolves!" the boy exclaimed. Jack's excitement was evident in his voice and his eyes and although he was eager, he stayed at David's side until he was given leave to move.

"They are called cubs, Jack," David said.

Jack nodded that he had understood, and asked to hold one.

"Yes lad, be gentle and watch they don't bite, they have needles for teeth at the moment. They are just getting ready for their supper, would you like to help?"

"Oh I would! May we stay for a little while, Uncle David?"

"We cannot, Jack. I am afraid we will be very late as it is and your mother will be very worried about you. I do not want her to think that I have kidnapped you."

Jack looked puzzled for a second but remembered the criminal slang and with reluctance, agreed with his uncle.

"I am sorry, Mr. Stafford, I cannot stay to help, but I would like to come back sometime, if I may?"

After extracting assurances from both adults that indeed he

16

would be able to return - and soon - they left the Zoological Gardens for the carriage.

David expected Jack to be asleep within minutes, but he was wide awake and eager to learn more about wolves and criminal slang. So David continued.

"Let's see. '*Canting*' is the criminal language I was using. When I told him that I '*tip the nod*' at more than one '*arch rogue*' can you guess what that means?"

"An 'arch' someone is a high-up chap, like an archdeacon in the church. So I would venture that would mean a king of thieves?"

"You are as smart as a whip!" David said, with evident delight. "To '*tip the nod*' or '*tip the wink*' is to be on good terms with someone. And when I said to him '*here's the grunt*' it means a similar phrase to 'a word in your ear'. Do you understand?" David smiled as Jack nodded. "I am known as a right '*Tarter*' in criminal terms because I would make a powerful and very dangerous enemy. My '*Bilboa*' ..." again, David slipped the sheath down his cane a little way to show Jack the glistening steel, "is my sword or other sharp blade. No do not touch it Jack, it is razor sharp." David pulled the swordstick out of reach of the curious fingers.

"So you told him that you would stick him with that?"

"Yes Jack, but please remember this, if you offer a threat to someone, always be prepared to carry it out. Otherwise, don't threaten. Do you understand me?"

"Yes sir."

"Good lad. Now, to '*gammon*' someone is to lie to or deceive them and '*flippers*' - as when I said 'keep your flippers to yourself' - are hands."

"How odd," Jack said. He was leaning against David and slowly passing into slumber land and it was with some relief that David did not have to explain that a '*hempen widow*' was

17

a hanged man's wife, *'monkey up'* would be a violent temper enraged and the *'resurrection men'* he had offered to hand the thief to before he was ready were 'body snatchers' - robbers of freshly dead corpses, the purpose of which was to sell to surgeons for their research.

It was long past dark when the carriage arrived back at Jack's home. His mother was not unduly worried, but Jack did not know this because he was fast asleep. She put him to bed, kissed his forehead and closed the door quietly before returning downstairs to her guest.

"I have sent the carriage into town to await my return. I was being presumptuous this morning when I imagined that I would be welcome to stay this evening, but I cannot help it." David took Amelia in his arms and kissed her with a passion.

She was flushed and panting as they parted but she held herself in restraint. "Of course you may stay the night, David, my darling. But first we must have supper so that I can send the servants to their beds. I cannot afford a scandal amongst them; I need servants to keep this house, for I could not manage it alone."

"I know, but it will be difficult to keep up the pretence throughout supper."

"But as ever, you must – brother," she laughed.

"One day, Amelia, one day soon, we shall be together without fear of scandal."

"I know. Until then, we must snatch our pleasure when we may. God help me if your family ever found me."

At her words, a dark shadow of sorrow passed over his eyes. "God help you, maybe, but there would be no help for poor little Jack."

They ate supper and then made a show of David leaving by the front door, calling goodnight to the cook and Florence, the young maid.

"Will that be all ma'am?" Florence stifled a yawn as Amelia locked the front door.

"Oh yes, Florence, thank you. I am sorry that you have been kept up so late. You be off to bed too, Mrs. Flint."

"That's all right ma'am. It's my half day tomorrow, so I can have a bit of a lie-in at any rate," Florence said.

Amelia nodded and said goodnight to them both.

David was already in her room as she arrived there. She was taken by surprise because she had not heard him.

"It was better that I immediately got back into the house so that Florence and Mrs. Flint did not hear me returning, especially without a very good reason."

"You seem to have a very good reason right here," Amelia said as her hand strayed to David's groin.

As they lay in the afterglow of love making, David beginning to doze, Amelia watched him fall asleep. Then she blew out the candle and went off to sleep herself, knowing he would be gone before she woke in the morning.

Though she awoke early, David was gone. She washed and dressed, then went to wake Jack. She was not surprised when he was not in his room and was less surprised to find him in the kitchen scullery, half way through his breakfast.

"Good morning Jack," she said, kissing the top of his blonde head. "Good morning Mrs. Flint, thank you for making his breakfast."

"Good morning mama," Jack said past his food. His cheeks bulged with bacon and sausage, a little dribble of egg yolk running down his chin.

Amelia was shocked at his lack of manners.

"Jack, put down your cutlery. Finish the food you have in your mouth," she said and waited while he did just that. "What is the meaning of these atrocious manners? This is not like you."

19

"I am a wolf, mama. We eat our food as quickly as we can, for we have to be on the move, ready to go at a moment's notice." He was eager in his explanation.

Amelia's face blanched as he made his statement. "You are most certainly *not* a wolf, young man!"

Mrs. Flint, watching as she wiped her hands, saw the look of shock pass over Amelia's face and the disappointment which crossed Jack's face a mere moment before annoyance replaced the expression.

"Ma'am, sit down. You look awful. That's the second plateful and the first went down in much the same way. I'm sorry ma'am; I figured he was hungry after missing his supper last night."

"No, it is all right, Mrs. Flint. I suppose I overreacted to his bad table manners."

Jack had resumed eating, but in front of his mother, he decided that he would be a polite little boy once more. He gulped down his tea and said "I have finished my breakfast, mama. Please may I leave the table?"

"Yes Jack, you may. Now go and wash and then get ready for school."

When he had left the room and pounded his way up the stairs, Amelia turned again to Mrs. Flint. "That is not like Jack. Where on earth did he get those manners from?"

"He certainly did not get them from you, or from Mr. David." Mrs. Flint said, "and not from me or Florence neither," she added her defence.

"Of course not from you or Florence, I never would have thought such a thing." Amelia said.

Their conversation stopped as Jack made a terrific noise on his way back down the stairs.

"I am ready mama," he said, interrupting the women.

"You have not had time to get ready! You have not had time

20

to wash and those clothes are the same ones that you had on yesterday, Jack. Whatever has come over you this morning?"

"I like these clothes, mama. They smell of the wolf cubs from yesterday."

"You must put on clean clothes for school Jack. Cleanliness is next to godliness. Now please hurry, you will be late." Amelia got up to go with him.

"I am not going to school, mama. I am practising to be a wolf."

Amelia blanched again, but recovered her composure well enough.

"Jack, darling, you cannot *become* a wolf. You are a little boy and little boys go to school."

"I won't go!" Jack said and he turned and ran to the front door. He was surprised to find it still locked because Florence had not yet unlocked it. Amelia caught up with him at the door and caught hold of his arm. She had to tighten her grip as he struggled. She almost dragged him up the stairs and she had to lock the bathroom door in order to prevent him escaping as she washed his face and hands.

The noise he made as he went up the stairs the first time had awakened Florence, and now she and Mrs. Flint stood at the bottom of the stairs, looking up.

"Ooh he's for it. He shall be late for school and you know how strict they are on punctuality." Florence said, folding her arms across her chest, emulating Mrs. Flint.

"Yes, but they're even more strict on cleanliness, Florence. If he turned up with dirty hands and face, with clothes smelling of wolf, he should be packed off for home with a letter and a flea in his ear."

"Smelling of wolf?" Florence was incredulous.

"So he says. He was petting them at the Zoological Gardens yesterday with Mr. David. Wolves, I ask you."

21

They ceased their commentary as the mistress of the house and her petulant looking son appeared with his face and hands scrubbed and clean clothes on.

"That's better, Master Jack, you're all clean and shiny like a new pin, ready for school," Mrs. Flint said smiling.

"I don't *want* to be like a new pin! I want to be like a *wolf!*" he shouted and both servants blinked their surprise.

"Would you like me to take him to school, ma'am? I'll drop him off on my way over to see my mother if you'd like."

"Oh thank you Florence, but I will take him, although you are welcome to walk along with me if you would like. The company would be nice."

The three of them set out for school, Jack was unwilling - almost to the point of being dragged.

"Jack, this must stop. You are a little boy and this make-believe is all very well but you have to be a little boy at school," then she paused as she thought. "I shall make a bargain with you."

"What bargain?" he asked after a short time.

"If you are a good *boy* at school, then you may be a wild wolf cub after you have done your home lessons. You may even be a little bit of a wolf at dinner time, but not too much, for you made a frightful mess at breakfast. So then, is that a bargain?"

Jack thought for a moment. "May I have raw meat?"

"No dear, you are not a wolf really, so your constitution cannot deal with raw meat, it would make you ill."

"May I make a wolf den in my bedroom and sleep in it?"

"Perhaps you may just for tonight and only if you promise to do well at your studies."

"Yes mama, I promise."

Amelia kissed him and gave him an extra hug as she left him at school that morning.

She walked on into the village with Florence and said goodbye at Florence's mother's door. As an afterthought, Amelia knocked upon the door that Florence had disappeared through. When she opened it, Amelia said "Florence, thank you for staying up late last night and for your help this morning."

"I hardly did anything this morning, ma'am."

"You offered to help and that has taken up time you would have spent with your mother. Take the whole of today off and return to work tomorrow morning if you would like."

"Oh that would be lovely ma'am, thank you so much."

"I shall see you tomorrow then. Goodbye."

"Goodbye ma'am."

Then Amelia walked on into the village to the inn where David stayed when he visited. He rose early as a rule, but with luck, he would still be around.

The inn was bustling with activity. People were hefting boxes and rolling barrels across the yard. Amelia went through the open back door and spoke to the landlord.

David was still in his room and the landlord allowed Amelia up to see him, thinking nothing amiss - they were well known as brother and sister.

Amelia sat in the large chair by the window as David lounged in his bed. He listened while she told him about the morning's events. David was not concerned.

"Perhaps he is just being uncharacteristically naughty for a change," he dismissed Amelia's worries in an offhanded manner.

"Of course he is being uncharacteristically naughty! That is why I am here; it is as though you brought back a different little boy! What happened yesterday?"

David told Amelia everything, including the incident with the pickpocket.

"Then why is he suddenly so obsessed with wolves?" she

asked, bewildered.

"Well there is the obvious reason, darling." He grew his teeth long and sharp and retracted them in the same instant.

"Did you show him that?" Amelia almost shrieked.

David threw back the covers and got off the bed to crouch down beside her, his arms around her shoulders. "Of course not, stop being hysterical. I would not show him, not until he is old enough - just as we agreed. Even then it would only be to reassure him before I made him full Wolf."

"David, you must help me. I am so lonely in the house. I have taken to Florence and Mrs. Flint far more than I should. I am beginning to talk more and more to Mrs. Flint, in an almost mother and daughter way. She is especially supportive."

"Well you must not. It is not safe for you to become friendly with your staff."

"David, can you not help us now, instead of waiting…"

"Amelia darling, we have been over this. I will never make you Wolf." He paused to listen for anyone eavesdropping. "It is not allowed. If I made you Wolf…" he continued almost at a whisper "I would not be allowed to let Jack live. If anyone found out about him now, I would be given the choice of killing him myself or allowing another to kill him."

"Please don't say that! I cannot bear the thought of it. He is my baby!"

"He is my baby too Amelia. Never think that I am not as attached to him as you are. He is my beautiful son. I would kill to protect him, you know that, but there are others who would kill us all for suffering a Throwback to live."

"And yet if you made him full Wolf now, he would be safe."

"I *think* he would be safe. There is an Irish Wolf by the name of Niall who was once Throwback. He was made full Wolf. He is on the council of elders now and it is no secret that he was born Throwback, but he is the only one that I have heard of that has made the transition - successfully."

The ominous warning seemed to have been lost on Amelia, she continued on the same tack.

"Well then, make him a full Wolf now and we can stop living this falsehood - this charade of me being a widow with adequate wealth and security. Do you know how many gentleman callers I have, sending their cards and invitations to my house? I am rapidly running out of excuses not to attend parties and functions. The women are all fancying themselves as matchmakers for their brothers and sons. One woman had the gall to offer her son, brother and widowed father to me, although she was not as indelicate as to offer them all upon the same occasion. I am thoroughly scandalised! I walk through the village in fear of talking to anyone, just in case they have a suitor lined up."

"I cannot possibly make Jack Wolf whilst he is so young. It is not an experience I would wish a child to go through. It is not exactly an experience I relish the thought of you going through, if truth be told. I have seen it happen. It is violent and terrifying, even for Wolves. Hume adults are scared witless when they see it, even if they have been forewarned. You would not be able to bear to watch Jack go through it, even if he were a strong adult. It would kill you to see him go through it as a child and I cannot imagine that you would allow it to happen without your presence.

"One other factor, a rather more deciding factor if I am honest, is that I am not entirely sure that we are allowed to turn children to Wolf. I do not know what would happen to him, for you see, Wolves that are born, never change until puberty and so even if Jack had been born Wolf, he would not be able to change at the full moon for a number of years yet. We must be patient."

"But I want to live with you. We are married. My family

25

know you as my husband. They would know Jack as our son."

David nodded as she spoke, to show that he understood. Then he said: "If we went back to our home town and I introduced you to my family, they would see you as a mere Hume. If they did accept that I wanted you as my wife in every aspect, not just as a pastime or a whim that I would soon become bored with, you would be treated with suspicion and in all probability, until you were turned, with disdain. My family are born Wolf and it was always expected that I would choose a wife from a family of the same stature in our society." He paused and moved her away from him in order to look at Amelia and try to work out if she followed what he was telling her. "You would be given two different choices. You would first be asked if you wished to be made Wolf. I already know your decision there and so the choice would be easy. The second choice would be so much more difficult. You would be asked if you wish Jack's parents to kill him or if you would wish a Sentinel to perform the execution on your behalf. Jack would not be allowed to continue living. There could be no debate, no plea or appeal. He would be put to death, by me or a stranger."

Amelia was crying now and he hugged her close to him once more. "Please stop it."

"No Amelia, you need to know the full extent of this."

"But I know of other Wolves in your family and pack that have married humans. How are they different?"

"It is only under exceptional circumstances that a human woman becomes pregnant by a Wolf. It is even rarer if a Wolf becomes pregnant by a male human. I suspect that it is because few females take human males as their lovers or husbands. But this is why we had to run as soon as I sensed that you were with child. If you had been near any other Wolves, they would have sensed it too and we would have been hunted, tracked,

26

followed until you gave birth - if indeed you had survived till then. By rights, I should have killed him the very day he was born, but I could not. He was so beautiful and I loved him immediately and I saw that you did too. I could not bear to kill him, to destroy our baby. I could not bring that to your door. I could not risk that you would hate me - for you would have."

"Make me Wolf!" Amelia blurted out between her tears.

"No. I cannot."

"Of course you can."

"No, I cannot and there are more than a few reasons." As he said this, he stood and walked away from his human wife and listened at the door. Then he crossed to the window to watch the proceedings in the courtyard.

"David, you are naked, there are people down there that know I have come to visit you. They also think that you are my brother."

"Oh yes, I forgot." He moved away from the window but paced the floor of his room as she continued.

"You have reasons not to make me Wolf now?"

"Yes, first of all, if I were the one to make you Wolf, then we could not have any more children."

"Why couldn't we?"

"Because any more children we had would be Throwback too, but in a different way to Jack. He is a Hume - human - Throwback. These would be Wolf Throwback. Whilst there is a possible remedy for Jack's condition, there would be none for the others."

"Who would know?"

"Ah my darling, we would know. Any Sentinel worth his salt would know and the worst about it is that the child would know. Probably not that he is a Throwback, but that something was different, odd, strange, something that set him apart from everyone else. Eventually he or she would be driven insane

27

and again, you would never forgive me."

"And if we were to have no more children?"

"Even if we could say that we shall never have more children, if any other found out that I had made you, then Jack would be in danger still - for they would assume he was Throwback anyway, and he would be a legal kill." David sat upon his bed and gazed at his wife, trying to make her realise the importance of what he was trying to tell her. "Another reason for not making you Wolf is that you would not be able to take care of Jack for three days in each twenty eight. You would be unable to even see him when the moon is full."

"But he is my son, if nothing else, my instincts..."

"Would count for nothing. Your human instincts for your human child would not even scratch the surface of your Wolf instincts. You would see him as a tiny morsel - a tidbit to whet your appetite. That is why we use such derision when we refer to humans. We call them Hume because they are less than us, not by a mere shade are they - you - weaker, but by a vast abyss."

"So Jack's fate looks grim whichever way we turn? And the only way is to make him Wolf when he is older and to have someone else make me Wolf at around the same time?"

David nodded. "Yes darling. Unfortunately, that is how it shall be. If something were to happen to me, I have left documents with our solicitor - a Hume. He is instructed to contact friends of mine - not family - who would be asked to make you and Jack Wolf - when he is old enough."

"Do not talk that way. Nothing is going to happen to you. But I do wish that we could do this now."

"I know. Hindsight is a wonderful thing. I would have had you made Wolf before we were married if I had even thought that it were possible that we could have a child before you were Wolf."

David drew Amelia to him and kissed her to reassure her. Then his kisses began to take on urgency and his breathing became more ragged as his passion increased.

Amelia pulled away from him.

"David, stop! We are brother and sister here and I will not take the risk of anyone discovering us - neither to discover that we are lovers, nor not siblings. I will not be forced to move home again."

"But Amelia, I want you so much."

"Yes, I know and I want you, but not now and not here. I will not take chances. I like living here. It is so much easier for you; you have no ties, not even to me and Jack."

David appeared wounded at that remark, but said nothing, not wanting to start an argument.

"I have a lot to think about, I must go. I would appreciate your help on the matter of Jack's new found distraction, however. Please give it some thought."

She kissed him fondly and left him to dress.

"I shall see you this evening, sister dear. May I come to dinner?"

"No, this evening is out of the question, *brother* dear," she said, pausing in the doorway. "I am afraid that Florence is at her mother's this evening and I am accepting an invitation to dinner."

Quick as lightning, David was at the door, her wrist gripped in his hand, none too gentle and he snarled a warning.

"Think hard before you play games with my affections, Amelia. Think *very* hard."

Amelia was concerned at his outburst, for she shrank back from his grip as though frightened that he would strike her but she answered him.

"There is nothing untoward in the invitation. In fact, you were also invited, but I had declined on your behalf as you

29

were intending to go back into town. If you would like, I will ask if the invitation stands and I shall tell Mrs. Broughton that you would like to accept.

"Do that," David snapped at her.

"I will let you know of the outcome by messenger later. I shall ask Mrs. Flint to watch Jack for the evening."

Amelia went down the stairs in a less than good mood and remembered the bargain she had made with Jack.

"Oh dash it all!" she exclaimed.

The landlady was passing and was quite shocked to hear Amelia come so close to bad language.

"Is something wrong, Mrs. Denton?"

"Oh no, it's just something I had forgotten, and my brother and I are going to dinner this evening. I apologise for my exclamation."

"Oh never you mind, Mrs. Denton, I've heard worse than that and from women who should know better too."

Mrs. Flint was more than happy to watch Jack for the evening, even when Amelia told her of the bargain. Jack would be a good little boy in exchange for a short time playing wolf and not forgetting his 'den' to be made instead of his bed for one night.

"Never you worry, ma'am, I can manage for one evening, I'm sure. I've had seven of my own, you know. Off you go now, Mr. David is waiting."

The evening was not as lively as David had been expecting. He was bored for the majority of the time. Of course, Amelia was kept from him - being her *brother* and all, he had no need to monopolise her company. The occasion would 'give her a chance to meet some eligible young men'. Eligible they may all have been, but young? For the majority - no, except of course, Mrs. Broughton's brother, Horace.

Still, David was not left out. There were a few single ladies

- chaperoned of course - who were introduced to him. One young girl caught his eye in particular. She was a little too young for consideration and she was too shy to flirt with him, so for decency's sake, he acted the role of a perfect gentleman - all evening.

As they were leaving, David could hear the gossip beginning before they were even out of the house. Most was not unfavourable, however, but the comment from one lady of "They are so close and supportive of each other, he has been watching her like a mother hen all evening," gave him pause for thought; he realised that he must loosen his grip and try to be less obvious in his attentions in future.

Then the familiar voice of Horace, whom David had spoken to a few times over the course of the evening, could be heard by David's acute hearing. "Oh yes, my sister organised this soiree in order that I might meet the delightful Mrs. Denton. I believe she is quite taken with me as I am with her. I don't doubt that she will be amenable to my dear sister's match-making."

His companion, a young man with an unfortunate complexion said "But what of her son? You know she is a widow with a child in tow?"

"Yes, I know, but he is easily got rid of, boarding schools are the best kind of education as we both know. And I am not exactly *inexperienced* myself." Horace bragged with indelicacy, thinking that they could not be overheard. "She obviously has means of support and as soon as she is married, control of that goes immediately to her new husband."

To say that David was in an ill temper as they travelled back to Amelia's house would be a distinct understatement. Amelia on the other hand, was full of gossip and either did not notice his black mood or chose to ignore it.

"Mrs Broughton's eldest daughter took such a shine to

31

you, darling. If she were not so plain, I should probably have been quite jealous. She kept asking questions about you. Her mother was becoming quite distraught at her openness."

David thought to himself that it was Mrs. Broughton's younger daughter that he was keeping his eye on, but said "I only had eyes for you and I think that was noticed. If I am to be the dutiful brother, perhaps I should think more carefully about watching you at all."

"Still, I cannot understand why we have to leave so early, you were enjoying the company, were you not?"

"You could not be further from the truth, Amelia. I was not enjoying the evening. The people were dull, the conversation was dull and the more I saw of the men fawning around you, the angrier I was becoming."

"Yes, I kept my eye on you too; I did not want all those young ladies turning your head after all." she giggled.

"No you did not watch me. You were happy to bask in the attentions of all those would-be paramours that had been lined up for you! If you gave me one glance all evening, it was to see me being introduced to Charlotte, Sarah and Ruth - only one of which was worth a second look, as you well know. And she was too shy to even speak to me."

"Charlotte is barely fifteen. Of course she is shy. I am quite annoyed that you were even considering toying with her affections in such a way, you know you are not available." Amelia became quite petulant.

"As do you, yet you still went there this evening!" David snarled.

"I only went there to keep up the appearance of being widowed and nothing more. If we could be a proper family, then…"

"I thought that you did not want to leave here?" David interrupted.

32

"Of course I do not want to leave."

"We cannot suddenly become a couple as you would like, in that case. It would be frowned upon as incest and quite rightly too." David smiled as another thought crossed his mind. "I think I shall move in with you, as your brother and become the eligible bachelor if you are insistent on being the eligible widow. I think I could quite enliven things around here if I wanted to, playing the scandalous rake and cad. That would soon stop the party invitations I think, although I do not think that Horace could stand that kind of competition."

"Oh, so now we come to the crux of the matter, it is Horace that you are jealous of, but why, darling? He is an arrogant and assuming creature. I know that Hester only invited me in order that I could be charmed by her brother, in the hope of making a match of us. Even if I really were a widow, I should rather stay on my own than marry such a man. He has no regard for me, except for the way I should look upon his arm in public, and he had the effrontery to enquire as to my means of support."

"Yet you were talking with him for the majority of the evening and so he could not have been such bad company." David snapped back.

They finished the journey in a chilly silence and David would have left Amelia to go into the house alone were it not for the fact that the door was flung open by Mrs. Flint as the carriage stopped. She was in an obvious state of distress; Mrs. Flint could not speak until they had taken her inside and settled her in the drawing room with a large brandy.

"Oh ma'am, it has been a terrible evening. I know that you told me that Jack was going to play make-believe this evening, but I could not control him. He became wild and even pretended to bite me. Well, I hope it was pretend."

"Mrs. Flint, are you quite all right? Please do not distress

33

yourself so. I am sure that we can put everything to rights." Amelia patted Mrs. Flint's hand as she spoke; the poor woman's complexion was almost grey.

As if on cue, a cacophony of bumps and howls emanated from above them and all three looked to the ceiling - above them was Jack's room.

"Oh my goodness, there he goes again!" Mrs. Flint wailed.

David flew out of the room with Amelia as close behind as was possible. David had gained the top of the stairs long before she was half way however, and she could only listen to what was happening as she struggled with her long skirts.

"What on earth are you doing, my boy?" Amelia heard David roar. Then there was a shocked silence, for Jack had not expected his Uncle David, but instead poor Mrs. Flint again, or his mother.

"Oh! Uncle David. I was playing make-believe wolf," Jack stammered.

"You were playing up poor Mrs. Flint is more like the truth of it. Look at the destruction here."

Amelia was panicked as Jack began squealing.

"Jack? David. What are you doing to him?"

As Amelia at last got to the room, she stood horror-stricken as she saw the scene of destruction and her secret husband holding his son at arm's length, seemingly about to inflict wilful damage upon his person.

Luckily, Mrs. Flint had not attempted to come to see what further carnage Jack had wrought and was still downstairs, clutching her brandy glass in one hand and her handkerchief to her bosom in the other as the uproar mounted above her.

"Please David! Put him down. Let him alone, you are hurting him, he is crying!"

"No Amelia. He has gone too far. He has been raised in a house full of women, with only a slight and infrequent male

34

influence to guide him."

"And whose fault is that?"

"The fault is mine and I fully accept the responsibility for it, which is why he is going away to school."

"Going away? No, I shall not allow it!"

"Your mollycoddling is to blame as well as my absence, Amelia, and now we must put that to rights."

"You cannot make me go away! You are not my father!" Jack shouted in defiance. "My father will return some day and you shall pay for this! He shall make you regret this! Put me down!"

"Listen to me, my boy…" David said as calm as he could manage.

"No! I am not your boy. You are not even my uncle!"

Amelia and David exchanged shocked glances.

"You do not even have the same name as us! How can you be brother and sister with different names?"

Amelia approached her dangling son and released him from David's grasp. Jack struggled but could not get free of his mother's grip either.

"When I married, my name changed, Jack," she tried to explain, but Jack was blinkered to any persuasion.

"Let me alone! I hate you! I hate you both!"

"Hate or not, Jack, you will clear this room and restore it to order or you shall have no supper. And after that, you will apologise to Mrs. Flint - and I do *not* mean at your earliest convenience, I mean directly you have made this room a little boy's bedroom once more instead of this pigsty."

"I shan't! I shall run away to find my papa and together we shall go to Africa to hunt lions… and wolves!" Jack's little chin was thrust out in absolute insubordination; somehow he knew that the mention of hunting wolves would touch a nerve in his Uncle David, and yet he did not realise to what extent it

35

would enrage him.

David leapt across the room, yanked the boy from his mother's grasp and began to slap his behind. The boy's squeals were renewed with vigour and as Amelia stepped forward to try to stop him, David shrugged her off. She was caught off-balance and stumbled on some of the debris that littered the floor, namely the mattress and bedclothes. She sprawled on the floor on her back and Jack became hysterical. David was sorry at once and set him down once more and he ran to his mother. David went across to her too, but she glared at him, holding Jack tight as he sobbed in her arms.

"Go home, David," Amelia whispered. "Just go home."

That night, Jack slept in his mother's bed. She stayed awake for a long time wondering what the morning would bring.

As Dawn broke, Amelia found that she had managed to get some sleep after all. She had been convinced that she would never be able to.

Jack was not at her side and so she got out of bed, pulled her robe over her nightgown and went down to the kitchen where she assumed Jack would be having breakfast and hopefully apologising to Mrs. Flint.

The kitchen was deserted and the fire had not yet been made. Puzzled, Amelia went back up the stairs to Jack's bedroom. Perhaps he and Mrs. Flint were friends again and restoring the room?

To her surprise, she found David there. He had cleared the bedding from the floor and put the bed to rights. The dressing table was moved back into its usual position from where Jack had managed to shove it and the drawers were replaced in their correct order.

The only thing out of place in the whole room was the large trunk which had always been stored in the built-in wardrobe at the far end of the room. It was now in the middle of the floor, the lid open.

"David? What on earth are you doing? I would have taken care of the mess before Florence arrived."

He stood up and his expression frightened her. "There is no need now. I have done it." His speech was clipped, almost curt. "Jack's behaviour worried me greatly last night. I got carried away and I apologise for that. That is why I returned to clear the room. Unfortunately, Jack is now getting out of hand. You cannot control him. I have made arrangements."

"What kind of arrangements? Where is Jack?"

"I sent Mrs. Flint away. She has been dismissed, but with a full year's pay and she said that she would take the opportunity to go and visit her sister in Devon. Florence has had a similar message, but with three months' pay, for she is young enough to gain other employment. I gave her a glowing reference. Jack is on his way to London. Fortunately he is used to your maiden name and I have enrolled him in one of the better schools. From there, he will go to college and university to learn to be a doctor or surgeon or lawyer. When he is old enough, he will have the chance to choose for himself. Now, you have the choice, would you be Wolf or not Wolf?"

"What are you saying? What do you mean?"

"You know what I am saying to you, Amelia. Do you want to join me as a Wolf now - or never?"

"In that case, if they are the only choices I have, then my answer is never, David."

"Very well, I shall say goodbye then Amelia." David turned to go.

"But what of Jack, am I to never see him again?"

"Do you take me for a monster, Amelia? Of course you shall see him, on every holiday at the end of each term. But he will go back to his schooling. It is I that shall never see him again. I shall never see you again either, my love," and his expression softened, if his voice did not. "You are now the widow that you have been playing for these last eight years. The house is yours. You are free to re-employ Florence, but as I told you, Mrs. Flint left. You shall need to find another cook."

"You have killed Mrs. Flint, haven't you?"

David did not answer his wife, but the wildness about him gave her the answer that he would not speak.

"And how shall I live?"

"Do not worry, *sister* dear. I shall of course, provide you with adequate funds annually. Your son shall never go without. Now, goodbye, and do not try to find me." He turned and picked up the trunk filled with Jack's clothes. "I have only one instruction, Amelia." He paused to look at her. "No word of my true nature shall ever escape your lips. This is not a request." Amelia took the full meaning of his words straight to her breaking heart.

She wanted to stop him from leaving, she had so many questions for him but it was past the time that she could ask him of his family or his heritage – it had got far too late, far too fast.

Amelia sold the house and bought one in London. This served more than one purpose. She was closer to Jack and he could return home on his holidays. The new house was not associated with bad memories for either of them. And now, David did not know where she lived - not that he would have a great deal of difficulty finding her if he wished to, the reassurance was purely psychological, but reassurance for all that.

The Graveside

Jack did well at his studies and worked very hard. As his father had hoped, he elected to become a surgeon. He studied hard to the detriment of any social life and when he qualified, he decided to specialise in gynaecology. Jack became an eminent surgeon, much respected and well sought after for his skills and knowledge. A workaholic almost, he spent his daytime at a more select hospital, counting amongst his patients duchesses, various princesses and countless titled ladies. On a few nights every week and even on weekends, Jack was to be found at the London Hospital and at a few workhouse infirmaries, giving his services for free in exchange for research potential amongst the poorer classes.

Tragically, Amelia became ill and died young and Jack despaired when he discovered that she had died from one of the very diseases that he was studying and trying so hard to discover a cure or at least a treatment for.

Before her death Amelia had become bedridden and Jack took time away from his work and research in order to sit with her as she slipped into delirium through pain and drugs.

It was during this time that Jack brought his work home,

and studied in the cellar, so that he could be home at the times that his mother was awake, without neglecting his research too much.

He took no notice of her ravings as she lay dying, except when she mentioned his father. "Mind your papa, baby Jack. You will grow up big and strong like him, you watch."

Yet Jack had always been led to believe that his father had died before he was even born - in military action in India. So, gently, he wheedled the name from his mother, the name was David.

Little by little, Jack began recalling childhood memories that had long been swamped by school and study - for Jack had been taken under the wing of many an indulgent tutor. Now that he thought with objectivity about it, they had probably been bribed to take an interest in him to encourage study.

One memory that evaded his every effort to recall was his very last evening at the country house that he had spent most of his childhood in.

Until at last, it came, along with the memory of the visit to the Zoological Gardens and the wolves.

He stayed by Amelia's side through her final days. He talked with her and to her. In her more lucid moments, she told him about her family - her mother and father - and it was only by a matter of days that he missed finding them before she died. The joy they shared at the reunion with their grandson was deeply marred by the news of the death of their daughter, lost to them for so many years.

In February 1883, Amelia died. It was a bright and sunny morning, but for Jack, it was dull and grey, he thought that the sun would never shine again on his life.

Jack arranged the funeral, refusing all offers of help from his grandmother. Six jet black horses drew the ornate hearse which bore Jack's beloved mother through the streets.

40

Passersby removed their hats and bowed their heads. People stood on their doorsteps to watch, for this was extravagant even for London.

Victorian ideals governed that a stiff upper lip was 'de rigeur' and Jack, true to his mother and her sense of propriety, had never allowed another single tear to fall since he had finished weeping on the day that she died.

He followed the coffin from the church, borne by hired pall bearers because Jack did not know many people, and none that he would have asked to bear his mother to her final resting place.

Jack's grandmother and grandfather attended and at least tried to give comfort to their returned grandson, but they were strangers, to all intents and purposes.

At the graveside, the ceremony was at an end when Jack saw someone that he recognised. He walked towards the tall, well built young man, debating with himself as he went. *No it could not possibly be him, yet it must be.*

The man had not seemed to notice Jack as he approached in a cautious and tentative manner, hesitating and even halting at times.

Jack drew near to him and noticed the man's shoulders jerk as he asked the back of the man: "Uncle David?"

The man's self-control returned just as he turned and so the loss of composure went unnoticed by Jack.

It was Jack's turn to be shocked as the man he had thought to be his uncle turned to face him. He was far younger than Jack had first thought as he saw him from a distance; this man was younger even than Jack.

He offered his hand to shake Jack's and said: "David was my father; he died a few months ago. You must be my cousin Jack."

"Yes of course. You could not possibly be my uncle; you

can only be twenty five at most. You are obviously younger than I yet you resemble my uncle – as I remember him - so very closely."

"It is often said so," the younger man nodded, a small smile playing at the corners of his mouth. "It causes great confusion at times, when old acquaintances of his appear, especially if they do not know of my father's demise. You gave me quite a turn when you addressed me by my late father's name." He smiled though and with such an ancient wisdom that Jack studied him with suspicion. Of course it was quite reasonable that this was his *cousin* and not his *uncle* but Jack was not entirely convinced. Certain mannerisms reminded Jack too strongly of his uncle. Then there was the fact that Jack himself had personally invited every person at this funeral. How did his *cousin* know Amelia when she had not kept in contact with even her parents?

"I did not realise that my mother had kept in contact with Uncle David or I would have attended his funeral. When was it, at Christmas time?" Jack asked.

The cousin's eyes narrowed at this question but he was courteous in his reply. "No, he died in October; the funeral was in early November. My father and your dear mother did not keep in contact, but whilst putting his affairs in order, I came across Aunt Amelia's name a few times and yours of course and I determined to track you down. Unfortunately, I found her whereabouts too late."

At the sound of her name being mentioned by what looked like his own uncle from years gone by, Jack was startled. He shook it off however and regained his composure. "Indeed, it was a tragedy for both of us, then. As cousins, I am sure that we could have been firm friends."

The man smiled and Jack was struck by how great the resemblance was between his remembered uncle and his newly discovered cousin.

"Will you come for a drink with me, cousin? I am afraid that I cannot offer a proper reception for my mother, for the only ones attending will be her immediate family. I sadly never traced the remains of my father's family for I never knew him. I believe that he died in military action in India."

"Of course I will. It would be a pleasure."

"Oh but I am forgetting," Jack said. "The other members of my mother's family are also your family. My mother and your father were brother and sister. Come, you must meet our grandparents." Jack took hold of his cousin's arm and began to guide him in the direction of the other mourners. "I am certain that they are as unaware of your existence as I was." Jack stopped pulling on David's arm because David had not made a move to go with him.

Jack at last let go of David's arm and instead, looked him straight in the eye as he spoke the thinly veiled accusation: "Come, *cousin*."

David waited a moment, seeming to weigh up Jack and his intentions. "Yes Jack, very clever. You obviously know. I suppose that your mother told you the truth of it. On her deathbed was it?"

Jack just stood facing David, silent as the grave in which he had just watched his mother's coffin being placed his face set as stone, waiting at last, for the truth.

"If you still wish to go for a drink and a proper talk, I can recommend my club; it is but a short hackney cab journey from here," David said.

"I would prefer my club if you wouldn't mind. I think that I would perhaps feel a little more secure there."

David grew angry then, yet his voice was kept under control and he spoke with a calmness that chilled Jack. "I mean you no harm Jack, but indeed if I did intend harm upon your person,

you would not be safe in the middle of Great Scotland Yard."
David's eyes glowed for a second and Jack saw a visage that he
could only hope he had imagined, a face which filled him with
terror for a split second.

"Yes, I believe you."

At the shock apparent on Jack's face, David realised that he
knew nothing of the truth after all, he had been fishing and
had almost reeled him in.

"On second thoughts, Jack, *I* believe that you do not know
the truth after all. Amelia kept her word, she took my - our -
secret to her grave. So on that note, son, I will take your leave.
Do not try to find me. It would prove dangerous for you," he
held up his hand to prevent Jack from voicing the comment
that was on his lips. "That was not a threat. I would not harm
you, but others of my kind would and if you did succeed in
discovering any of us, you would not survive long enough to
make use of the information. I have already told you more
than it is safe for you to know. Goodbye Jack. I loved your
mother, I still do, but this was her choice, goodbye, son."

Before Jack had chance to react, David was gone. He did
not disappear in a cloud of smoke, he moved, but he was so
swift that Jack could not have even told which direction he
had taken.

As the weeks passed, Jack grew angry. He thought back
to the graveside conversation often and wrote down what
he remembered, not only about the conversation, but of the
whole day. His father was David, he knew that already, but on
meeting him, he now knew that his own father was younger in
appearance than he was. He had passed himself off as his own
son with great success.

Going over and over the transcript of the conversation, a
few phrases continued to bother him. "Others of my kind".
Jack shuddered as he recalled the transformation that David's

44

face had performed. Jack did not need his extensive medical training to know that it was purely supernatural and that it was not physically possible for a human to transform in that way. That could only mean that David was not human, yet, Jack countered, he had appeared human. In this case, could it mean that he himself was at least some part of whatever this new species was? David was his father, he had called him 'son' - of course he was partially of the same species.

"This was her choice" was the other phrase that bothered Jack. What exactly did that mean? It was her choice for what, to produce a semi-species? No, he could not imagine his mother experimenting like that. What then? He forced himself to recall his last evening in the old house, before he had been sent away to boarding school. They had argued, his mother and David. He remembered being cradled in his mother's arms and she told David to go home. He did as she said and left, but in the night, he had returned, taken Jack from his mother's bed, wrapped him in a blanket and then he had given him to a man - the carriage driver. Yet there was someone else, another person who had stayed inside the carriage and taken Jack's drowsy form and made him comfortable so that he would go back to sleep. Jack tried hard to remember, but he had been a child and half-asleep.

What choice would she have made? For David to go - that was certain - but never to make contact again? David never had made contact so that question was answered.

Jack sat many a night wondering, pondering the puzzle that he had set himself. He never felt that he had solved the mystery of his mother's choice. He resolved to put away these thoughts and questions that were torturing his mind and distracting him. Jack went back to the hospital and threw himself into his work and studies.

On a routine post-mortem, Jack found the same symptoms

that his mother had suffered. He went through his old notes and other records. Soon Jack was back to his old self, single-minded and relentless, pursuing a cure for the disease that had killed his mother.

His patients in the workhouse hospital enabled him to study live sufferers of the disease, but they came his way too infrequently for his thirst for research potential and so his research progressed slowly. Still he could not find a cause for the disease. He tried to find a common denominator amongst sufferers but it affected rich and poor alike. He even resorted to unscientific reasoning and tried comparing the sufferers' looks but again he was thwarted, ugly and beautiful and all shades between were apt to become victim to this disease.

The only absolute fact was that the disease could only affect women because of the reproductive organs but that was obvious too.

In sheer desperation to find a way out of the stalemate that he found himself locked in, Jack wandered into a bookshop late one afternoon, his mind distracted by the constant puzzle he had set himself.

Perusing old medical books with long-discarded theories was a habit he had picked up whilst at university and he indulged in this practice when he was at an impasse. He happened to pick up a book that did not seem to belong in the medical section. The book was large, heavy and ancient. It was bound in leather it seemed; yet the texture was odd to the touch. The front cover was embossed with a large circle enclosing the outline of a star which was raised a touch more prominently than the rest of the design.

Jack turned the book over in his hands; there was no title on the cover or on the spine. The back had no decoration of any kind. Inside, on the front page, a title of sorts was faded and to his surprise, hand written. Perfect and neat, the ink was a barely legible title - Grimoire.

Intrigued, Jack read pages at random. A list of cures for warts, of all things, was listed on the page facing him. He read on.

One instruction said to rub the wart with a black slug and then to impale the slug on the spikes of a Hawthorn in the light of a New Moon. How on earth that would cure a wart, heaven only knew.

Another cure stated that the hair from a horse's tail tied tight about the wart would cause the wart to drop off. Jack thought about this for a moment. Cutting off blood supply to the wart would indeed cause it to die off and he supposed that the natural oils in the horse hair would aid the process. "Not quite as ludicrous as I first imagined." Jack muttered to himself.

Jack flipped backwards and forwards through the pages, stopping to read a couple that took his fancy.

Chewing the bark from a willow could cure a headache, as could feverfew. Then Jack became yet more interested in the writings in this ancient tome. Evening primrose, crushed and distilled could help alleviate "women's problems - the monthly kind".

This was an interesting book, not only for the cures but also for the handwritten script that was as uniform and constant as though it had been printed mechanically - yet that was clearly not the case. The book had been painstakingly written in a perfect, legible hand - it must have taken years.

Jack was quite tempted to purchase the book, if only for the novelty value. Then he happened upon a page that captured his attention and had him enthralled.

The cure for a Weerwolf is difficult and filled with danger. Preparation and aforethought is essential. Silver is widely thought to be the only metal which can harm or kill such a beast but to cure it, there are many methods.

Jack closed the book and took it to the rear of the shop. The shopkeeper looked surprised as Jack placed the book on the scarred wooden countertop before him and asked for him to wrap it.

"Are you quite sure sir?" The man raised his half-moon glasses with one hand whilst holding the book at the optimum distance from his eyes in order that he could appraise it with more care. "It is not your usual type of medical book. I confess that I placed it in that category only because I had not the slightest notion of where else I could put it."

"Yes I am quite sure." Jack said, trying to keep his tone light and pleasant, his impatience rising with the delay. "I do not wish to use it for my medical research; it is more for the novelty if you understand."

"Ah then it should be perfect for that purpose, sir."

Jack took the package straight home and searched for the page that had captured his attention. There were a great deal of pages on the subject of curing 'Weerwolves'. There was a great deal more on how to discover if a man - or a woman - was indeed such a creature. Jack read long into the wee small hours and had not finished even when the book slid into his lap and he began to slumber.

Jack woke late and had to rush in order to get to the hospital on time. He was so distracted during the day that at last he handed over the tools of his trade to a colleague and admitted that he had spent a terrible night and therefore it would be best if he did not perform operations that day.

For the first time that he could remember, Jack left the hospital early. He took a hackney carriage home rather than his usual walk and as soon as he could, he picked up his new book.

When he had finished reading the very last page on how to discover and reveal a 'Weerwolf', he forced himself to wash and change and to go out to eat. He did not linger at the club however, he returned home straight after finishing his meal, electing to smoke his cigar in the carriage home.

He was excited because when he had forced himself to put the book down and go to eat, it was because he could foresee not having the willpower to do that later on, once he had begun to read the next section – "How to make a Weerwolf of you or of some enemy for purpose of revenge".

The book advised that though it may seem a good way of getting rid of an enemy, changing such a person into a powerful and unrelenting beast was not a good idea in the long run. For, warned the author, the enemy would then be a stronger and more powerful foe than he ever was before and unless you were planning to change him in order to then denounce him as a 'Weerwolf' and so have him (or her) burned at the stake, it was best not to. Even if your plan was denouncement, it was still filled with great risk to one's person and community as a whole.

As Jack read on, the book told that the easiest method of becoming a 'Weerwolf' was to have one bite you, for if you survived, you would become a beast at the very next Full Moon. That method was simple but filled with great risk, for you may die and be destined to walk the earth as undead, rotting as a corpse would, able to communicate with humanity, saving the one, the 'Weerwolf' that killed you until at last, the 'Weerwolf' was driven insane by your haunting and committed suicide.

Jack read the passage again.

The least complicated way to become a Weerwolf is to cause such a creature to bite you. This would immediately result in

49

you becoming a Weerwolf at the very next Full Moon. Though why any person would choose to put him or herself in such great peril is beyond comprehension as the dangers...

Jack stopped reading and instead brought forth a memory from his mother's graveside. David had said "I loved your mother, I still do, but this was her choice."

Jack realised what David had meant at last. It had been her choice to *not* be bitten by him all those years ago.

Almost frantically, Jack read to the end of the section devoted to 'Weerwolves'. There were methods on becoming a 'Weerwolf', some which were permanent - such as being bitten - and others by using magical items.

A Wolf Belt for example, bestowed upon its wearer, the form and power of a wolf but as the wearer removed it, he would gain his usual form. That would seem the most ideal method but for one detail. A Wolf Belt was very difficult to come by. It was usually given only by the Devil himself and so was not widely available.

However, there were other means at his disposal. Given the right circumstances, with the correct use of ingredients and complex potions prepared to exact prescription, a person could use the pelt of a wolf to become a wolf. Jack's questing mind then took that theory further. Using the same potions and ceremonies and the pelt of a werewolf rather than an ordinary wolf, would he then be able to hold back the ravages of time, as his father seemed to be doing? In effect, become immortal?

The very next day, Jack informed the governors of the hospital that he was taking an extensive leave of absence and would inform them upon his return, but his advice was for them to find a more permanent replacement for him rather than a temporary one.

50

Employing an agent to take care of his affairs in England, Jack had his possessions put into storage, packed a large trunk and left for Europe.

Jack became as a man obsessed. He followed every lead, every rumour, legend and story that mentioned werewolf, man-wolf or even tame wolf. He sought men and women who were purported to have the power to alter their form - to wolf or other. He soon discovered were-bears and were-foxes abounded, especially in the dense forests of Germany.

Jack sought Wolf Belts - and found none. He became an expert on wolfbane and deadly nightshade and began studies on the foxglove - all of which are lethal poisons and yet can send the user into a delightful, if oft-times fatal trance.

His studies took him into the Black Forest and Bavaria and beyond even those remote countries. He filled notebooks with his findings and had to purchase an extra trunk in which to carry them. Jack discovered entire villages that lay claims to werewolf infestation yet on arriving at said village; he found that they had invariably 'cured' the werewolf by burning it at the stake. There were many such stories - far more than he would ever have guessed at - too many for mere coincidence. He became frustrated with tales of murders blamed upon werewolf activity yet to his civilised mentality, it was more likely the murderer was nothing more than vicious, greedy or lustful.

Eventually, Jack's enquiries brought him to a village, much the same as any other, where a few coins bought him information on a woman who was so skilled a healer that other villages knew of her also and sick and ailing people were brought from far and wide for her help. She was not thought of as a werewolf and because of her success in healing, had escaped being burned as a witch. Jack paid her a visit.

He stayed for three months.

51

Soon after leaving Bavaria, his quest took another direction. Tales of shamans and powerful medicine men who could change their form to any animal reached Jack and he extended his tour to America - the New World.

It seemed to prove an unfortunate waste of time for Jack, the shamans he sought were either on reservations and unwilling to talk with him or more often than not, untraceable because of the nomadic lifestyle that the Red Indians - as they were called - led.

By pure chance, Jack heard a rumour. Up in the Canadian mountains, an old Indian had been seen with a captured wolf in his camp. This was cause for speculation because the man was alone and yet he had captured and caged the biggest and fiercest wolf ever heard of. Of course in tales such as these, the animal in question was bound to be the largest specimen ever - otherwise the tale would have lost the point of its telling. Yet how could a frail and ancient man have captured the wolf by himself? If he was not alone at the capture, why was he alone afterwards? And, most puzzling of all, why was the wolf bound tight with ropes? Not to mention the question of how on earth did they manage to get the ropes on it? They could hardly have waited until it was sleeping.

The tale was that three trappers had found it, but only one was left for the telling of it.

Jack had a new quest - to find that man.

Jack was not an unintelligent man and so realised that asking strangers for information about his intended quarry could prove hazardous to his safety. Although he was wealthy, he did not have unlimited funds (and those which he had started with were dwindling after his extensive journeying) but he was willing to pay a private detective to do the searching for him. The private detective, a man named Syndhurst was thorough and efficient and had located what seemed to be the

52

correct man after only a few nights searching in the poorer parts of Boston. The detective informed his client that the man he had found was willing to meet with Jack for a price. Jack surmised that the price had been hiked up by Syndhurst but in his excitement didn't bother too much about that.

Syndhurst escorted Jack to the seediest bar that he had yet been inside and stood close by whilst he conducted his business with the whiskey-soaked trapper.

For the cost of a good hangover, Jack found the information that he needed but when asked if he would act as a guide back into the mountains, the trapper declined and no amount of alcohol could induce him to rethink his decision. Jack left, a little disappointed but determined to find the shaman the trapper had told him about, as well as the shaman's grandson whom the trapper had begun to talk about and then refused to elaborate on. If nothing else, Jack could tell that the trapper had 'clammed up' when he realised what he was saying. Jack was curious about the things he had been told. He was more than inquisitive about the things that he had *not* been told.

It was quite possible that if the trapper had agreed to guide Jack into the mountains, he could have arrived earlier, but as it happened, he missed his goal by a matter of weeks. The winter camp was abandoned and it took longer yet to find the new camp. By this time, the tribe's shaman's grandson had departed.

It was only by more good fortune that Jack was able to glean the information he needed. Jack used a cane, not to help him walk, but purely for fashion. On the tip of the cane was a carved wolf's head and a boy from the camp saw it and assumed that he was a friend of another visitor - one that had left a few weeks earlier.

"Friend of Anton?" The boy asked with an innocence that beguiled Jack, pointing to Jack's cane.

53

"What? Oh yes, friend of Anton," Jack agreed.

The boy pointed to a group of men and went off again, playing with his friends.

Jack approached the group that had been pointed out to him with an instinctive caution. The men turned to look at him after a few moments, a scowl on each of their faces.

"I am trying to find the man called Anton. Please could you tell me if he is here?" Jack asked, tipping his hat towards the men.

"Who told you that he was here?" the more ancient looking of the men asked.

"I have followed him from Europe. It is of great urgency that I find him," Jack said.

"He returns to Europe. You have had a wasted journey." The old man turned his back on Jack to show that the conversation was at an end, but Jack persisted.

"Was he successful in his quest? Did he get what he came here for?"

"Go away stranger. You are fishing. I do not know how you know Anton, but you know nothing of his quest here. Leave. You are not welcome." The expression on the old man's face made it clear to Jack that the discussion was closed but still he tried.

"And the caged wolf; is that still here?"

An angry silence descended and Jack at last decided that discretion was the better part of valour, bowed with respect and left, hoping that he could keep his skin intact until he could get back to his own camp and his guide. Jack had an uneasy feeling all the way back and he felt no easier the following morning, nor the morning after. Not until they had left the harsh mountainous country did he begin to regain his ease.

Jack was impatient to be home but navigating his way across America was still a long and arduous task. All he could be thankful for was that his guide was knowledgeable of the terrain.

Jack arrived back in Liverpool with as much knowledge on werewolf lore as any one person alive, he guessed. Add to that the fact that he was part werewolf already; he now thought that he was an authority on the subject, second to none. He knew how to kill a werewolf, how to prove that a person suspected of being a werewolf was one and then how to force it out of wolf form and into its true human form. He even had certain methods at his disposal to force a man into his wolf form against his will and since his three month stay with the healer woman in Bavaria, he also had the knowledge on how to make himself wolf at will. What he did not yet realise was that he also had the inherited ability to sense such creatures.

Jack took it upon himself to begin experiments to draw the elusive creatures to him. He knew that the full moon was when they were at their most active, and therefore it made perfect sense to search out a creature at the time close to a full moon.

On a whim one Saturday evening in February, Jack strolled out to see if he couldn't utilise the knowledge he had gathered.

He found himself in the area where some of his patients called 'home'. These patients were not duchesses or ladies however, they were more likely to describe themselves as 'seamstress' – which happened to be the term used by most prostitutes if they were required to give an occupation, either to the magistrate, the police or the workhouse infirmary.

As he continued his stroll, he was aware of a woman watching him. He altered the direction of his path and went towards her. She straightened up as soon as he changed direction and adjusted her bonnet. Her smile seemed forced to Jack but he continued towards her. She had been leaning on a fence and she brushed the dirt from her sleeve.

"Hello," Jack said, tipping his hat. He saw the disdain in her eyes then and some part inside his mind took a dislike to the woman. "Are you alone?"

"Yes, I am and I have a little time, if you would like to stay and talk for a few minutes."

Her voice grated on Jack's nerves; it had a nasal whine about it and sounded as though she was perhaps just recovering from a cold – or was about to come down with one.

He didn't like her eyes either; they were shifty and had a sly cast to them. She would look over Jack's shoulder as she spoke to him, rather than looking at his face. Jack liked to talk with people who looked him in the eye as they spoke, he could tell if they were being truthful with him – with unerring accuracy. He could tell that she did not want to be here, talking to a stranger, but perhaps that was because she was being forced into this life of prostitution. Then Jack heard a sound off to his left and behind him. Suddenly he had the impression that he really was not safe in this place. He had outstayed his welcome and he decided to beat a hasty retreat.

He tipped his hat, betraying his manners and said: "I beg your pardon, madam; I appear to have mistaken you for an acquaintance of mine. I must apologise, I shall leave you to your assignation. Good night."

Then, before he could be accosted by her companion or pimp, he made his departure.

He heard a whispered argument begin and he ducked into the shadows surrounding her chosen area of work and listened.

"What did you say to him to make him leave?" A gruff voice snarled at the woman.

"I didn't say nuffin! Why would I warn him?" The voice which had been grating on Jack's nerves, grated even more as she became angry and defensive. "You made a noise as you made your move."

"You must 'ave given him a signal, I didn't make no noise to warn him."

"Well it weren't me neither!" She stuck her fists onto her hips and thrust out her chin.

He lifted his stout and rough-hewn walking stick as though to strike her and she ducked her head. "Don't you hit me, you bastard! I've told you before, I'll go along with you as long as you never hit me and the takings are split equal like."

"Yeah and I told you, we're partners as long as it suits me. I've had enough of you, Annie, you're a greedy trollop and you're not getting no younger, neither. You don't draw 'em in like you used to. I shan't hit you but you just stay away from me now, you 'ear?"

Jack heard the footsteps walking away from him. He waited for a few moments, to give the pimp time to vacate the area and he was about to move away when he heard her wheedling voice once more.

"Hello sir, are you looking for a companion like?"

The hairs on the nape of Jack's neck bristled and he watched as Annie spoke to another man. Her partner must have passed the client as he left for he had not passed Jack, but what was the cause of the eerie feeling that had begun to make its way down his back and up across his scalp?

The illumination from the street light was diffused and pale, it gave everything a washed-out appearance but Jack could see their breath as they spoke, though he could not hear what they said.

He watched, fascinated as they talked, and he gave out a gasp of surprise as Annie doubled over because the man had punched her low in the abdomen. He punched her again and again and Jack's instinct was to turn to her aid but something held him back. The hairs on the back of his neck were still raised and it was something about the phenomenon that gave him pause for thought. The man bending over Annie's prone form was suddenly aware of Jack's presence, perhaps because of Jack's gasp of surprise and shock. He straightened up and stared into the shadows and as Jack made a move forwards, the attacker looked over Jack's shoulder, just as Annie had done, and he fled.

Jack went to Annie's prone form and lifted her skirts to assess the injuries. There were a few stab wounds to her legs and lower abdomen and Jack was worried. His instincts as Doctor came to the fore and he did what he could for her before leaving. Fortunately she was wearing her hefty winter clothing and that had prevented her from being more seriously injured. Jack did not want to attract attention however; it would not be good for his reputation as a respected surgeon if he were to be seen with an injured woman here, it would be difficult to explain why he was in the area.

As he left her, she was coming round from her faint and he was certain that she would be able to get herself the short distance to the workhouse infirmary without his help.

What distressed and disturbed him most were the noises of interest in the surrounding area. His hearing seemed to be more acute than usual. He could hear someone close by, sniffing the air as though the scent of blood was appealing to them.

When Jack passed close to the place where he thought the sniffing person was hidden, he looked into the gloom and saw a flash of amber light - twin orbs – at head-height. Realising what he had seen, and that he had had a very fortunate escape, Jack tipped his head forward and fled.

The Revelation

Because from the age of eight, Jack had been compulsive in his studies, he had been blinded to his own burgeoning instincts.

The proximity of his father at his mother's graveside had kindled the flame of those instincts, but he had not, as yet, had opportunity to realise that. He remembered, from time to time, the horrifying and instantaneous transformation that David's face had undergone but he had no way of knowing that David had not consciously performed the transformation, nor was he aware that Jack could see him in his Wolfed form. From that precise moment, Jack's instincts had been waking themselves up to the full power that should have been a gradual process over the years from the onset of puberty onwards. Therefore, he had in excess of twenty years to catch up on.

The next time that Jack encountered a werewolf, the effect on his instincts sent him into paroxysms of panic.

Whilst working in his laboratory at the hospital, Jack had been performing an autopsy and dissecting a woman who had been brought in under unusual circumstances. She seemed to have been the victim of a horrendous attack. Her face was sliced open, as was her neck and chest. She had been very healthy prior to her demise and had a strong musculature – she did not seem to be the usual specimen that Jack had to work upon. He took his time in examining her but it was obvious that her injuries were what had caused her death and he was only going through the motions of the autopsy. He had already decided to finish up because he had an appointment later when a knock on his laboratory door caused his wandering mind to snap back to attention and his scalpel slipped. He sliced his hand with the scalpel that had removed the larger than average adrenal gland moments before. Cursing under his breath, he unlocked the door and allowed his colleague access.

He gave instructions to his colleague and left him to finish the autopsy. After a few moments of cleaning himself up and dressing his wound, Jack left for home.

He had a relaxing bath, changed his clothes and made his way to his club for an early dinner. From there he caught a hackney carriage and went on to the theatre.

In the foyer of the Haymarket Theatre, along with three hospital governors (who were delighted by Jack's return to them), their wives and a young lady whom Jack found to be most agreeable company, Jack suddenly had the queerest of feelings. His scalp began to tingle and that tingle wandered down his neck, across his shoulders and down his arms to the very ends of his fingers. The tingle also travelled down his spine and spread out at the base of his hips to make its way down the outside of his legs, becoming most uncomfortable at a point just below his knees as it continued down the outside of his calves. As this was happening, his palms began to itch and rapidly became all but unbearable in the sensation. He resisted the overwhelming urge to scratch them both only with a great deal of self-restraint. Jack was then compelled to look up towards the balcony - straight into the eyes of a man that was not a man. He saw the eyes of this stranger flash with amber light and for an instant, his features changed to and from wolf in the same manner that his father's features had, over five years before.

Jack could not help but let out a low moan. His companions looked to him and were at once concerned. The man who had inadvertently brought about Jack's plight was also concerned, for he had not the slightest idea that it was he who had caused the problem. Jack realised that he was the centre of attention and dropped his cane, gloves and hat to clutch at his chest. This brought forth renewed cries of alarm from the ladies and shouts for aid and assistance from the governors. Of course, one cannot be involved with a hospital and not know what to do in the event of a probable heart attack. Jack furthered his cause by dropping to his knees. Attendants rushed to help the distressed group. The man who had frightened Jack moved prudently away and Jack sat on the floor of the foyer, protesting to everyone that he was perfectly all right - or would be in a moment or so.

"No, Sir Matthew, I shall be fine. Just give me a moment to be sure," Jack said, waving away the attendant closest to him.

"I can have you taken across to the London; that is by far the closest hospital. You will be in good hands there," Sir Matthew assured him.

"No. I promise that I shall be all right. A carriage home may be a good idea however."

An attendant rushed outside to call up a carriage and informed the group when one had arrived.

"I shall go with you," Sir Matthew insisted.

"Do not miss Lillie Langtry on my account, Sir Matthew."

"Nonsense, I insist. Everyone else shall go in and I shall catch up with her performance later. I will brook no argument."

Jack nodded and gave a feeble smile for the benefit of the ladies. "I feel such a fool. I beg your pardon for spoiling your evening. As soon as I feel better, I promise to make this up to you all."

Cries of 'nonsense' and other protests and 'goodnight' and one of 'make sure that he is safe in bed before you return' followed the two men out of the foyer and into the street where the carriage was waiting.

Once inside the carriage, Sir Matthew needed further reassurance that Jack was indeed not playing heroics in front of everyone so as not to spoil their evening.

"I am fine, Sir Matthew, I assure you. I just had a dizzy spell."

"No chest pain?"

"None, just a slight flutter, but I shall have a check-up on my return to work in the morning. I promise not to be foolish."

"Good man!"

"And I can also manage to tuck myself up in my bed too. You go back, your wife is waiting. It would be a shame to spoil her evening. Please apologise to everyone again, especially to the lovely Juliette. Such a shame," he sighed.

"There will be other evenings, Jack. I seem to think that Miss March, Juliette, is as enamoured with you as you seem to be with her. Goodnight Jack." Sir Matthew clasped Jack's hand and shook it with genuine fondness.

Jack waved as he mounted the steps up to his front door and let himself into his house. However, once inside, he made his way through the house to the back door where he let himself out again.

Through the door in the wall that separated his garden from the back alley he slinked. He went past the other doors in the row, cautious and swift, keeping to the shadows where he could. Then he made his way out of the better area and into the seedier parts of the city. Not far in distance, but a whole world away in privilege.

With his hat pulled down and the collar of his cloak pulled up about his ears, he watched those that were hidden from the society that knew theatres and soirees – the society that embraced him and his profession – he watched from the shadows and he saw deprivation combated by drunkenness and wantonness fed by lust.

He had seen these types of people before, when he treated them at the workhouse, when at last their bodies had given in to the ravages of illness and they could no longer scrape together the few pennies it took to subsist in these places. At last, he saw the cause of the alcohol-induced and sexually transmitted diseases – this is how some people lived in a day by day and hand to mouth existence.

He moved on, toward a quieter area and he found a semblance of peace even in the midst of the squalor.

He looked up to the sky in between the crowded buildings and the sky was bright with stars. On a whim, he moved from his vantage point and out into a more open area. A breeze caught his white scarf and he tucked it inside his cloak so that it wouldn't draw attention to him. The breeze was helping to clear some of the smog and he looked up to see the sky again. The full May moon - or 'Hare Moon' - shone down upon him and he studied the face of it. He thought that the moon was not a pure white after all, it was more a very pale blue and it seemed to have eyes and an open mouth - as though something had surprised it. A pale misty light surrounded the moon, almost as though it was draped with a veil of the thinnest chiffon imaginable. Jack was lost in the beauty and the simplicity of the scene above him.

Jack was aware in the back of his mind that he had an erection.

Just then his elbow was touched, bringing his consciousness back to the filth and squalor he was surrounded by. He looked around to see who had disturbed him.

A very pretty face peered up at him. The girl was very tiny, but not a child – her curvaceous body proved that. Her breasts peeped up over her corset and were less than covered by the blouse she wore, their paleness shining with a hypnotising luminescence to rival the moonlight. Unusual for inhabitants of these slums, her face was clean and unmarked by dirt or bruises.

The effect was spoiled somewhat when she opened her mouth to speak. The unmistakable local dialect tumbled forth from her pretty mouth and quite broke the spell that she had cast over Jack.

"Ere mister, want some company, do yer?" she asked and looked up into his eyes in as close an impression of coyness as he supposed she could manage.

Jack only then noticed her sway as she stood.

"No, go away."

She looked once more at his face, seeming to study him and then she lowered her gaze down to his groin. Her hand whipped out from her side and she felt his erection through his trousers.

"What the devil!" Jack exclaimed, knocking her hand away.

She placed both fists on her hips, faced him square on and said: "I don't offer twice, mister. It seemed to me that you weren't quite sure what I meant. I hope you're under no such illusion now?"

"I…" Jack stammered. His gaze rested on the tops of her breasts once more and his mouth opened and closed without sound.

"Yeah, I thought as much. Listen to me," her voice was no longer soft and imploring, she seemed more *real* somehow. This was no act; this was how she was for most of the time. Jack didn't need this explaining to him, he realised as soon as

64

she began talking. "I'm clean, I am. I was brought up proper and I don't do too bad for myself. I got a proper lodgin' an' everythin'. I charges a bit more, you see, but I'm bloody worth it, I can tell yer!"

"Yes, I am quite sure that you are, but…"

"Well if you're lookin' for better, you'll have to go a long way from Whitechapel mister, cos there ain't no better 'ere. An' from what I felt just then, it'd be an uncomfortable long journey, if you get my meaning." Her eyes never left his and he got the impression that she was telling him the truth not just for his benefit, but because she *was* the best and she was damned proud of that fact.

After a moment of pause, he replied, "Yes, I do get your meaning. What I meant was that I had no intentions…"

"Yeah, I know, you're a proper gentleman you are. Come on, love," she said as she took hold of his arm and began to guide him back the way he had wandered. She turned down an alley and almost at once turned again to a door that was not locked. Inside, there was a hall with seven doors and a staircase. She led him down the hall, past the staircase, to the very end door, directly opposite the one that they had entered the building by.

Inside, the room was not very dirty - she had not been lying. The bed was made, the floor swept and a fire in the grate kept the room from getting damp, though he did notice that a slight breeze blew through a broken window. Jack took a look around and once satisfied, closed the door behind him.

The girl smiled. She pulled back the sheets on the bed and approached her latest customer with a slow and seductive sway.

Jack allowed her to undress him; she was very careful and folded his clothes neatly, putting them on a chair. Then she gently pushed him onto the bed but he resisted and moved towards his clothes. He fumbled in his jacket, but she stopped him. "No sir, you pays after, cos you might like it the once and want to stay a bit longer."

She pushed him back to the bed and he sat on the edge, watching as she teased him. She at last stood naked in front of him, the glow from the fire adding to the ambience.

She approached him, her fingers tweaking at her nipples, making them stand to attention. By the way his eyes boggled on stalks, she could tell that he was a novice and so she determined to make this experience one that he would want to repeat - with her of course.

He did indeed want to repeat the experience - twice more that evening - and promised to return another time.

"I'll find you then sir, never you fear. But if you do come round 'ere, just be ware, I share this room with someone, so don't think that I've scarpered if she's 'ere an' not me. She'd sort you out nice enough too, though not as good as what I can," she glanced down at the money that he offered. "Oh thank you sir. That's very generous of you. An 'ole five pounds! You're more than welcome again sir!" she said as she made the note vanish from his sight.

Jack had enjoyed his first taste of a prostitute and his second, and indeed, his third but the following morning when he awoke in his own bed, naked for a change, he felt disgusted with himself.

In reality he had very little to feel guilty for. He had no wife and so was not breaking any marriage vows, nor betraying a loved one. He had not abused the girl in a physical or verbal sense and he did not follow any religion and so would not have to suffer the wrath of any supreme being. Yet he loathed himself. He stripped his bed; found clean linen - a task he had never undertaken for himself in all his years. He made his own bed and drew a bath. On hindsight, he would have been better staying at his club the previous night, at least he would not have had to change his bed sheets or draw his own bath. He caught himself thinking "Well I shall have to do that the next time it happens then," and he answered himself out loud: "What are you thinking of? There will never be a next time!"

Jack was still at home later the same day, he had not gone to work. He sent a hastily written note to Sir Matthew that he was still not quite up to the mark and he would be back on Monday, it being Friday would mean that Sir Matthew would have to find someone to cover him over the weekend. It would mean an inconvenience for Sir Matthew and for the person covering, but Jack had other things to think on and he did not dwell on the nuisance he had caused.

So he decided to try to relax and not think about the events of the previous night, but he was restless. He sat down to read, and then changed his book. Then he decided to fix himself a drink, then something to eat. Then he lost interest in both novels and decided to study instead. The light was not quite right. His chair was uncomfortable. He was thirsty again. In sheer desperation he stood and then paced. Though the house was not small, Jack could not find a room in which he could settle. Eventually he took to the stairs and paced the bedrooms. Still not satisfied, he took to the other set of stairs and went up into the attic. From the smallest window at the top of the house, he looked over the tops of all the houses. A sense of peace descended upon him and he stood still and quiet, the calmness washing over him like the gentle lapping of waves on the shore.

All at once he seemed to awake and he was startled because it was dark outside. Had he watched the sun set and not even noticed? He was in the same place as he had been to begin with and yet he seemed to have been asleep. How could he have slept so soundly and not moved or fallen?

It had been early afternoon when he had ascended the stairs to the attic. The sun had been shining through his little window but now it was the moon, so full and bright, giving a different kind of light to that of the sun. The refreshing cold light had him lifting his face towards it to bask in its coldness, the same smoky, blue, misty quality of light that had captured his attention on the previous night and made him unaware of the girl until she had grasped his elbow and led him away to her bed.

Again he was aware that he had an erection but it was different this time. He could feel the blood pulsing through his penis. He could feel every heartbeat. As he closed his eyes and concentrated, his pulse beat throbbed through his temples too. He could feel the blood coursing through every part of him. The arteries in his neck were throbbing in the most uncomfortable way. Even his eyes felt as though they were beating. He placed the tips of his fingers on his closed eyelids and could feel the tiny throb through them. He put a hand to his chest and counted his pulse rate. There was no racing of his heart, no variance, it was beating strong and regular - but it was beating so that he could feel it throughout his entire being.

Then Jack was distracted. His scalp began to tingle, just like it had the previous night at the theatre. The sensation continued down the back of his neck and along his shoulders. Down his arms the sensation travelled but slowly - not like a shudder, which is instant - this sensation took a full minute to reach his fingertips. Then, as it had the night before, it reached the palms of his hands. Oh how they itched. A deep seated and crawling itch beneath the skin on his palms and he knew that even if he scratched them raw, they would still itch, almost enough to make him go mad. He nevertheless leaned forward to scrape the palms on the window ledge and closed his eyes in ecstasy as the itching was relieved a little.

As he opened his eyes he looked out of the window to find himself face to face with a nightmare countenance.

A large creature was on the other side of the glass looking in, right at Jack. Its eyes glowed for an instant and Jack's own eyes widened further yet - if that were possible. The beast's face had transformed for a moment into that of a man and back to the horrific features of a wolf that was not quite a wolf, one that was wilder, more feral than even a wild animal could be. Jack screamed and leaped back, the beast smiled and then it was gone.

Jack found himself sitting upon the bare boards of the attic floor. His palms were red and sore where he had scraped them, his hair was a mess where it had stood on end and the erection was still pumping inside his trousers, almost as though it were a separate entity, determined to make its presence felt.

He scrambled across the attic floor and down the narrow stairs in sheer terror and hid himself under his bed, shaking so hard that he feared he may loosen his own teeth. After a short time he calmed down a little and decided that if he had not been murdered by now, the danger was most likely past and he emerged from under his bed. Jack went downstairs to the drinks cabinet and poured a large brandy. He downed it almost in one and reduced himself to a coughing, shaking wreck as the spirit burned its way down his throat. He decided that he had had enough of a fright for his quaking heart for one evening and went straight back to his room. His clothes were dirty and dusty from his refuge of earlier and he again slept naked.

That night he had dreams of running naked alongside a pack of wolves. They seemed to ignore him for the most part and he kept up with them very well as they loped across the open countryside. When one turned to face him, its face changed to that of a beautiful woman and he was taken aback to the extent that he missed his footing and stumbled. He regained his gait at the next step he took but he was further back along the length of the pack as it ran. The next wolf to look at him was the same man that he had seen at the theatre and at his attic window and he again was taken by surprise but he did not lose any ground. The wolf to the side of the familiar young man glanced in his direction and again the face altered to that of a beautiful woman – one that he could not recall seeing, yet she was familiar somehow.

A young male wolf caught up to him, running alongside the young man he had just recognised and the face of the new wolf turned to another young man, but this time he had a resemblance that Jack recognised at once. It was the younger face of the old shaman he had encountered whilst in Canada. The face did not revert back to wolf right away and Jack studied him as they ran. All at once the young shaman's face turned back to wolf and he snarled at Jack and made as though to bite him. Jack swerved away from the jaws and became frightened of further attacks.

He made a concerted effort to regain his original place at the head of the pack – or at least alongside the front-runners.

The beautiful woman-wolf was still at the head of the pack but alongside her, closest to Jack was another wolf; this was a magnificent creature, larger than the female with sleek glossy black fur. Jack thought that the fur also shone with a deep purple undertone and as the wolf turned to look at him as the others had, its jaws opened wide and caught Jack's throat and chest in the most violent attack. Though on one subconscious level, his mind knew it was a dream, Jack was terrified and began thrashing at the wolf's head and face to try to make it let go. It did at last let him go and dropped him at the side of the trail where the rest of the pack flowed past him like a river in full flood, the fur of the beasts slowly changing to waves on the surface of a fast moving river and Jack knew that the wolf had injured him beyond human endurance and that he was dying.

He woke up in his bed with sweat running down his chest. He was soaked through. His bedding and the slickness of his skin made him panic once more until he realised that it was not his lifeblood that had soaked him through, but the sweat of his exertions. He tried to remember what he had been dreaming about but each time he grasped for the answer, it faded; it was like trying to grip smoke in both hands. Each time he thought he had it in his grasp, it evaded his every effort to recognise and comprehend it until at last even the most slender of memories was gone, faded back into dreamland.

He got out of bed to hear Lizzie coming in through the back door as she usually did on Saturday morning. He dressed quickly and felt disgusting under his clothes. He assumed that it was the residual perspiration on his skin that made him feel clammy and wretched and made a mental note to take a bath once Lizzie had finished her work and gone home.

At last she did finish, though she seemed to be concerned about her employer and was kind enough to make him a nice breakfast and then lunch before she at last left.

Jack did not know what he was going to do. He could not live in utter terror for three nights out of each month and his curious scientific mind was clamouring with questions that he needed to answer.

At last, late in the afternoon he made a decision. He took an hour or more to prepare but once his mind was made up, he went about his task in his usual methodical and efficient manner. He searched his study for a notebook that had not yet been written in and took it down to his basement laboratory. Then he set about removing the old experiments and prepared the entire area for some new ones. When he deemed himself ready, Jack dressed in older clothes and though he had none that were shabby, he thought that his attire was not quite as conspicuous as it had been forty-eight hours before. Satisfied with the way that he looked, he went out of the back door. This time, however, he kept away from the street where he had met the girl. He did not want to chance running into her again. He had already decided that he would keep her for special occasions.

Tonight, he would watch and wait.

He became aware of his scalp prickling, but the sensation did not become any stronger and nor did it make any progression along his neck and shoulders. While he was waiting - for what, he did not yet know - he mused upon this phenomenon.

In the theatre foyer, his scalp had tingled, as did his palms. Just like last evening they had become unbearable with the itchiness and upon both occasions, he had seen a terrible vision. He could only have described it as thus. He did not wish to go down the path of thinking that they were hallucinations or delusions – or dreams. On both occasions, the eyes had glowed but the visage was different on both times - or was it? He forced himself to clear his mind and to concentrate on what exactly he had seen. He tried to remember every detail of the man in the theatre. A handsome and young face, but no real distinguishing features apart from the fact that his face had altered into a wolf's face - turned purely feral. Then he thought of the face at his window earlier, a wolf face to begin with, a Werewolf in all probability, the face of which had also altered, changed to that of a man, but were they the *same* man? Jack could not be sure. He wanted to be certain but he was a man of science and needed proof and so could not draw any conclusion as yet.

On both occasions, his head, neck, shoulders, arms, fingers and especially palms had tingled with a static shudder and then his palms had gone further and began to itch. Both times he had been frightened out of his wits but of course, he had not been expecting the encounter. What would happen then, if he *was* expecting the encounter and how could he ensure that it would happen under controlled circumstances? Could he entice a werewolf into a controlled situation? Not to trap it but to watch. He knew everything it was possible to know of the creatures; surely it would be a matter of simplicity itself to attract one? It was a bright full moon, the most likely time to find a werewolf and he knew that there was at least one in the vicinity, he had seen it and sensed it. Now he had to try to make one come to him. Yet he knew that this was a dangerous experiment that he was planning to undertake; not only was his personal safety at stake, but also the reputation that he had built up over many years of hard work and hard study. His reputation as an eminent surgeon would not be given up easily. If he were discovered, all would be up with him. Still, the stakes may be high, but the rewards were even higher.

Though he loathed rushing an experiment, he knew that tonight was the optimum time. The full May moon was beginning to wane; it was the last night that he would be able to conduct this experiment for twenty-six days.

Thinking quickly as he spied a lone woman, he had to make his move. She seemed to be very drunk and she staggered along holding onto her shawl with one hand and the wall with her other. Her gait was unsteady and her clothes were dirty, shabby and dishevelled – even more than what seemed to be the norm. He took one swift look about him to assure himself that there were not many others close by and none that were within a number of yards of her. Steeling himself now that he had made his decision, he stepped out of the shadows. He approached the woman with confidence and took her arm. He led her, unresisting, out of the alley and through another.

"Are you available dear?" he asked her as soon as he was certain that he had not been noticed.

"Eh? Yeah, yes sir, I am at that," she said as she grinned up at him and he realised that she was older than he had imagined and by God, she smelled rank.

"Good," he forced his voice to sound amiable, his special and practiced tone - the one that he used on his better class of patient. "But not here, I know a place not far from here."

"I gots me a place, lovie," she began to lead him in another direction.

"No, this way, I have the perfect place." He did not have the perfect place, but he could find it. His scalp was tingling again, but it was becoming more insistent. His neck and shoulders felt the needles running down and now they had gone past, down his arms but no further than that. Jack stopped before the sensation arrived at his hands.

"Are we 'ere then lovie?" the crone asked.

"No. Shut up."

She looked up at him and something about his concentration must have cut through her gin-sodden brain. She pulled from his grasp. "I ain't stayin' 'ere. You're up to summink. Be off, let me alone!"

In desperation, he drew the cane from its sheath and as she turned to stagger off, he sliced at her back, cutting through the clothing and into her flesh. The blade was as sharp as his surgeon's tools and for a moment, she thought that he had just grabbed for her and missed. Then with a small groan, she fell to her knees, dropping her ragged shawl as she tried to reach around the back of herself. Blood was soaking her clothes and she was whimpering as she sank onto her front. Her hands were still fluttering around her sides, trying to reach her wound.

Jack watched all of this in a detached and clinical silence

and then he was aware that the tingling sensation had begun to move again into his hands and his palms were itching once more. He managed to block out the sensation with a great deal of will-power and he melted into the shadows to observe.

Then he saw the beast. It was watching him, sitting in a puddle of moonlight as though by intent so that he could see it better. The light slanting from over the rooftops was made almost palpable by the smog which was beginning to thicken. Then the wolf - which Jack knew to be a werewolf - spoke. Jack almost jumped out of his skin. He never imagined that they could speak.

"Well finish it then. Do not let it suffer so. Do not worry; I shall not steal your kill." The voice was deep and velvety. Jack could imagine that voice talking to him whilst he allowed its owner to tear out his throat; it was almost hypnotic in the alluring timbre. Jack thought of deep silky fur enveloping him as he sunk into unfathomable depths to meet with ecstasy, delight and... blood. Jack stayed silent but he did move closer to the beast. Then, as before, the eyes flashed and its human form was revealed to him. This one was a woman, and he had a glimpse of recognition, but could not place where he recognised her from. Jack gasped but waved for the wolf to go forward.

The wolf looked puzzled - and Jack was bemused at how an animal *could* look puzzled. Then it shrugged and moved on past him. She positioned herself on the opposite side of the woman's body so that she could keep a wary eye on Jack as she devoured the unexpected prize.

"I do not recommend that you stay too long to watch, my friend. I shall be finished here very soon and my appetite is but whetted. Of course, I much prefer the easier prey such as you have kindly furnished me with but rest assured that your blade is no match for my weaponry."

75

Jack took the hint and fled. He became happier once he had reached a populated area and he slipped inside the first public house that he came to, to imbibe some spirits to steady his jangling nerves. He was thankful that all he got from the barman was a dirty glass full of whisky and an odd look. Jack did not want conversation and the barman seemed to share that sentiment. Jack did not trust his own voice to be steady at this moment.

He did not think that he could face going into the all but deserted streets again that night but after a few glasses of the amber spirit, he mustered his courage and felt that he ought to try. The barman was beginning to take too much notice of him, as was a large woman who Jack could not quite decide whether she was looking at him or the barman at the other side of the bar, so bad was her squint. Before she could proposition him, therefore, Jack made a move.

He had not realised until now just how much of the whisky he had downed, but he was not too drunk to walk – not quite.

Once outside in the narrow street, he realised that the chances of calling a hackney cab were slim to none. He shook his head to clear it and set off back for his own neighbourhood. Trying to keep to the better lighted streets if he could, Jack made unsteady progress.

He leaned against a wall in order to get his bearings, just as someone approached. He stayed still and quiet but the person was by now directly in front of him and through his drunken haze, he could only just tell that this was a woman.

"Ere, you look in a frightful way. You got any money?" she squawked at him, making him wince.

"Not much. How much will it cost?"

"Kinda forward ain't ya?"

"Look, I need a companion to walk with me. I shall pay you when I arrive home safely. I do not have more than a few pennies with me, I have been drinking you see."

"I can see that, darlin'. Come on then. Which way is 'ome?"

Jack nodded as she pulled him upright and propped him against her hip whilst she got a better hold of him.

She prattled on all the way to Jack's street, barely pausing for added direction from Jack - or for breath.

Jack was more than relieved when he at last recognised his street.

"You can stop now. Wait a moment," he fished in his pockets and drew a florin, a sixpence and three pennies. "Will that do?" he asked.

"Do for what? I don't want your money. I didn't 'elp you for money."

"What did you help me for then?" He stood looking at her, his hand still outstretched to her with the coins in his fingers.

"Listen doctor," her voice had lost the squawkiness of earlier and was now altogether more pleasant to his ears. "You 'elped my 'ole mum when she was in that work'ouse hospital. She died all the same but you 'elped 'her before she went."

"That's my job, but why did you not say so when you first saw me?"

"I weren't sure it was you. And 'sides, it weren't safe to announce that you are a doctor. What on earth you were doing down that part of town, I don't know, but you're not safe, dressed like a toff an' all, there. Someone'll skin ya, soon as look at ya even if all the money you have on ya is a florin and nine pence. Go on; get off home before your neighbours see you talkin' to the likes o' me."

He grabbed her wrist and forced the money into her hand. "It really is all that I have on me, but thank you. I have been silly and reckless this evening."

"Yeah, you 'ave," she said as she disappeared back into the shadow lands that she inhabited.

"That was lucky, doctor," a nightmarish growl of a voice came from the shadows that the woman had disappeared into moments ago.

"Oh good God!" Jack said and sprinted for his front door. Mocking laughter followed him as he fumbled with his key.

He locked the door and ran into the kitchen to ensure that it was also locked. Then he stumbled to his dining room and made straight for the brandy to calm his nerves. He eventually fell into a fitful and disturbed sleep in his chair. More nightmarish figures assaulted him in his dreams and when he finally awoke, his head was thick with a hangover and his stomach was heaving.

He had awoken with a start and in his dazed and hung-over state, thought that he was late for work until he remembered that he was recuperating until after the weekend. Hearing bustling about in the kitchen, he called out for the maid. "Lizzie!"

"Ooh, yes sir. I was thinking that you must have gone to work already. Oh sir, you do look awful, can I get you anything?"

"Yes Lizzie, please could you get me a pitcher of water; I am quite unwell and cannot bear the thought of food at this time."

"I shall get it right away sir," she bobbed her head and left him.

"Now, can I get you anything else sir?" Lizzie said as she placed the pitcher of cold water on the table close to him.

"Not just now, Lizzie, I shall go back to bed I think."

He didn't catch the look of disdain that his maid gave to his retreating back. She said to herself: "I think 'go back to bed' you've not even *been* to bed yet and you smell like a brewery. No wonder you don't want to go to work. It's the start of ruin if you ask me." She shook her head as she went back to her

78

chores, thinking that though her family were poor as church mice, none of them drank too much of an evening - well not so that it stopped them getting up and going out to the work that they were lucky enough to have.

Jack was very ill and slept through the day and on into the evening. Lizzie did knock on his door as she was about to leave, telling him that his lunch had been prepared but not completed, giving his state of health she doubted that he would be able to eat. He muttered in his sleep which she took as an answer and she left.

As the window began to grow darker and his room was enveloped by the growing dusk, Jack improved. He had consumed nothing but water all day and his head was beginning to clear. He decided that it had been the whisky that had made him so ill, it had definitely not been 'the good stuff' and was probably distilled around the back of the pub which he had been drinking at.

A trip over to his club would set him to rights. He would have to make a good show of his recovery to Sir Matthew on the morning and he determined to curb his drinking so as not to get into the same state as he had been that morning. He washed and shaved then took a hackney cab to the gentleman's club where he dined on a regular basis.

The next day as he got to the hospital, Sir Matthew was waiting for his arrival. Jack was perturbed at the sight of him but could not think that he had anything to worry about, the older gentleman was probably curious as to his health from the scare he had given them at the theatre.

Sir Matthew did ask after Jack's well-being but that was not the reason for his reception as Jack arrived at work. He had disturbing news.

"The young woman that you were autopsying on Thursday, what did you do with the body?"

"What did I do with it?" Jack repeated the question in puzzlement. "Why, Gregory took over from me as I went home early that evening, to get ready for the theatre. Sir Matthew, what is wrong?"

"It is disturbing news, I am afraid. Gregory has not been seen since Thursday and to all appearances, he has made off with a cadaver."

Jack thought that he had somehow misheard the other. "Gregory is missing and so is the corpse?"

"Gone, and so is the autopsy report that you made. I take it that you wrote everything in the ledger?"

Jack nodded and said "Yes, I did everything as I usually do. I wrote as I worked." They were walking towards the pathology labs as they discussed the puzzling episode and as they inspected the ledger, Jack realised that the autopsy report that had been recorded by him had been removed from the large book with expert skill, using a sharp blade so that the sheets that pertained to that one particular autopsy would not be seen to be missing unless they were searched for.

Sir Matthew was at a loss.

"What should we do? I have never known anything like this before, a surgeon stealing a body and going missing? Whatever next?" Jack said, half to himself.

Sir Matthew was in much the same state of bewilderment and he assured Jack that it would be dealt with and not to worry, especially after the health scare that he had gone through over the weekend. So Jack left it all to Sir Matthew but wondered about the corpse; he recognised the wounds and realised that he had felt the same wounds in his dream. To disguise his shock at that memory, Jack turned away and went right to work.

It had been almost four weeks since his first adventures in the

80

slum lands of Whitechapel and Jack was once again walking home from his club, he had said goodnight to the doorman and declined his offer of calling him a cab home, the mid-June evening was pleasant enough and the walk would settle his dinner.

He lifted his hat to a couple walking in the opposite direction and said "A good evening to you," in reply to their greeting. Jack was enjoying the walk. The air was not cold and not smoggy for a pleasant change. The gaslights illuminated his way and he felt satisfied from his meal and he continued to be able to appreciate the excellent brandy in sharp contrast to the gutter water he had been unfortunate enough to have been served a month before – that hangover was one he did not plan on repeating.

A young lady with a pretty hat on caught him up. He heard the tip-tap of her heels as she walked. He gasped in surprise as her arm slipped into his and he looked around at her. She echoed his gasp and put one gloved hand to her mouth as she let go of his arm. "Oh I do beg your pardon sir. I thought that I recognised you as my fiancé and meant to surprise you."

"Well you succeeded there at least," he said laughing.

"Oh I am sorry sir," she looked around with an anxious frown on her brow. "Oh where can he be? He was going to fetch us a hansom cab but he has been an absolute age. I thought that you were he and I have been trying to catch you up. Oh dear."

"It is no matter, my dear. Please do not concern yourself. I am not harmed nor frightened so you really have nothing to worry about on my behalf."

"That is as may be, but I do have something to worry about on my own behalf for now I am quite a way from where I should have waited and must now make my return alone."

"I shall find you a cab and then instruct the driver to take

81

you back."

"Oh but I see my fiancé now," she pointed down the street to a figure that did indeed bear a resemblance to Jack in the fact that he also wore a cloak, a top hat and carried a cane.

As the young man approached, Jack grew uneasy. He recognised the young man, but from where? The man was almost upon them when it dawned on Jack. He was the man from the theatre when he had his 'seizure' – the one that had been the cause of it.

"Good evening Doctor. I trust that you are quite recovered from your illness of the other evening?" The smile he wore was one of pleasant good humour but Jack also detected an underlying cunning.

"I am quite well, I thank you, yes. I shall leave your fiancée in your capable hands then." He tipped his hat and made to leave to continue on his way.

"You did not recognise me, Doctor?" the young woman asked.

"No, I do not think so." He realised that the pair were playing games with him but could not imagine why.

"You offered me a meal last month, Doctor. I am curious as to why."

"And you had an opportunity to indulge in conversation with me on the previous evening – the night before you invited my fiancée to dine. The night that you fled from your attic to spend an uncomfortable evening underneath your bed."

"That was you? I did not realise." Jack ignored the goading which implied his cowardice.

"We know that you didn't and we also know that you are watching us. We would like to know the reason for that too."

Jack thought on his feet. "I know the legends of superhumans such as werewolves and vampires and I study. I had thought at first that the myths and legends were just stories but I have now seen two werewolves."

"You will never see a vampire, no such thing exists," she said.

Jack nodded in acceptance and continued: "I did not imagine that so beautiful a lady and so handsome a gentleman could become such magnificent beasts and yet, for all my studies, they are as nothing." He sighed in what he hoped was a wistful manner, hoping to catch a romantic nature in either of them.

"How so, Doctor?" the young man answered, surprising Jack as he had assumed that the lady would have been taken by his act sooner than the gentleman.

"You know sir, surely?" Jack gasped. "You are an avid theatre-goer and who has not heard of the trials and tribulations of one Dr. Jekyll and his - ah, associate - Mr. Hyde? Who does not thrill to the sheer blood curdling story of The Vampire? Not to mention of course, Dr. Frankenstein and his monster, another lamented man of science. How would my own studies be received if I were to publish them? Why, I would be at best, thought of as a would-be novelist and at worst as a madman. No, dear sir, kind lady, my studies are worthless, except to me." He sighed again and removed his hat to mop his brow. "I apologise if I appear crude to such perfect creatures as you but I have longed for such a meeting."

"You had such a meeting just last month, Doctor, but you fled." The lady smiled such a wicked smile that Jack shuddered at the memory of their meeting.

"Dear lady," he recovered his composure fast enough so that they perhaps hadn't noticed. "You had warned me to flee. I would not have stayed because of your blood lust, but I did so want to."

"For what purpose?"

"Why, to conduct an interview of course."

"An interview? To what end?"

"Again, for my own selfish reasons. Your beauty beguiles me, for as a species, yours is the stronger by far. You have the grace, the beauty and the magnificence. By God! You have lethal power. Puny as we humans are, I as one can only admire and envy you." He paused as they looked at each other. "But let me assure you, I wish not to learn your secrets, only to ask of your past. Not to learn how you are able to conceal your inner wolf, more to ask how you enjoy your lives. Do you have a similar constraining society as ours is or, as I hope and dream, is it free of rules and petty, unimportant regulations on how we should live and conduct ourselves in public and even in private?"

They looked at each other in quiet bemusement and he continued, hoping for at least a stay of execution, for he was in no doubt as to why they had waylaid him in such a manner; it was to kill him - after they had the answers to their questions.

"Oh blessed beings, fortunate creatures, please, I implore you, divulge your secrets to me, even if they be the last things that I hear. It has been my life's work and all would be for nothing if I do not know." Jack seemed so impassioned that the two werewolves in human form again looked to each other.

"No," the woman said.

"No?" her mate asked.

"I do not want to. Why should we tell this Hume our secrets?"

"He does not wish to know our secrets. He cannot glean from us answers that we do not wish to give. Come, it would be such sport."

"You *want* to do this, Marcellus?"

"Indeed I do," then he turned his face away from Jack, dropped his voice so low that it was impossible for Jack to hear and added: "and after we have delighted him, we can

84

devour him."

"You are insane, Marcellus," she smiled and then said to Jack: "very well. We will indulge you, but I will not answer questions that I do not wish to. Do not press me on any that I refuse to answer."

"That is understood, dear lady."

"My name is Almyra."

Jack nodded and smiled as he dipped in a polite bow.

They stood for a moment until Marcellus took the initiative. "Shall we then?" he held out his arm and the lady took it, then they accompanied Jack along the pavement for the short distance to his front door.

Jack maintained an excited babble for he realised that he must keep up the pretence of adoration, if only to mask his sheer terror.

He held open the front door for his guests and the couple preceded him. They were all in the hall and Jack locked the door and then invited them to "a tour first?"

He took them all the way up to the top of the house, to the attic where Jack had seen Marcellus before he had realised whom Marcellus was.

Then they went back down the stairs and Jack said, "may I offer you a drink, perhaps tea or brandy? I have an excellent wine cellar. Oh, I also have my collection and my work on werewolf lore and legends if you would be so kind as to give me your more enlightened opinion upon it?"

"Of course, that is the reason that we are here, is it not?" Marcellus said without waiting for his fiancée to give her affirmation.

"It is all down in my cellar," Jack fished in his pocket for the key to the door. "I keep it locked for my daily maid is quite inquisitive. I also keep my research down here so that she does not get too suspicious. I allowed her to find the door unlocked

85

once and I spied on her as she came sneaking down. It took great self-control not to laugh out loud as she screamed. She almost fainted when she saw this particular specimen jar." He indicated a large bell-jar which contained the wrinkled form of a grotesque and vaguely humanoid foetus. The colour of its skin was distorted by the liquid that it was immersed in but it did not look to be the usual pale pink colour of a new baby and it was covered in two inch long thick black hair.

Almyra gasped in surprise and gripped Marcellus's arm. "Is that…?"

"Ask him."

Jack looked back to his guests realising what they were questioning.

"No dear lady that is not a werewolf baby. The mother was also exceptionally hirsute, to the extent that she did indeed resemble a wild animal but I assure you, she did not alter during the full moon."

"You watched her?" Almyra asked.

"Of course I did. I had as much protection as I could possibly get. I had a large pentagram, cloves of garlic, a silver cross and deadly nightshade, so I was perfectly safe."

The two werewolves looked at each other with knowing smiles. They looked at Jack's notes and documents, his books and the experiments that were set up and then Marcellus paused. He beckoned Almyra over and showed her a book, the very book that Jack had purchased from the bookshop that had set him on his studies.

"Where did you get this book?" Marcellus asked.

"Oh, from an ordinary book shop, the one in Whitechapel Road, I believe."

"You are a mortal; you are not permitted to possess this book. It is a Grimoire."

"Oh, I did not realise. You see I bought it, I did not steal

86

it."

"It should not have been sold. I must take it," Marcellus picked up the book and held it to his chest as though protecting it.

"Oh dear, but I suppose, if you must, then you must."

"And is this where your information has come from?"

"Well yes, for the most part, but also from my travels to Europe and to the New World." Jack hung his head as though sad that the book must be taken from him but he did not argue.

They then made their way back up the stairs back into the main body of the house.

"Oh, I almost forgot the wine," Jack said and went back down the stairs to where they had seen the vast array of wine bottles in one corner of the cellar.

Jack rejoined them at the top of the stairs where they had waited for him, entering neither the drawing room nor the sitting room. Jack motioned for them to go into one of the rooms off the hallway. "I think that we shall be most comfortable in here," he said as he followed them into the sitting room. "Please sit down."

Jack made himself busy uncorking the wine and allowing it to breathe whilst he put the glasses ready. He then poured out the wine and as he sat down, he swirled his wine around in the glass, making up for the lack of time he had given it to breathe in the bottle. He held up his glass to his guests and said "to immortality," then he took a sip and savoured the taste. His guests glanced at each other and also held up their glass to him, clinking them together just between the two of them. "Immortality," they said in unison.

Jack picked up a pencil and a notebook and looked expectant, waiting for Marcellus or Almyra to begin.

"You expect us to allow you to write down this interview?"

Almyra asked.

"Why yes, I did rather."

"There must be no written record of us even being here, let alone having given an interview."

"I see, in that case, I shall not write anything down. I suppose this is more like conversation between friends then?"

"Yes, exactly so," Marcellus replied, smiling.

"Now then, introductions first, I think. I am Doctor John Coupe but my friends call me Jack," he waited for a moment until the other realised that Jack wanted the other to introduce himself and his companion.

"This is my lady Almyra and I am known as Marcellus. Or at rather, we have been known as such for this century at least."

"I am delighted my lady Almyra. I shall remain your servant sir," Jack gave a small and polite nod towards them both. "This leads me directly onto my first question. It is not yet full moon, are you out hunting already?"

Macellus smiled as though to reassure him. "No, of course not, but we do not like to waste the three nights of the full moon on socialising and so we came to visit you beforehand. Also, Almyra imagined that you would be far too cautious to allow us to approach you when the moon was full."

Jack nodded at the explanation, they were correct, he would not have allowed them to get anywhere near him if they had made the same approach a few nights hence. "Of course," he smiled and without appearing alarmed or distressed, continued with his questions. "How old are you and to what age can you expect to live?"

"You should never ask a lady her age, Jack," Almyra said and laughed. "I am one hundred and sixty six years old."

"And I am but a whelp at one hundred and twenty six years," Marcellus said. "I do not know to what age a *werewolf* -

as you call us - can live but I have heard of the ancients being in excess of five hundred years and older."

"My goodness!" Jack exclaimed. "Truly immortal and yet you look so very young, barely out of your teens I would have guessed at, the both of you. Remarkable." Jack stood up to pour them more wine, topping their glasses up as well as his own. "Now, this is rather an indelicate question and I fully apologise for it beforehand my lady, but how do werewolves procreate?" he had the decency to blush at his own question.

"Why, in the same way as Humes!" Marcellus said.

"*Humes,* now is that a pet name?"

"If you like," Almyra said, smiling.

The conversation continued, the wine flowed, and some questions were ignored, such as "how do I become a werewolf?" Yet most others were answered and with as much detail as possible.

The next bottle of wine had been finished and Jack had gone to the cellar for another bottle.

"This is all very civilised Marcellus, but I grow tired of answering his questions. I cannot see that he would do us any harm, but are we going home or are we staying here for supper?"

Marcellus smiled at his love. "The choice, as ever, is yours, my darling."

Jack returned and they ceased talking for the moment. He pretended that he was not chilled to the marrow by their overheard conversation as he passed them their glasses once more, both were refilled and he again took his own and held it up.

"Another toast if you please, to long life and eternal beauty," he sipped his wine as they were holding up their own glasses and again echoing his toast. Then he smiled and sat down.

"One last round of questions and then I believe it is supper time," Jack said as he sat down in front of his guests. They had not noticed, but Jack's bearing had altered as the evening had worn on. He was no longer the excited student, he was more calculating now, asking questions which were far more prying than he had at first. Soon his veneer slipped completely. "My lady, almost a month ago, I had the greatest pleasure in meeting you for the first time. I did not realise that it was you until you mentioned it earlier this evening but nevertheless, the pleasure was all mine." Jack paused for affirmation, she nodded.

"Then, a little more than a week after that meeting, I again encountered a werewolf. I saw where he was spending the evening and I managed to procure the services of a streetwalker close to where he was. I also managed to attract his attention, by way of stabbing the woman in the chest. Yet he only watched. I know that he saw everything and that he was exceedingly intrigued, yet he neither changed his form, nor did he leave. I do not know what happened to the body of that woman, I have scoured the newspapers for reports of the discovery of it but I have not found anything that resembles the attack."

"Why are you telling us of this? I thought that you were questioning us."

"Yes dear lady, but I am explaining the problem. The question is relative but you need the background first. As I stabbed the woman, the werewolf, as I said, was only mildly interested. I thought that piercing the heart would arouse his inner wolf, but the wound to her breast did nothing to make him change. I am quite perplexed. Can you shed some light upon this mystery?"

"This is no mystery. It was not full moon. An older *werewolf* or even one not so old but one that was *born* Wolf, will be more able to resist the urge to change into a wolf, even with

90

such a great temptation. I must ask you a question now, Jack. How did you know that he was a Wolf?"

Jack looked at Almyra for a little while, seeming to mull over her answer. Then he went right on to another question of his own, ignoring hers.

"Were you both born werewolf or have you been made?"

"We were born *werewolf*. I am from a long bloodline, but not pureblood. Before you ask, purebloods have only ever mated with other born *werewolves*; none that were made are allowed to produce offspring."

"Does that practice not make for interbreeding and weakness associated with incest?"

"It most certainly does not!" Almyra snapped, her usual composure slipping for a second. "You know nothing of our ways, Hume."

"This is exactly the reason for all of these questions," Jack replied with great patience. "If a werewolf is killed whilst in the form of a wolf does he - or indeed she - automatically revert to their human form as in the legends?"

"Don't be ridiculous. How could a dead animal change appearance?" the anger in her voice was evident.

"So it is conscious effort to alter form? That *is* interesting."

"Marcellus, I think I need to feed now," she ignored Jack's conclusion.

Marcellus was still watching however. He then began to look a little puzzled.

"Marcellus? What is it?" Almyra asked.

Jack ignored her anxiety and Marcellus's by now apparent lethargy and continued.

"This shall be my last question then. How would I kill a werewolf?"

"Do you really expect an answer to that question, Hume?" Almyra's voice dripped with venom, her attention diverted from Marcellus for a moment.

"No, I suppose not. I think perhaps that was rather insensitive of me. May I rephrase it then? Would distilled aconite render a werewolf helpless, if for example, it was administered slowly over the course of a few hours in and on glasses of wine?"

"Aconite?" Marcellus asked in a voice that was slow and languid.

"Aconite is distilled wolfsbane, Marcellus. It is a poison. It coats your glass which is why you are in a more advanced state of poisoning than Almyra. She is wearing gloves and so it would not have affected her, but the aconite inside the glass would." He drained his own glass. "You have been quite helpful. I cannot say that you have been extremely helpful for I knew a lot of the information that you have divulged to me, but your bloodlines were of great interest. I do wonder though, how vindictive can your respective families be? Will they mourn your passing as a 'Hume' would, or as an animal? Also, will they wish to exact a terrible revenge upon your murderer?"

Marcellus seemed to have slipped into slumber but Almyra was still conscious although she had to fight hard to stay awake, drowsiness was overtaking her.

Though she was battling to stay alert, she roused herself to berate Jack once more. "You have ignored my question Hume. I grow weary of your invasive questions. You have not yet told me how you knew the other was Wolf."

Jack thought about it for a moment then came to a decision. "I shall answer your question. I could tell that he was a werewolf by the same means that I recognised Marcellus as a werewolf a while ago and indeed your very good self last month. My father was a werewolf - one of your own kind. My mother was a human - Hume - and I seem to have inherited his legacy."

"You are a throwback?" she whispered, her eyes widening.

"Oh I have a pet name too do I?" he said. "Still, it is no matter. I suppose that you are wondering how long this poison will take to pass through your body so that you are again well." He paused as though expecting an answer, but Almyra was beyond answering, in fact, she may have been beyond hearing by this time but Jack was biding his time, there was no point in rushing now, not when he had been so patient all evening. No, he would wait until he was certain that he would not be injured by a Wolf playing possum. He continued to tell her about his poison.

"Unfortunately, it is not called wolfsbane for nothing. You are dying, Almyra. The poison is cumulative. Your organs, especially your heart, are affected and are dying. Soon your strong heart will slow down, your blood pressure will drop and your heart will falter and soon after, you will die. The problem that I shall have will be in disposing of your bodies in such a way so that you are not recognisable, but I think I have that problem worked out. Oh, I see Marcellus is already gone, will you join him?"

Jack did not turn his back on Almyra once in all the time that he was talking to her. It would not have mattered, she was incapable of moving, but Jack did not wish to take any chances.

Once he was certain that they were both dead, he began to work. He lifted the body of Marcellus onto his shoulders and carried him down to the cellar. There he laid him onto a mortuary table. He sliced off the clothes and dropped them in a heap to be burned in the incinerator.

Curiosity got the better of him and he touched a small silver cross to Marcellus's cheek. The flesh sizzled and burned, melting away from under the silver, almost in the same way that it would had Jack poured acid upon the flesh. Jack wrote the findings in a notebook and went back to the task of removing the clothing.

Once the body was naked, Jack then shaved Marcellus. He removed all the hair from the head down, even the backs of the hands and the tops of the toes were shaved with extreme care. When all the hair was removed, it was bagged and labelled.

Then an incision was made in the vein at the ankle and the blood was collected. As the flow slowed, another incision was made just below one of his ears.

Jack studied the musculature of Marcellus's whole body. He was so engrossed that he did not realise the time. Only sunlight spiking through the tiny cellar window right into his eyes reminded him that there was still work to be done upstairs.

He brought down Almyra's body with a great deal of difficulty as she had begun to succumb to rigor mortis during the hours that he had been studying Marcellus.

He dropped her without ceremony onto the cellar floor and went back upstairs to put everything back to rights in time for the maid's arrival.

He made certain that the cellar door was locked and then went upstairs to bed, knowing that Lizzie would be arriving in a matter of minutes. He folded his clothes over the back of the chair, put his nightshirt on and got into bed, ensuring that he disturbed the covers and made the bed warm so as to look as though he had slept in it.

When he at last heard Lizzie, he got up, dressed in his day clothes and washed and shaved. Then he went off to work as usual with only a perfunctory greeting to Lizzie in passing.

That evening, he returned home and continued his work on the werewolves. He discovered that they had a different number of teeth to humans and that their glands were a little larger. Density made the bones heavier, muscles were also denser and joints were more flexible. The heart was a little larger but for his claimed age, Marcellus did not have any ravages which age usually visited upon a body. All organs were healthy and free from disease. Fatty deposits were non-existent anywhere on the body. And the eyes were clear and free from any trace of cataract or impending blindness.

All in all, Jack admired the body for its health and apparent vitality - right up until the point of death, which would most certainly not have occurred for a great number of years if not for his intervention.

He had found just one tiny imperfection – a scar on his abdomen. On close inspection, it had looked like a burn. Jack was puzzled and then cursed himself that he had not thought to ask if anything could harm a born werewolf. Of course a werewolf that had been made could have scars on the body, due to a human's inability to heal with the efficiency of a werewolf - but a born werewolf should have no scars. Jack thought; still, that was one question to ask if the opportunity ever arose again. Jack could only assume that the scar had been caused by contact with silver but because he had not acquired the fact of it, he decided not to note it in his documents.

Jack took the same care and attention to detail with the body of Almyra. Again the body was shaved. He was surprised to note that she was not as hirsute as he had expected her to be but she was very young in appearance, smooth skinned and devoid of blemishes, including moles.

After the blood was drained, collected and labelled, Jack got down to the task of disposing of the body. He had decided not to do a full autopsy on her remains but almost on a whim, he removed her uterus and placed it in a jar of formaldehyde.

First Jack dismembered the body, leaving the torso. Then he immersed the parts in a weak solution of arsenic so as to preserve them and prevent noxious odours.

Once the parts had had time to be suffused with the arsenic solution, he then wrapped the parts in some of the cloth that he had taken from the body and tied the 'parcels' with string. The arms and legs were dismembered further at the elbow and knee joints and also wrapped in cloth and tied with string. The head was put into a large bell jar containing a solution of formaldehyde. It looked nothing like a woman's head without the hair. He labelled this 'Text book case: 8 yr old boy. Source: Russia' and he put it to the back of his other specimens.

For the body of Marcellus, he dug a pit close to the incinerator and part filled it with lime. He placed the body on top and then shovelled lime onto it to fill the hole.

As the weeks passed, the hole would be filled and tamped down as the lime did its job of decomposing the body and the ground level dropped.

The trunks were placed in the far corner of the cellar to await travel arrangements.

Now that everything was tidied away, completed and all evidence disposed of, Jack wrote down all the new details that he had discovered – including the accidental discovery that aconite prevented the werewolves changing to Wolf. Therefore, he surmised, it would also have a similar effect and prevent a werewolf in wolf form changing to human.

Now all that was left for Jack to do was to finish his potions and ointments for the culmination of his work.

In August, Jack decided to repeat the experiment that he had described to Almyra and he took to the streets with exactly two weeks to go until the full moon. He deemed it necessary for the Wolf to be at its weakest to prevent any harm coming to his own self.

Jack went out in his shabby clothes once more. He located a male werewolf first and did nothing to attract its attention but made certain of its location before going off to find another willing companion. He followed a woman and her three companions to George Yard buildings in Whitechapel and became disappointed when he thought that he had missed his chance at the experiment. Only as he was leaving did he hear one of the couples move off, leaving the other couple a semblance of privacy to perform a quick and sordid sexual act.

The woman was making adjustments to her attire and the young man – in uniform, Jack noticed – left her without looking back, his obvious and base needs fulfilled. Jack made certain that his test subject was still in the area and was delighted to find that he was some kind of voyeur; he had been watching the couple as they had swift and business-like sex.

Jack approached the woman from behind and made a pantomime of embracing her and caressing her, pretending that he was her erstwhile lover who had remained to escort her back. Whilst the unsuspecting young man watched, Jack proceeded to first pierce the woman's heart and when the Wolf neither reacted nor retreated, became angry to almost a frenzied pitch and he at last dropped the woman's body when he became exhausted by his exertions.

The Wolf watched for a few seconds more, seeming curious as to Jack's motive but he retreated before Jack could ask any question of him.

Jack had decided to leave the body of the woman where it had fallen but he heard a muted conversation from the other end of the covered alley and he realised that the soldier had not left his companion alone, he had merely moved away to allow her to rearrange her clothing and to Jack's dismay, seemed to be talking with a policeman.

Thinking quickly, Jack gathered up the woman's body and cast around for a suitable hiding place. He found a door leading off the yard unlocked and he thanked his lucky stars that it led onto a stairwell rather than into someone's living quarters. He dropped the body on the lower stairs and arranged it so that she was to all casual glances, sleeping. Then he left the same way the werewolf had gone, he hoped that his luck would hold and that he would not catch up with the werewolf, for he did not like the idea of having to answer awkward questions about his activities.

During September, the remains began to become bothersome to Jack and he took the trunk, late at night and deposited it close to the area where he lived for he could not carry it far without drawing unwanted attention. He hid it in the cellar of a disused building and hoped that it would be undiscovered for a while at least. A few pieces that would not fit in the trunk were buried close to the river in the soft mud which is left at low tide. Jack was not entirely comfortable with the hiding place but he thought that for the majority of the time, the remains would be covered by water and so should be safe from inquisitive dogs. The only danger was from 'mudlarks' – scavenging children (and destitute adults sometimes) who scoured the banks of the river for anything that could be used or sold.

He did become worried that his studies had somehow drawn the beasts to him. How had his learning about werewolves attracted the creatures to find him? He determined to find out more.

Chapter 1

One year, towards the latter part of the nineteenth century, summer was just beginning to go into decline to autumn in the English countryside – not that many could tell in that particular corner of England. There the weather was usually cloaked with smog and the only way to differentiate between summer and winter was by how the residents shivered, or didn't. As is the English quirk, the weather was of the utmost importance – even through the stinking, cloying pollution.

On most evenings, visibility was but a few yards in some places. The smell was much, much more bothersome. Coal soot hung in the air, mixing with the dampness of that particularly wet summer. The product of the soot and damp made for clinging, cloying smog hanging like a pall over the streets and alleys that made up that chosen city of habitation.

The additional stench helped to make that part of the city a miserable place to exist for the majority. Sewage and rotting slaughter waste were regular aromas – and obstacles to be avoided. Little wonder at the population of rats - they thrived. The air just a few feet above their level was almost too thick to breathe.

Fog enveloped shapes and absorbed the scant illumination given off by the gas street lamps. Figures loomed into view suddenly and were just as swift to disappear. To be certain of recognition, a person would have to be almost on top of another – unless there was another means of identifying them.

On that night, visibility was worse than usual - if that were possible. A large warehouse had been burning with a fierce intensity since the early evening and was only being brought under control in the early hours of the morning. People were amassed on the South Docks, watching the conflagration.

It was little wonder then, that the woman standing a mile or so away from the burning building was alone - for the moment.

"You are late – very late," she snapped.

"I realise this, madam and I apologise, but I lost my way. I am not yet familiar with this town."

"No excuse, I left adequate trails. If you had practiced your techniques as you were instructed, you would have picked me up even before I reached here." She was not placated by his apology but she was not angry either. Her voice was calm and even, though her words and tone were harsh. She was softly spoken even though they were alone, and though the hour was late, she did not chance being overheard.

"I also had a small difficulty to overcome, madam. I take it that it was not an obstacle devised by you as I first imagined."

"I left no obstacles. As I explained at your first lesson, until you are reasonably adept at tracking, I will leave only the plainest of trails for you."

"Ah then I think that you need to follow me back to the obstacle, madam, I can show you rather than try to explain my difficulties."

She nodded agreement and they retraced his steps.

As they walked, she noticed his manner altering. He began looking behind and scenting the air, choked though it was by the smoke from the destroyed warehouse. She had noticed the smell of fresh blood begin to mingle with the soot and grime and sewage perhaps even before he had. Not that the stench of slaughtered animals was not prevalent – it was – every other work yard seemed to be a place of slaughter for cows, sheep, pigs and horses. Yet the smell of human blood is far more interesting and it was that that she noticed now. She hung back a little and allowed him to approach first. She knew the place that he had brought her to; it was called Bucks Row, though the street signs - if there were any - were obscured by the smog. The couple were now between rows of houses – slums filled with too many people too poor to get out into semi-decent accommodation.

Her companion had slowed his pace and had almost stopped before she saw what he had come back here to show her. She looked hard at the large bundle lying in a closed gateway. If it were not for the smell of blood pervading the whole area, she would have assumed there was nothing of interest.

"As you can see, madam, this is a fresh kill." His voice shook her from her reverie, she had allowed the scents to swamp her for a moment but his voice had broken into her daydream state. "I had to use all of my concentration to avoid my change. Unfortunately in doing so, I lost your trail and it took a while before I managed to control myself and to find it again."

"By your explanation, I take it that this is not your work," she stated rather than asked. "And in the face of this, you resisted change?" Her tone belied the fact that she was impressed at his restraint even if her words did not.

He nodded affirmation.

She paused to think for a moment. "In that case, I am pleased. You have done well, but come with me. I hear footfalls and I do not think that you would hold up to much scrutiny.

Your teeth are again murderously long and sharp and you are beginning to salivate. The smell of this is invigorating, is it not?" Without waiting for his answer, she turned and melted into the shadows. He took her lead and stood beside her as they watched in silence.

A man approached and noticed the murdered woman's body, but he did not seem to be shocked, could this be the murderer returning to the crime? They watched with growing curiosity.

The man got closer and she realised that he did not yet know that it was a body, he could not see as well as they could.

The moment that he realised what he had discovered, he leaped back with a horrified exclamation and then he looked about him in fear.

From the same direction that he had arrived, another man approached. The first man called to him: "Come and look over here! There's a woman lying on the pavement."

Together, both men bent to take stock of the woman. She was lying on her back, her skirts pulled up indecently high, almost baring the full length of her legs.

The first man whispered to his companion "I believe she is dead."

The other had bent his head to her chest and was trying to hear if she was breathing. He waved a hand for his companion to be quiet.

"I cannot hear her breathing," the first said after a moment's concentration. "But I think that I can feel her breathing, but very little if she is." He lifted his head from her chest. "We should sit her up."

"No, I don't think we should. She has been assaulted. We should get along to work, I'm already late and we will inform the police on our way."

As they left, the second man glanced back as though to

reassure himself, but the two watching saw that he was not reassured at all. Instead he turned back to his journey and made a swift exit from the bloody scene. Had the workman seen something in the shadows? The hidden observers both looked but neither saw anything, although she felt a little uneasy.

"Madam," the young man whispered. "He saw something."

"Yes, I thought so too."

"I am beginning to wonder if this kill is an ordinary murder after all."

"Exactly my thought, continue."

"I begin to think that perhaps this is a Wolf kill, but how can that be? We are more than a whole week past full moon."

"I am puzzled also but lower your voice still further. If this is a Wolf kill then he must be an Ancient to have the power to change without the moon's influence and therefore, it is quite likely that he can hear our conversation as clearly as we can."

He nodded and then stiffened as he heard something else. "Another approaches."

The newcomer proved to be a policeman with a lantern. They again watched in silence as he approached with obvious caution. He held out his lantern at arm's length as he got closer to the body so that he may perhaps see the further extent of the woman's injuries. The light from his lantern glistened on the blood and upon the open eyes of the victim. He bent down to touch the woman. He felt her hand then upwards, higher up her right arm, which was closest to him.

He straightened as he too heard yet another set of footfalls close by. Signalling by waving his lantern, the two watching in the shadows realised that this was a colleague, another policeman.

"Here's a woman with her throat cut. Run at once for Dr. Llewellyn," the kneeling policemen said with urgency.

As the policeman ran to do the first one's bidding, yet another arrived, he was hurrying, either because he had heard the call for the doctor or because the two men that had first found the body had informed him.

As he approached, the first said: "see if you can't find an ambulance will you?"

The watchers found that they could now not move from their observation point without being seen, so they continued to watch as this depiction of human tragedy unfolded before their eyes.

The doctor arrived at the same time as the ambulance. He bent to examine the woman but did not have to spend a great deal of time before he concluded that she was beyond help in this mortal realm.

"Move her to the mortuary. She is dead. I will make a thorough examination there."

Two officers lifted the body onto the ambulance, which was no more than a coffin sized box mounted on carriage wheels.

The procession of police, doctor and a few curious passers-by followed the push-cart-cum-ambulance and at last, the two that had been observing all of this could move from their hiding place. But they moved with caution. They were still cautious that the murderer could be still in the vicinity, watching just as they had.

They did not speak again until they were back at the dockyard. The sun was just beginning to rise, giving a slight glow to the dark and chilly sky, highlighting the underside of the pall of smoke that furled from the wreckage of the warehouse.

After looking out over the slimy water for a time, she turned to her pupil.

"I do not give compliments lightly. I meant what I said

back there. You did extremely well to retain your composure and resist the urge to change in the face of that blood and gore."

"Thank you, Madam Hazel. I appreciate your guidance as much as the compliment you paid me."

She chuckled. "You do realise that the woman had been disembowelled as well as having her throat cut?"

"No, I did not but is that detail important?"

She nodded and her smile widened. "You did better than even you think then. Your instinct to change would have been very powerful, almost irresistible even without the moon's influence and yet you did not fully change. By disembowelling the body, new scents are released; the scent of organs, glands and other juices all force your instincts to overcome your will. These are all tools of the Hunter. I will explain more fully another time. You have passed a test that I did not set for you, one that is more advanced than I thought you to be. Well done."

"So you have changed your mind about not wishing to tutor me?" he said, with hope and eagerness in his tone.

"Hmm, we shall see."

He seemed about to say more but then thought better of it, bowed and turned to walk away.

"I shall see you tomorrow evening then?" she said to his back.

He stopped for a moment and then turned to face her. He removed his stovepipe hat and said: "If it would please you madam, I would be most grateful."

She allowed herself another smile and nodded. "Goodnight, Keme."

She was further impressed when he left so fast that she only just managed to follow him with her eyes.

"He has potential. It is a great pity that he was not tutored

105

from the very beginning, by the one that made him."

"That is but one reason that you were given the task and he is correct, you did not want to tutor him."

"You know that is true and I did not. I can find other things to do with my evenings, thank you."

"As can we all, but you of all people know that an untutored Wolf is by far more dangerous to us on the whole than even a Wolf intent on wholesale slaughter. He can make mistakes, be caught and not know how to escape or avoid detection. We have a good living here in these modern times Hazel. The public in general are above the superstitions of their forebears. They do not believe the old myths and legends, therefore we cannot possibly exist. Science is our ally, at least until one of our kind is caught, killed and examined. Then we would surely be in trouble."

"Was it you who killed the woman?"

"I? No of course not. Why would I?"

Hazel seemed surprised at his answer. "I felt sure that you did."

"But why would you think that?"

"If only because you once tested Nichasin and me in a similar manner," she reminded him.

"Not really, I used animal offal and human urine. That was a controlled test. I would never perform so volatile a test in such a dangerous situation – where the Wolf could be observed by Humes and even caught."

"Yes, I understand now, but it certainly looked as though someone had done this for a reason."

"I agree it does look that way, but whatever for?"

"I am afraid that it is a mystery to be left for another time. I am tired. I am going to find a bed and sleep for a few hours. I have to tutor your protégé again this evening."

"Ah, unfair, you try to make me feel guilty."

"How is it unfair when it is the truth? He is your protégé, your find and yet I tutor him," she said with only the ghost of a smile upon her lips.

"I am supervising though," he said, trying to placate her.

"Only from a distance, yes and I know that you are there, but it is still me that has to have my instincts on full alert at all times, not only watching for danger to myself but also for him, and to assure myself that he is not about to do anything silly or dangerous. That is why we work during the waning moon."

"I did wonder at that. It is a very good idea."

"Yes, now I am away to a bed."

"I ask just one thing more, if I may?"

"Ask while we walk then." She nodded and started off.

"You did not seem surprised that I am here."

"I was not surprised; I knew that you were here."

"You mean that you assumed that I would be here?"

"I *mean* that I knew. I sensed you. I could even identify you positively and without guesswork. I just knew that it was you here, Anton, and no other."

"I was cloaked against such detection," he argued.

"Yet I still knew. You know that I cannot explain how or why. Perhaps it is another skill?" She sounded weary and for a moment Anton regretted pressing the point.

"Indeed, can you sense all Wolves in the vicinity?" curiosity overcame his regret and he pressed again.

"Not as I sensed you, but I can tell you how many there are. I presume that I sensed you so well because we are close, familiar."

"You could be right, amazing." He shook his head in wonderment then continued. "How did he fare this evening?"

"Hah! Why don't you tell me how he did? You followed him, did you not?"

He smiled. "Yes I did, clever minx."

"So you know of the problem he had when he tracked me."

"And you know that is not exactly fair. He had an obstacle to overcome."

"I know that he told me he had an obstacle. I also know that he told me how he had dealt with it. What I do not know is if he told me true. Did he cause the obstacle? If not, did he do as he claims and resist change, even in the face of all that gore? Then, most importantly, did he become confused or did he stay to either plunder the kill or to watch?" she asked, all traces of weariness gone, replaced by her own voracious curiosity.

"He did not cause it, I can verify that he happened upon the body purely by chance and was quite shocked by it. I know that he was shocked, for he did lose control for a moment and his transformation did begin but he recognised the change and halted it swiftly, even though he could not reverse it at that time." He waited to see if she would ask anything more and when she did not, he continued. "As for your last question, he did seem confused but not in the manner I think you mean. He was looking around, not for your trail – for some*thing* - but it seemed to me that he was searching for some*one*. Perhaps he thought that you had placed the body in his path to give him a tougher test and were observing his reactions. Still and all, Hazel, his progress is rapid. He listens to your guidance and he practiced what you instructed him to practice all last evening. He is a willing and eager pupil. Have more patience, you may yet enjoy this."

"Yes I know that you are right – as always. I promise to try. It is just that I sense something. Sometimes I get an uneasy feeling that I can neither explain nor rid myself of then suddenly it disappears."

"It is perhaps another Wolf, a stranger?"

"It could be, but not at this time of the month, surely? And it seems Wolf and yet not Wolf. Perhaps we have a Throwback here."

"We may have but as you know, by their nature they are unpredictable and mostly secretive, especially if they can sense Wolf, their instinct is usually to avoid us. It is only the exceptional one that turns Hunter of Wolf and even they are not the true exception. All Throwbacks are extremely dangerous to us. Keep a weather eye out for it, just in case, though I do not advise informing your pupil for the moment, you do not wish to alarm him or warn the Throwback that you are aware of their presence."

"Quite right and now if you will excuse me, I really must sleep." Hazel had stopped. They were standing next to a very high brick wall with no windows. Just a little farther up the street was an imposing wooden gate, large enough to allow passage of a four-horse cart.

She turned and he saw that she was very tired. She went towards the smaller gate cut into the right hand half of the larger ones.

"What is this place, Hazel, a warehouse?" He caught hold of her arm to stop her. She looked down at his hand as though daring him to keep hold of her and he let go of her arm as her temper suddenly flared.

"Yes it is a warehouse; it is a very well guarded one. I am completely safe here. There is no need for your concern."

"Safe you may well be but you cannot be comfortable."

"It is somewhere safe to sleep, that is all."

"No, you are tired because you are not getting sufficient rest. How long have you been here?"

"A week or so, I move often. I am fine."

"And I tell you that you are not. You are tired and weary.

Your temper is frayed and you have no patience with your pupil. It is because you try to sleep in a place that allows no quiet. I dare say that you have to fight rats for your bedding?"

"Not quite, but you are right, it is noisy. I could do with a bath."

"We go to my hotel then. Go and gather your belongings. I shall wait." She was back in just a few minutes. She waved farewell to the little old man that opened the gate for her and they went to the hotel.

"When you said 'my hotel' I did not realise that it belonged to you and that it would be quite so magnificent."

He smiled at her admiration but asked: "Why on earth were you dossing in that place?"

"It was an easy alternative. I always find similar accommodation and I move frequently; I do not like the fancy trappings of establishments such as this one. Besides, if you live in hotels you have to keep up appearances. I do not enjoy fancying myself up each time I leave the place. Sometimes I like to blend in with the ordinary people, you can learn a lot by doing that."

"It is time that I spoiled you Hazel. This afternoon we will go out shopping."

"I do not want to. I like these clothes, it doesn't matter if I tear or dirty them. With new and fancy clothes, I must take care not to splash them with mud or catch them on anything so therefore, I cannot be myself."

"Hazel, listen to me. You are a beautiful woman; you draw attention no matter what clothes you wear. Admiring glances are yours whether you wear rags or riches but you look suspicious in these rags."

"Why do I?"

"You do because people wonder why such a beauty with such bearing as you carry yourself with is not the mistress

110

of a wealthy man. They wonder why she has no sponsor. Well I shall be your sponsor and by allowing this, it will be so much easier to tutor Keme. Now I shall have you shown to your rooms, a bath is waiting. In the morning I will have a seamstress visit you and you *will* be civil towards her."

"Yes Anton I will and you are right as usual and I am too weary to argue."

He whispered as they were shown upstairs to her rooms: "Just because you are Wolf does not mean that you cannot be *civilised* too."

She realised that she had been living wild and that Anton had forced Keme's tuition onto her in order to bring her back into society.

She bathed and then crawled into the bed, the soft sheets and mattress were a luxury to her and she fell asleep, safe and secure – with no rats to bother her for the first time in months.

111

Chapter 2

Gentle tapping on her door awoke Hazel the next morning. Unthinking, she rose from her bed and opened the door. Anton stood alone in the hallway.

He said: "I thought you might answer your door this way." He kept his eyes fixed on hers. "You need to remember that you have servants now and they are not used to the naked female form, not even the other females."

She stepped back to allow Anton entry to her rooms, then turned back to her bed chamber for find her clothes. She could not find them and was just beginning to pull a sheet from the bed when Anton called from the sitting room.

"There is a robe hanging on the back of a door somewhere in there, I suggest that you use that."

Locating the robe, she put it on; tying the sash as she got back to Anton.

"Morning Anton," she muttered.

"Good morning Hazel." He seemed rather too joyful for Hazel's frame of mind for the moment and she scowled but Anton was determined and he persevered in his niceties. "You look well rested and dare I say, clean?"

"I do not feel particularly well rested. I have had far too much sleep and slept too deeply. My mind is fogged, I feel thick-headed."

"Do not worry. I have asked for coffee to be brought up as well as a decent breakfast. Then the seamstress will come to see you. I do not know how long a dress takes to make but if needs be, I dare say that I could borrow one from one of my lady acquaintances in order that we may step out this evening."

"I have a prior engagement this evening if I recall. I will be tutoring Keme once more."

"Yes, he may join us."

"I would ask something of you, Anton. Who is Keme and where is he from?"

"I am not sure that I should be gossiping about him, Hazel."

"I do not ask for gossip, I ask for fact. I would feel a little less uneasy if I had good background knowledge about him. So if you would not mind, please enlighten me."

"Very well, he is a Native American Indian. He is the descendant of a great and wise shaman of my acquaintance. He was made Wolf, I suppose, by accident."

Hazel's eyebrows lifted at the statement. "How is someone made Wolf 'by accident'? I have never heard of such a thing."

"Ah it is very infrequent but it can happen. The shaman I mentioned, he tutored me many years ago. He had great shape-shifting powers and as you may recall, I had just begun to experiment on my own such ability. I searched for one such as he that could help me. I lived amongst them for many years and saw some of his children grow. When I left them it was not for good. I did return, once just before the Shaman left this mortal plain and a few times since. My eternal youth is not questioned. I am always accepted and the last time that I visited was at a request from the present shaman, Keme's grandfather. He had been tutoring Keme since he had come

113

of age and Keme's lessons had progressed so well that both were certain that Keme would be able to lead his tribe as their shaman. Then a visitor came to their lands. They made him welcome as they do most often. The tribe was just getting used to the stranger when he disappeared. He just went missing without a word and the tribesmen were concerned.

"One evening he was seen in the forest by a hunting party. They hailed him but he did not reply. Curious, they followed. Keme was in the party and he was concerned. From a distance, they heard horrible screaming and noises of tearing and snapping followed by growls and snarls. By the time they had found the source of the noises, the screaming and shouting had stopped. The cause for all this screaming however was evident. A large wolf was standing before them. It was alone and had obviously killed the stranger. Usually the native wolves do not approach man. Of course, living in the same forest, the tribe saw them from time to time but usually in a small pack. Lone wolves are very rare indeed. This one was yet more so. He was a very large wolf and he stood his ground as they approached. They thoroughly expected him to run so that they could take the remains of their friend, but instead of fleeing, it attacked. There was no other choice. The hunters had to kill it or it would be a continuing danger to their tribe.

"What they did not know was that this wolf was one of *our* kind. He was ferocious, very strong and could also think, unlike the wolves that survive on their instinct. This Wolf took down many of their finest hunters but Keme had a magnificent spear, his ceremonial spear, given to him by his grandfather. The spear tip was made from silver. It pierced the Wolf's heart, and even Keme will admit that he was extremely lucky. But what was even luckier for the tribe – though they did not know it – was that there were no surviving injured. That is to say none were wounded – bitten - by the Wolf and left to become Wolf at the next full moon."

Anton stopped and Hazel was about to ask him a question when she sensed someone approaching her door. A knock and then the door opened. A maid entered the room with a slight bob of a curtsey, the door held open by a liveried manservant. Anton thanked them both as they left.

"Ah breakfast. Good!"

They ate in relative silence and no more was spoken about Keme until they had finished breakfast.

As they sipped their coffee, Hazel asked Anton to continue.

"Ah yes, there were no wounded left for the Wolf legacy to continue. I suppose then that you are wondering how Keme became Wolf."

"Don't be so smug. I have a fair idea, it concerns his shamanism I suppose," Hazel said, smiling.

"You could never settle for being just a pretty face, could you my dear?" Anton said. "You are right in a small way. The tribe people carried back their dead and the Wolf body. They did not find the remains of the stranger, but did not concern themselves with that for the time being, they had other matters to deal with. The ceremonies were begun for their fallen brothers and because it was Keme's spear that killed the beast, the kill and therefore the pelt were his. He set to work, skinning the beast very carefully. He had had practice in skinning animals but this was very important, it had to be exact. His father and grandfather both gave advice as they watched but neither helped. Once the skin was off, the meat was stripped from the body and dried in the traditional manner – on frames in the sun having first being heavily salted. But Wolf meat is not very appetising and members of the tribe consumed none of it. It was to be used for the camp dogs in the coming winter when times would be hard. This was yet another fortunate occurrence of course for even I do not know what the result of a Hume eating Wolf flesh would be. The skin was stretched on a hoop and dried. If it were left like that, it would become hard and unyielding, so Keme used buffalo brains to tan the skin to make it supple, stamping the brain mix into the skin with his toes. Eventually the pelt was ready. The head had been left on and Keme had a new ceremonial gown to wear, a Wolf pelt." Anton paused again, he seemed to be thinking and Hazel didn't interrupt his thoughts.

"As you can imagine, Hazel, the tribe had been exceptionally fortunate in the whole business so far. Regrettably, the good fortune was about to desert them completely. By mere coincidence, the next ceremony was held to honour the moon – the full moon that helped the hunter. There were a few unhappy coincidences that contributed to the ensuing tragedy. One was that the pelt was no ordinary wolf as they thought – it was of course, a werewolf pelt. The ceremony of the moon – held at the most powerful full moon, the one closest to Feralia or Halloween and the final ingredient for disaster – the last coincidence - was that the one that had killed the Wolf would be the one to wear the pelt. Keme had offered the pelt to his grandfather in tribute to his shaman but he declined the offer in view of the fact that he had one already and Keme did not.

"Now, some of the legends of Werewolf lore are complete tripe, others are based in fact. You once asked me if a man that was killed by a Wolf would return to plague his killer - that is tripe, as is the legend that states hairs growing on the palms of one's hands denote a werewolf. Tell me, do you have hairs on the palms of your hands? No? Neither do I. However, the legend which tells that if you kill a werewolf, skin it and use its pelt under the bright full moon then you will become werewolf yourself – now that is based upon truth. Although it is not quite as easy as it sounds, the legend began because of shape shifters such as my shaman teacher. I had heard of it

116

but as you can imagine, the practice is not widespread because of its obvious limitations. For one, there can be no going back. Once you have become Wolf, then that is how you remain – a man-wolf."

"And I assume that is what happened to Keme." Hazel said.

Anton nodded; he waited while Hazel pondered for a moment and then smiled as he saw the question forming and she asked:

"But how did they overcome him? It must have taken a while before you could get there, weeks if not months.

"You are quite right Hazel; it did take months of travelling but more of that in a moment. At the ceremony of the moon, Keme began his part and his grandfather noticed that he was altering. His manner had changed to one who was more aggressive than Keme usually was when performing ceremonies. His voice had changed timbre and both of those things are attributes that we know so well, but that had only been spoken of to the Shaman, yet he had the presence of mind to know what to do. He gathered his wits and before the transformation had fully completed, he wrapped leather thong around his grandson and stopped the ceremony. Leather cord would not hold you or me but as Keme was a fledgling, it was just enough to hold him in his struggles. He had enough humanity left to not try to attack his grandfather, which happens to be the only good fortune that occurred that night.

"The shaman sent out the women to collect wolfsbane and he spent the next day preparing potions and stronger bindings for the coming ordeals. As darkness fell, he did not rely on his shamanist knowledge alone; he also took great care for his own safety. He had fashioned a muzzle and much as he hated to use it, it was fixed firmly in place before the transformation began."

"Now as the name implies, wolfsbane is deadly to us but it

117

is also a poison to not-Wolf too. The shaman knew this and took as much care as he possibly could to avoid poisoning himself or his grandson. Over the next two nights the shaman battled with his grandson, finding out that when the first full transformation occurs, the Wolf cannot change back to Hume unless a kill is made. But he also found out something equally important – wolfsbane, in its distilled form prevents Wolf from altering shape so that a Wolf in human form could not change to Wolf and vice-versa. It inhibits the muscles so that they cannot perform the metamorphosis. Because Keme had not killed or eaten human flesh, he was still Wolf on the next morning."

"The same as I was on my first time."

"Ah yes, exactly then. The shaman was distressed at the thought that he could not reverse the change in his grandson. The rest of the tribe were not rejoicing either, but they stayed with them both and supported the shaman in every way possible. A strong cage was made and Keme was forced into it, weakened by the wolfsbane and muzzled and bound, but he was still exceptionally strong in his misery.

"They carried him a long way from their camp and left the shaman alone. Every day, a parcel of meat was left for them as well as other food. Given that this was in the beginning of winter and the tribe had lost a number of their best hunters in the Wolf attack, this was a very difficult time for all concerned. At the approach of the next full moon, Keme was becoming stronger still and the shaman was becoming increasingly concerned for his safety as well as his grandson's sanity. He did not realise that his grandson's mind would be safe because the Wolf cannot reach the human psyche at such an early stage in his Wolfing. Although I do not recommend that a Wolf stay as such for a full month in ordinary circumstances, this was no ordinary Wolfing as we know it."

"I agree, to be forced to remain Wolf is a painful and terrible experience, I do not recommend it."

"You can remember the experience?" Anton asked with ill-concealed eagerness.

"Yes, it haunts me. The hunger seemed to be consuming me from the inside, my gut felt like it was trying to turn itself inside out and there was a scouring sensation on the inside of my skin. It felt as though there were sharp claws scraping the very flesh from my bones as well. I suppose it would be almost the same sensation as the Wolf that Keme skinned would have felt were he still alive when Keme skinned him."

"I really must talk with you in depth about that experience. I assume that you can remember it because of the foretold prophesy; you were even then far more advanced than usual."

"I assume then that the practice of keeping a Wolf from feeding on his first Wolfing is not as unusual as I first thought?"

"It is. I know of a handful of Wolves that have suffered such a first Wolfing but none can remember the experience, only you."

"Then I must be the lucky one." Hazel rolled her eyes at Anton and gave a half smile.

"No, you are the Prophesised One. You are gifted but unfortunately, some gifts are more like a curse. It was necessary; you do understand why they had to keep you from making the kill on your first Wolfing?" Anton's tone had grown tender and he took her hands in his.

"Anton, do not worry about me. The memory is all that is left, I sometimes have dreams about it but nothing to worry about, believe me." She smiled to reassure him and pulled her hands from his, patting his arm.

"I still want to ask about that night."

"Yes and I shall tell you everything I remember, including how I tore my friend to pieces without knowing." She turned

119

her head away then and wiped away a tear that had welled up; she hoped that Anton had not noticed. He had but pretended that he had not.

Anton poured Hazel another cup of coffee to make it clear that that part of the conversation was at an end.

"Eventually the shaman realised that Keme was no ordinary wolf and that he would need human flesh in order for him to be released. His grandson's agony did not overly concern him for he was feeding. The muzzle had been cut off when they knew that he was safely caged but he was still tightly bound. One day, the shaman had a visitor; a tribesman arrived with the woman that brought the food parcel. One of the hunters had seen traces of white men, which was unusual at the time of year in such a wild and desolate place. The hunter bid his shaman be careful in the event that the white man found their camp. It seems that fate had taken a hand once more as the white men did indeed discover his encampment. Although worried for his grandson and protégé, he had to think first of himself and he hid, but close enough to keep watch."

"To begin with, the two trappers seemed decent enough men, they did not touch anything upon finding the fire embers still hot and they "helloo'd" a few times. When they realised that it was not a white man's camp, their demeanour altered somewhat and they then began poking around, looking at everything that belonged to the shaman. Keme had become silent which was what had alerted the shaman to the men's presence, but now he set up a snarling, drawing attention to himself. The shaman told me that it seemed very deliberate of him; he lured the men to him. They were curious of course, but were also very cautious – for Keme makes a large Wolf and they had a healthy wariness of him.

"As the shaman watched, Keme became calm. His eyes flicked to his grandfather briefly and then the ropes and leather thongs that had bound him for a little under a month snapped as though they were rotten. The cage disintegrated, it exploded as Keme made his escape and then he was loose. The shaman did not know how safe he was of course, but because Keme had resisted making his escape – even though it was now blatantly obvious that he could have, at any time – he took a chance and stayed to watch. He was brave but not foolish however, he did keep out of plain sight so as not to be noticed by his grandson.

"The Wolf circled the two trappers who should both have known better, I suppose, and instead of parting and making it look as though the wolf was being hunted or staying together and making enough noise to put the wolf to flight, I can only guess that they fancied their chances at recapturing him. As it happened, nothing that they could have done would have set Keme to flight and they had absolutely no chance of capturing him, neither could they have escaped. From the moment that Keme had decided they would be his prey, they were doomed.

"As the first was taken down, the second pulled his gun and shot Keme but as you know, unless it is silver and an exceptionally lucky shot, killing a Wolf is never instantaneous, the trapper would have died anyway. Keme was too far gone by that time, probably even his grandfather would have been slaughtered, but as I said, he is wise and kept low while Keme completed his kills, plundered the carcasses and found the glands. Then because it was daylight I suppose, Keme began to change back to his human form. Still his grandfather held back, which is again very fortunate because it seems that Keme was very feral at that moment and very unpredictable. Eventually he came to his right mind and fell asleep soon after. He remained sleeping for a full night and all the next day, waking at sunset. Unusually, Keme can recall every detail of his first kills as a Wolf. He has spoken to me about his first experiences. He was visited on occasion by Wolves and though he has difficulty in translating, he could understand them in his Wolf Psyche."

Hazel had listened in almost complete silence and continued in that silence after Anton had finished.

"What are you thinking, Hazel?"

"Only that Keme's experience was worse than mine. I had to endure just one night and one day of that agony and he suffered through a whole month of it. Can he remember it?"

"He has not said that he can, he may remember at some point in the future, he may not."

"How different is it for the Wolves that are born to this? They must have a first time too, is it different?"

"No, it is much the same. Of course, a born Wolf can never be quite sure when he will change for the first time. They are a little like Humes, they mature at different times and so it is with Purebloods. It does seem to be that the more ruthless and bloodthirsty a Pureblood is, the sooner he or she changes, but it could also be the opposite – an early change makes for ruthlessness. My bloodline for example, we are exceptionally early." He gave Hazel a grin, which was far removed from the civilised man that she was talking with; it was so feral that she gave an involuntary gasp of surprise. Anton laughed and Hazel joined in.

"How did you arrive with the Shaman so quickly?" she asked once the laughter had died.

"I was sent a message that it may be in our best interest to go and visit with the Tribe."

"Who would send such a message? And, moreover, who would have that information beforehand?"

Anton didn't respond; he held her gaze and she answered the question for herself.

"The Scribe? But I always thought that he could not interfere in our affairs."

"No, he cannot and he did not send me a message telling me to do anything. It was, in fact, very cryptic and by the time I had deciphered its meaning, valuable time had passed. No matter though, I did arrive in time and fortunately for all involved, Keme was intact, both physically and mentally."

"But what of Keme's family; his tribe, did they allow you to take him away?"

"Not immediately, no. I was in discussion with them for a good few days. I had brought with me some of the purple flower that helps in these situations. Do you remember the flower?"

"Yes, wolfsbane. Of course I remember it; its properties are invaluable, even to an Ancient."

Anton nodded and smiled. "I showed Keme how to utilise its power to prevent change and I believe that he used it until recently, as a matter of course." Anton saw the question arrive in Hazel's mind and pre-empted it. "No, he did not use that method to prevent his change last night. He is exceptional and very much in control. I tutored him all the way here and he listens and learns very well. I would even go so far as to think that he would make a very good Sentinel at some point."

"Really?" Hazel was impressed by Anton's faith in her new protégé.

"Indeed. He has a great thirst for knowledge and he would certainly always keep what he learned to the forefront of his mind. His grandfather taught him that much at least."

"Do you plan to keep him under such close scrutiny, Anton, or am I to be allowed free rein with his lessons?"

"Both my dear. I trust you implicitly and yet, after last night, I have a feeling of dread hanging over this matter, like the pall that hangs over the city. It is inexplicable at the moment but I have a feeling that it will soon come to a head and I'm not sure that I relish that thought."

Hazel said nothing, but sipped at her coffee and contemplated.

Anton recognised her mood and questioned her. "What is it, Hazel? Something disturbs you."

Hazel looked at him over the lip of her cup and waited for a long time before she answered.

"The warehouse that was burned last night, do you know it?"

"No, but I am guessing that you do."

"Until a few nights ago, I was using it."

"When did you move, and was there a reason for you moving?"

Again, Hazel held her counsel for a long moment. "I spent just one sleep in the building that I took you to. I don't know exactly why I moved, I had a feeling and I have learned to take heed of those kinds of feelings."

"Do you think the fire was set deliberately then?"

"No - I know it was."

"Did you see anyone?"

"No, but I think it was Wolf."

Anton's eyebrows twitched in surprise at this information. Hazel's instincts were honed sharper than he had seen them, she had come on in leaps and bounds in the years that they had been apart and though he tried to keep in contact with her, the nature of her work meant that it was not always possible – or safe – for her to do so. If Hazel suspected that another Wolf was trying to kill her or at the very least, drive her off, it boded ill for the structured, if somewhat tenuous, peace in their society.

Chapter 3

One early October evening, Keme and Hazel were to be found awaiting Anton. They had become closer as friends over the preceding days, but not so close as to be able to forego the formal civility dictated by Victorian standards and so they waited in the foyer of the hotel, passing pleasantries as would be expected about the weather and the more palatable items of news. They avoided discussing the news about the latest murders – especially the '*Double Event*' - for fear of becoming engrossed in the details and allowing Keme to become overexcited.

Frustrated, Hazel took to her feet and paced.

"He is more than an hour late, with neither word nor message. This is becoming increasingly worrying." Her hands were flung up, gesturing as she spoke, emphasising her impatience and concern.

"I agree, Madam Hazel, yet what can we do? We cannot go out looking for him; we are already at his home. Where would we begin?" Keme sat waiting with a calm that irked Hazel.

"In London? I do not know. If we had been in Rome, I would know where we could possibly look for him, but here?

125

Your guess is as good as mine."

Hazel glared as Keme's stomach growled audibly and a passing servant turned her head to him and blushed as she frowned in disapproval. Though he had been in London's Society for a good many months under Anton's relentless tutelage, Keme's newly learned manners and etiquette still could not overcome his ingrained habits. He did not apologise, as a gentleman would have done. Anton had, fortunately, been successful in disabusing Keme of the notion that breaking wind loudly was an acceptable method of showing derision and for that, Hazel was thankful.

Keme did not grasp the concept of apologising for naturally occurring bodily functions over which he had no control, and so didn't.

He was exceptionally charming in all other aspects however. His manners were impeccable, his charm and grace were natural and easy. Society ladies – Wolf and Hume alike – were flattered by his merest attention and yet male Humes did not become jealous.

Of course, Keme had been formally introduced to Wolf society long before he was let loose amongst the delicate Humes. Wolves could forgive a slight faux pas a new Whelp could make, whereas sharp teeth and glowing eyes would cause somewhat of a panic amongst the 'cattle' as some of the Wolf snobs were wont to call them.

Keme was unique in Wolf society and it was entirely due to Anton's influence that he was regarded as a fascinating novelty rather than an anomaly to be ostracised without a chance of ever fitting in. It was because of this influence that everyone – not just Keme, Anton and Hazel, were taking Keme's tutoring seriously. Wolves respected Anton and not just on the basis of his age, wisdom or power. Most knew that he had abdicated in favour of his granddaughter, Victoria, but even those who did not know of his status in Wolf hierarchy, were aware of his prowess on and off the fields of combat. Anton may appear old – in Wolf terms at least - but not even age could mask his bearing and the manner in which he carried himself, or, for that matter, his ultimate confidence. To the Hume eye, he was a dignified, middle-aged businessman who enjoyed the company of younger members of his acquaintance – in reality he was more than a thousand years old. Hazel was approaching five hundred years, yet she could pass as someone in her early thirties – easily. Only Keme represented his true age.

It was because Anton commanded such vast respect that any protégé under his wing could be guaranteed any amount of guidance – especially if the protégé in question would have made a fool of himself in view of Humes. No one likes looking foolish and any student of Anton's would be helped to avoid appearing as such.

Of course, often there are also those who would wish that such a privileged and high-profile protégé would fall 'flat on his face' and would possibly even be willing to aid in such a fall but who would dare? A penalty for angering Anton in that manner would at best, be a painful and humiliating experience and at worst, terminal.

Hazel decided at last, that Keme's stomach had the right notion.

"Come, Keme, we cannot wait any longer. Anton may well have great influence with the maître d', but I doubt that he will hold the table for very much longer, if indeed, it is still available to us."

The doorman hailed a cab for the pair and they travelled to the restaurant. Hazel waited for Keme while he paid their driver, and when she saw the grin break across the driver's face, she made a mental note to have words with Keme about over-tipping.

The maître d' was very put out at the lack of punctuality, especially as he had other customers waiting to be seated but he did not give voice to his annoyance.

Hazel and Keme were led to a table and a wine list was placed before them. They were just about to order their meal when Anton arrived, quiet and subdued.

Hazel frowned but Keme greeted his mentor as usual, with a polite nod.

Anton sat down, neglecting to greet Hazel. She ignored this slight and waited.

The waiter appeared and asked to take their order. Anton ordered for all three without asking. The waiter glanced at Hazel as though to ask if the choice met with her satisfaction. She allowed a strained smile and handed the menu to him.

Anton began to speak even as the waiter left.

"Almyra Willoughby and Marcellus Salter are missing."

Hazel was puzzled by this news. "Why would they go missing?"

"There is the mystery." Anton sighed. "They were due to announce their engagement this weekend, with a celebration two weeks hence, on the full moon. So why would they go missing?"

"Obviously not to elope," Keme said. "If they were not hiding their love and everyone was in celebration, there would be no need to run away."

"You are right, Keme, apart from the fact that Almyra just loves an excuse for a celebration, their respective families were delighted at the match," Anton said.

"There has been no feud between the families?" Hazel asked.

"Not for centuries, as you know. Not one Wolf opposed this match – which is nothing short of miraculous in itself.

The fortunate thing is that no one will be throwing wild accusations of foul play around."

"Could they have been killed, do you think?" Keme asked.

"I seriously doubt it, Keme, but stranger things have happened," Anton said.

"But both of them? That is a great coincidence if they have been killed separately and it does not bear thinking about if they were dispatched together." Hazel looked at her companions in turn as she said this.

"Indeed it does not. Yet we do not know where they are. The last time anyone recalls seeing them, they were together at the last full moon which would be on or around the 21st of August."

"Would that date be significant?" Keme asked.

"Not especially, only that they had gone out hunting together," Anton explained.

Hazel was quiet as she contemplated what Anton had told them.

"Your view then?" Anton asked Hazel.

She wrinkled her nose and shook herself from her reverie. "It could be a Hunter."

"Nonsense!" Anton's voice had raised and he lowered it again as people around them glanced over. "Sentinels have virtually eradicated the Hunter!"

"How do we know? How do you know? Sentinels are a breed apart almost, loners who don't keep in touch with each other, and the pariahs of Wolf society."

"What are Hunters and who or what are Sentinels?" Keme asked quietly.

Anton looked to Hazel to answer him.

"Oh no! This one is yours," she said.

"A Hunter is almost always a Throwback. More often than not, it is a Hume Throwback rather than Wolf."

"What is a Throwback?" Keme interrupted.

"Ah, *'Throwback'* is an anomaly of our species. It is something that should not have been born. A Wolf mating with a Hume or a Wolf making their own mate, the offspring of both come under the term 'Throwback'. A Wolf/Hume Throwback is exceptionally rare – but possible. It is usually a female Hume, which means that the birth will go undetected, for unless the male Wolf keeps in contact, he will not know of the child. If a female Wolf were to become pregnant by a Hume male, she would know to kill the child – if indeed, she carried to full term." Anton explained as best he could but Hazel could see that Keme had not quite grasped it.

"If you were to fall in love with a Hume and wished to be with her forever, she would have to be bitten by another Wolf, for if you made her, and then mated, your children would be Throwbacks. Our First Laws state that a Throwback shall not be suffered to live," Hazel helped Anton with his explanation.

"Is that not callous?" Keme asked.

Hazel smiled as she watched Anton explain further.

"It is to protect us all. I am loath to use the term: 'for the greater good', but it fits. A Throwback is defective, it will eventually go insane and our society relies upon total secrecy in order to survive. Man is ingenious; the inventions of the last century alone would make your head spin, for it certainly does mine. Man is vicious and can be unnecessarily cruel. You know little of our culture or history yet, Keme, but I can assure you that there have been far fewer wars between Wolves in our entire history than those between man and his brother in even the past half a century." Anton paused to make sure that no one was able to listen closely to what he was telling Keme.

"Of course, we utilise those wars to our best interests, and why shouldn't we? We become strong on the glands of the war-dead, but we do not fight with each other. Our hierarchy is set. Our Leader, to all intents and purposes is immortal. We do not reproduce with such abandon as do Humes. Planning – careful planning is necessary. Even to make a Wolf by biting is now forbidden without permission. We must protect ourselves."

"But surely if we can create another Wolf so easily, we could overrun the human population?"

"Exactly so, but think, if one Wolf made one other on every full moon and on the following full moon, those Wolves each made one other and on and on; in less than half a year, there would be an army of Wolves, all new and hungry and wanting to feed. In less than a decade, what would we eat? We would need wars between ourselves to keep our numbers in check. Perhaps that is the real reason for Humes going to war upon each other?"

"Am I then, a Throwback?" Keme said after a moment of contemplation.

"No. You are different and as yet, we do not know how different you are, but you are not a Throwback. You were not born, you were made – and not by the usual method, by being bitten. We have sent for The Scribe, another Ancient who records all. Every prophecy, every deed or misdeed of note, he has knowledge of it all."

Hazel saw Keme's confusion and explained to him: "We are almost certain that your particular circumstance is unprecedented, but the Scribe will know for sure. Either way, your studies continue but this is perplexing. We must remain vigilant, there is something in the air and it is beginning to smell like danger."

"Does any of this mean that I shall be given the opportunity of a hunt soon?" Keme surprised Hazel with the eagerness she heard in his voice. She had not realised that he was quite so in control of his bloodlust and, until then, when his guard

131

slipped for a moment, he had appeared almost nonchalant about his tutoring.

"Anton, have you given Keme leave to make his own kill yet, or have you always provided prey?"

"He has made kills," Anton replied. "But, oh, do you mean have I tracked them down for him to take? The answer is yes, I have tracked all of his kills so far and he followed."

"So Keme has not chosen his own prey?"

"No, I did that for him."

"In that case, I see the reason for your impatience. When we next hunt, we shall discuss your choice of prey and if it is a good one, made for the right reasons, I shall stand back and give you full rein."

"Really?" Keme was unable to conceal his delight.

"I think that you are ready," Hazel nodded.

Keme came as close to excitement at her reply than she had ever seen him. He excused himself with the correct propriety and went outside for a moment; Hazel assumed it was to get a breath of fresh air, until she heard the distant howl. She stopped talking and looked to Anton for his reaction. He was as astounded as she was. When Keme returned to the dining room, flustered and flushed in the face, she expected an apology or explanation but was surprised when he seemed as shocked as everyone else in the restaurant was.

"Was that you, Keme?" Hazel asked in a hushed voice.

"No," he answered and then again: "no, really it was not. I heard it as I was thinking on your decision to allow me to choose my kill. It came from quite a distance, how could it have been me?" Keme reasoned.

"I accept your denial but you had time to go that distance and howl your delight and get back here, but if you say it was not you, then I believe you." Anton said.

Hazel said nothing.

They ate the remainder of their meal in silence and as soon as they had finished, they made their way out and onto the street once more. The walk to their destination was a short one and they continued their silence as they progressed, each contemplating their own thoughts. Keme had no idea where they were going or for what purpose. Anton and Hazel knew that they were going to a meeting of Wolves and that questions would be asked of the three of them.

The meeting had been called by a number of families, two of whom were missing a child. Marcellus and Almyra's families had reported their disappearances to Anton and were hoping that the meeting would bring good news.

Anton met with both families before the meeting began and received the news that there had been no sightings of either. Then they went on into the large room where a number of Wolves were gathered already. Anton recognised one Wolf, the presence of whom gave Anton good reason to frown. He had not been invited and he should not have been there. He pointed the Wolf out to Hazel and whispered, "here's trouble."

Hazel understood Anton's annoyance and the reason for it and shook her head. "Let him alone, we shall deal with him if and when he becomes a problem. If we cause a fuss now, he will be further filled with his own importance and will martyr himself in the eyes of his group," Hazel said in a whisper. "Better to allow him to watch and listen to the proceedings so that he can at least give the warning."

"I doubt that he will give any truthful report, but I shall leave him alone as you ask."

There was no stage to speak of but the assembly had been provided with seating, so all could see the three at the head of the room if they remained standing. Anton began by thanking them for coming.

"We are gathered this evening because we are missing two

133

youngsters. Marcellus Salter and Almyra Willoughby have not been seen for a number of weeks and their parents and families are becoming worried. This is not the only reason for the meeting, however; we also have another, equally disturbing dilemma. There would seem to be a serial murderer at large in the city of Whitechapel." Anton allowed the gathered assembly to voice their opinions to one another for a few moments and then held up his hands to appeal for silence once more.

"There are other factors of which we think you should all be aware. I shall allow the Sentinel Exemplar to tell you of these factors."

Hazel stepped forward and waited for the room to become silent.

"I have a theory that the murders are being carried out by a Throwback." She paused to wait for the hubbub to rise and then held up her own hand to ask for silence. "I shall take questions later, but at this moment, please allow me to speak. I believe there is a Throwback loose in the area of Whitechapel."

She stopped speaking as the furore erupted from the audience. Many voices asking questions at the same time made for a row that she could not interpret into one discernible question or another. She held up her hands in a plea for silence but it did not come. Men were beginning to rise from their seats and arguments had broken out.

Anton stepped forward and roared. The sound, unlike any that the assembly were used to, stopped their squabbling and though they did not all sit down, they were at least quietened.

Anton waited, glaring at individuals until they sat once again, then he spoke. "Sentinel Exemplar is by no means obligated to keep you informed; she can go about her business without any of you knowing where she is or what she is about. She has called this meeting to inform us all of the very real danger that we face. She did this to keep you safe; I suggest that you give her at least the courtesy of listening to her. If that courtesy is not forthcoming, then she will leave you to it – and so shall I."

Hazel took the front once more. "As I was trying to tell you all, I believe there is a Throwback and I believe he knows what he is doing. His actions seem to be deliberate and calculated and he uses some techniques designed to lure a Wolf to change."

"There is no such technique!" a voice from the back of the room interrupted.

Hazel stopped speaking and looked directly at the person who had spoken. He shrank at her gaze and sat back down.

"I am not here to argue. I am here to tell you what I have discovered and what I believe to be the cause of this trouble. I care not if you disagree with my theory or me, and whilst that may seem arrogant, again, I care not. There *is* a Throwback, it *is* murdering streetwalkers in Whitechapel and as yet, I do not know why, but I shall execute it and if I find out the reasons behind its actions, then I may or may not inform you. But, in the meantime, it may be a danger to us and therefore, I am warning you all to be vigilant and to warn your friends, family and other Wolves of the danger. Please do not take this lightly, do not underestimate the Throwback, it may have limitations of being only part-Wolf but I know from bitter experience that it could also have inherited skills that we cannot measure. I believe it is targeting Wolves on purpose."

"With all due respect, Sentinel, I do not understand your theory. If these murders are the work of a Throwback, why are none committed at full moon? There have been women slaughtered, more even than the press have got hold of and emblazoned across the pages of their so-called 'news' papers – none of these were Wolf so what is the explanation for this?"

The older gentleman did not sit back down after speaking and the uproar around him proved that most in the gathering agreed with his questions.

Hazel waited until the hubbub had died down before beginning her explanation.

"Sir, my theory, for the moment, is just that – a theory. If another Wolf has a better explanation for these murders, then I am most willing to listen and, if necessary, act upon them." This seemed to placate the gentleman somewhat and he retook his seat.

"I know that you have other things on your mind, I gather there is yet no word of your son or his fiancée?"

No, there has been nothing from either of them since the summer."

"And they would not have eloped?"

"I clutched at that straw for a time, but the fact that Almyra herself had organised the engagement party speaks volumes. She would not have missed it, and Marcellus indulged her every whim. No, they were both looking forward to the engagement, and the wedding, which as you know, would have been a celebration of massive proportions."

"As I thought, yet I had to ask the question," the Sentinel said. "Now, as far as my explanation to my theory goes, I believe that this Throwback is murdering women – prostitutes for the most part – because they are willing to accompany him at the promise of a few coins. They are also weaker than he is and are obviously expecting that he becomes intimate with them at some point and that would enable him to get close. He has enough knowledge of our behaviour, I believe, to cut his victims to allow the Wolf to scent blood, but anyone with a basic knowledge of mythological creatures would know to do the same. If he were hunting vampires, he would probably perform a similar ceremony. The reason that I believe he is

136

targeting Wolves is because he also disembowels his victims. He steals organs, and the scents that the victim then emits are far more intoxicating to Wolf senses. Believe me, I know, I saw the first of his victims, and Keme here," she indicated to the young man next to Anton, "was probably the first to see her, he may have missed the murder by only a matter of moments." She waited for silence to descend once more after the shocking statement.

"I believe that this Throwback is not a Hunter in the conventional sense. He does not necessarily wish to track us in order to slaughter us for a bounty, I believe he has a more nefarious reason for tracking us, and he uses the murders to identify who is Wolf, but he does so at such a time that we are not at our strongest. That is why none of the murders have taken place at full moon. I believe that he also targets newer and younger Wolves, those who have not achieved their full potential, those such as Keme. He has been Wolf for less than a decade. I think that this could be the reason that he has seen half of the murders, the very first one and another just over a week ago."

A man, positioned towards the back of the room stood and waited to be acknowledged before he spoke. Once Hazel had nodded to him, he began his statement. "Earlier, in the summer, I had a strange experience and if I may, I shall recount it to you." Again he waited for Hazel's acknowledgement before he continued. "I was passing through one of the slum areas after midnight and I caught the sense of another Wolf. I was then set on hurrying through his territory for I did not wish to appear to be trespassing and I did not – I still do not – wish to explain my reasons for being in that place." He paused again, seeming to wait for a signal to continue or at least assurance that no question would be asked as to the reason for his being in that place at that time. Hazel smiled at his secrecy, as did

Anton.

The man nodded and continued his tale. "I watched as four Humes came close, they were in a state of drunkenness and it amuses me to watch them as they fumble in their prelude to sex," his face broke into a smile as he heard murmurs of agreement. "One of the couples walked on and past me, out of the yard where they had wandered for privacy, but the other couple performed as I had expected them to and I watched as they indulged in their performance of sex. I admit that I am constantly astounded at how fast they can perform this act." Again, his comment was met with amused agreement.

The man's voice became more serious as he recounted the next part of his account. "As the female was adjusting her clothing, the male left her, I assumed that he had finished with her and had no more use for her. It would appear that the other that I had sensed earlier, assumed the same as I did. I had thought that this was perhaps an Ancient who could mask his presence from me because I did not sense him very strongly, but now, as I have listened to the Sentinel Exemplar, I shall assume that it was perhaps the Throwback."

The man could not continue for the furore he had induced with his tale and until it died down, he stood, silent and waiting. "The Throwback took the female from behind and leaned forward and stabbed her in the heart. She died almost immediately but he did not stop his frenzy; he seemed to become angry and I could not count the times that he stabbed this woman. All the time he was attacking the female, he was looking at me. I scented the blood but as you know, I am no whelp and such small encouragement does not affect me in the way that it would now appear he was wanting. I left the yard area quietly and without fuss, I believe he showed a certain disappointment when I made my move to leave. If anyone should doubt my tale, I believe it was reported in the newspapers, the Throwback had moved the body into a stairwell where it was discovered early in the morning by someone who assumed that she was sleeping. The newspaper reported that she was stabbed thirty nine times."

Once he had finished speaking, the audience took a moment as though to catch its collective breath. Then the tumult began, questions were asked of neighbours and opinions and theories were shared. Hazel allowed the hubbub to continue until one by one the amassed audience turned their faces toward the front of the room once more and waited for either Anton or Hazel to say their piece.

Neither had time to formulate and voice an opinion.

"Sentinel, one more question if I may?" The gentleman who had spoken before stood again. He waited for acknowledgement before continuing. "My son and his fiancée, could they have fallen foul of this Throwback?"

"Two Wolves? It is very unlikely that he could overpower them, yet I cannot discount it. We can see that he is extremely sly, by the methods he already employs. I have one question that I cannot answer, however. Why is he doing this? I believe that if we are to find him, we need to all be on our guard and because of the serious nature of the situation, more sentinels will be joining me very soon, from Europe."

"That could prove an unpopular move," a voice from the back of the room interrupted - its owner hidden in the shadows. "One Sentinel in London is one too many for most decent Wolves to stomach. If you bring in an army, you may turn the tide of acceptance – what little you have – against you."

"On the contrary, David," Anton stood to speak over the growing clamour of agreement for the Wolf's statement. Anton had anticipated this kind of argument the moment he saw David, which is why he had pointed him out to Hazel as

139

an insurrectionist. "The 'decent' Wolves have nothing to fear from the Sentinels. As ever, it is those with something to hide who fear their presence." Anton held up his hand to prevent David's retort. "And before you get up on your high horse and reply in righteous indignation, I will say this: the majority of Wolves have a little something to hide. We all have secrets, the ones who fear the Sentinels most seem to be the ones who have not had dealings with them and so do not fully realise exactly what they do, or how they benefit our society. The ones that do not fear the Sentinels are either foolish in their belief that they can escape detection for their crimes, or are dead. I know that you have no affection for the Sentinels, David, I do not know - or care - why this is, but I request that you leave your campaigns outside any meeting called by Sentinel Exemplar. She did not have to warn every Wolf in London to be wary of this present danger, she could have allowed this Throwback to carry on doing what he is doing and waited until she was certain of his intent before even bothering to find him. The fact that she is keeping you all informed is surely proof of her good will, even in the face of animosity from you and your group. There has been a select few Ancients invited here tonight, you were not invited as you are neither Ancient nor influential enough to be widely listened to, yet you were not refused entry and were not ejected. You may either go forth and tell those few in your group of these theories, and help to warn of this possible danger, or not. I personally care little either way. The Sentinel Exemplar on the other hand, has proven that she does care that there may be a Throwback – a potential Hunter of Wolf – on the loose in London and she wishes to prevent it from harming any Wolf – including you and your group."

"You misunderstand my reasons for being here, sir," the Wolf named David began. "I heard of this meeting and instead of assuming that it was called so that the elite can further force their changes to our society upon us all, I came to listen to what was to be said. I listened and fully appreciate the grave situation. I merely mentioned that if we were to bring a large influx of Sentinels to our city, there would be many who would assume that the story of a Throwback is an excuse, a ruse to bring Sentinels in and once they are here, how would we send them back? We would be under martial law, would we not?"

"I think, sir," Hazel stepped forward and placed her hand on Anton's arm to hold him from further reply. "That you came here because you share belief in the assumption that Sentinels wish to conquer Wolf kind. Believe me or not, we certainly do not. We are loyal to our Lycaeon and her ancestors. I do not need to reiterate that, it is a fact - oft-times proven by action and deed. I *will* reiterate the fact though, if only because you seem to either not know or have forgotten. Sentinels are ultimately loyal to our Lycaeon. If I were to decide that your presence here is nefarious, I could execute you here and now and face no recrimination or reprisal. Instead I allowed you to stay and hear the discussion. I allowed you to question my motive and I will allow you to leave, unharmed and unhindered and I sincerely hope that you will go back to tell everyone in your group – and indeed, anyone that will listen – of this possible threat to our more vulnerable Wolves."

"You will allow me to leave unharmed?" David sneered. "Am I supposed to be grateful for that concession?"

"Yes, I think that you are," Anton said, despite Hazel's hand on his arm, squeezing tightly. "Sentinel Exemplar has acted with decency, openness and civility towards you, towards every Wolf invited here this evening. There is a very real danger to our society which will only be exacerbated by denial or ignoring of the facts."

141

"These facts, my Lord, seem to be corroborated by the Sentinel's own lap-dog. No one else has been witness to any of the murders..." he was interrupted then by a man sitting next to the gentleman that was missing his son.

"Actually sir, I have also spoken to one who has seen the victim of such a murder. My daughter came home in a most distressed state. She saw the victim's remains over at Mitre Square not a week since. It was referred to as the 'Double Event' or so I am led to believe. She said that she was compelled to change because of the odours caused by the severity of the mutilations. The woman's face had been sliced open and her throat cut such as to almost sever the head. She had been hacked open, as one would gut a slaughtered animal. The intestines were pulled out and laid over one shoulder. The smell of all of this so excited my daughter - who as all of you that know her, is the most genteel lady when the full moon is not upon us – that she almost changed to full Wolf there and then."

"Yes, it seems tragic that your daughter should have witnessed such depravity, yet it also seems all too convenient."

"Sir, I protest! Do you accuse me of a lie, or my daughter?" The man stood, pushing his chair backwards, his expression furious yet he struggled to remain calm.

It seemed then, that sanity had returned to the Wolf named David, for when he was confronted by the snarling and angry Wolf whom he had insulted, he made his apologies and left the room.

The hasty departure of David opened up the dialogue in the room and if the intent was to encourage scaremongering and objection to Sentinels coming to the city, the actuality was the reverse. The Wolves voiced nothing but support of any measures deemed necessary by the Sentinels and furthermore, declared their intent to inform every Wolf even throughout the country if necessary. All Wolves would be protected in this time of uncertainty, they vowed, even to the extreme measure that each Wolf would be forbidden to go out alone until the state of emergency was resolved.

The debate went on long into the night and many subjects were covered. From speculation of who the murderer could be, to the very real danger of the police being drafted into the area in huge volumes and what it could mean to Wolf society if the police ever saw one of their number in a state of 'wolfishness'. They all knew that the more the police were drafted in, the greater the danger that one would be seen and discovered.

Hazel was disturbed that neither Anton nor Keme were as concerned as she was about the possibility of an extra police presence in the area. She tried a number of means to bring the subject up for discussion again but the assembly was less concerned than she was and she was frustrated in her attempts.

It was a very contemplative Hazel that made her way back to the hotel rooms alone. Anton had not noticed her leave, but Keme did. He allowed her to go without asking why she was leaving early and did not mention it to Anton until they left the meeting.

"Hazel left a while ago so we should not wait for her to come out," Keme said as he walked past Anton.

"When did she leave?" Anton turned to voice the question toward Keme's departing back.

Keme just shrugged and kept his back to Anton.

"Keme! I am speaking to you, please turn around and show some courtesy. Your manners are better than this."

There was no hint of belligerence in his manner as Keme replied to the admonishment. "I cannot be certain of exactly when Hazel took her leave; it was an hour or more since. She did not say goodbye or offer any explanation as to where she was going. I saw her leave and that is all."

"You did not think to mention it to me?"

"I thought of it, but I saw that you were busy with other Elders and did not wish to interrupt." Keme made to walk away again and Anton caught his arm for an instant, giving Keme cause to turn.

"I do not know where it is that you go of an evening and it is not my business, but I would ask that you are careful. You do not have skills yet to navigate the city streets as you did back home in your mountains and forests, and I worry for your safety."

Keme looked Anton in the eye and said, "I may not be fluent in the language of these streets but I shall get by. I will be careful as you ask – I always am - and I understand your concern for my well-being. Thank you Anton, you are a good friend." Keme turned to leave once more. As an afterthought he turned back to face the older man, removed his hat and bowed towards Anton in a mark of respect for his mentor.

Anton smiled as he watched Keme saunter away and his grin broadened with sheer pride as Keme was enveloped by shadows and then moved so fast that he all but vanished.

Anton had a fair idea where Keme was heading – or at least the purpose for his journey, and he thought that perhaps it was not such a bad idea, and altered his own course and went to visit one of his *acquaintances* – perhaps he could persuade her to lend Hazel a nice dress for the theatre.

Hazel had gone back to the hotel for only a brief time, just long enough to change out of her smart clothes and into the clean but ragged ones that she had been wearing before moving in to the hotel. She kept them for occasions such as this. She wanted to go out into the slums and to not stand out like a jester at a graveside.

She didn't think of Anton or of Keme, her immediate

144

priority was for the whole of the community, not individuals. She would be more able to indulge in her close companions after she had investigated what was troubling her right now.

When she had changed and left the hotel, Hazel made her way to the area where they had witnessed the murder a month before. Once there, she scaled the fence easily and dropped down into the yard.

Too much time had passed, it seemed, for she could not sense what she was searching for. Too many footfalls had been made in the area in the time. She cursed herself for not thinking of this earlier, but it couldn't be helped, she was too late here.

She was not certain of what it was that she needed to find, but there was an insistent nagging of something that she had overlooked at the back of her mind and she knew that until she had found what it was, she would not feel at ease.

Hazel wandered the area, casting around in her head for the point that she was missing. She did not know what time it was and she did not know where she was heading but she was always aware of her surroundings in the fact that there were sometimes others close by – mostly Humes, and just one or two Wolves. No one took any notice of her.

Then someone did.

Her elbow was caught hold of – not in a harsh manner, but not gentle either - and she turned to face the one who wanted her attention. She heard him gasp in surprise when he realised that the woman he was about to proposition was his tutor and he let go of his hold on her arm.

"Is there something I can help you with, Keme?" Hazel asked with humour in her tone.

"Ah, Madam Hazel. I did not realise it was you."

"I would say that was perfectly obvious," her smile was widening, and he grew more flustered. "I repeat; is there something that I can help you with?"

"No, most certainly no. I must apologise, Hazel," then he gave up with pretence and confessed. "There is no point in lying to you madam, I would not insult you by trying. I was enveloped by a need, I am afraid it is one of the baser desires and I am sure that I need not go into details."

Hazel at once felt compassion for Keme; he must be very lonely, so far from everyone that he knew and everything that was familiar to him. "I understand and please do not feel ashamed or embarrassed about this. We all have those kinds of needs but I believe that Anton would have introduced you to someone who could help alleviate the problem?"

"And indeed he has, but sometimes… if you would please excuse me, I feel uncomfortable in explaining. This is most odd. I think that I have become a little too close to you to be able to discuss such indelicacies with you now. Please accept my apologies."

"Why Keme, I do believe that you are blushing." Hazel laughed and took Keme's arm in hers and led him out of Whitechapel towards an establishment that she knew of that could take care of his particular predicament.

When she had shown him which door to knock upon and whose name to drop into the conversation, she said goodnight to her pupil and allowed him to compose himself before making use of the brothel that she had led him to. She was still smiling as she let herself in to her rooms at the hotel, her own problem, for the moment at least, forgotten.

Hazel drifted to sleep feeling safe and peaceful. She was aware of Anton as he returned and his presence arrived on her mental *radar* but the awareness did not disturb her.

Out beyond the walls of the hotel there was a figure looking up at the windows, wondering which room Hazel was sleeping in. He knew she was back at the hotel - he had followed her.

By chance, he had spotted her as she left Keme at the brothel and had taken advantage of her good mood and therefore her uncharacteristic complacency and kept out of sight and out of range of her senses.

Before morning broke, the yard at the back of the hotel was again deserted until the kitchen servants began their daily grind, starting their workday by preparing breakfast for the guests. Hazel knew nothing of the one that had followed her and her breakfast was served earlier than most of the other guests, and she was out and about long before Anton went looking for her.

When Anton finally caught up with Hazel, she was relaxed and refreshed. She had spent a very pleasant morning, strolling around the park, watching children playing and feeding ducks. She had even indulged in conversation with a polite and well-to-do young man who had picked up a glove that she had dropped and returned it to her. His mild flirting had put her in an excellent temper and on spotting Anton, she waved to him and he couldn't help but notice the glow in her cheeks and the nimbleness of her step.

"What have you been up to?" he asked, smiling because her mood was infectious.

"I was just walking, watching people going about their daily lives. I sometimes feel a little sad for the Humes; they have but a short time to enjoy this life."

"If you have never had it, you never miss it, Hazel. They do not know and so cannot mourn."

"I suppose so, but still, I am glad that I can enjoy it – all of it, for I have seen both sides of the coin."

Anton nodded agreement. Then his face clouded for a moment and he asked her about what was bothering him. "Now Hazel, I must ask, why did you leave without saying anything last evening?"

147

"It wasn't last evening, Anton; it was past evening and well into last night when I left. The meeting had fizzled out into a reunion of Ancients. I was bored, Keme was bored and I had things that I needed to do. Which reminds me, I went out to try to understand what it is that's bothering me and on my travels, I met Keme. He was in Whitechapel, close to where he had his first lesson with me, where he encountered that..." she paused, "that problem."

Anton looked up when she paused. "What was he doing there?"

"He was looking for 'entertainment' of the female variety." She was smiling as she explained.

"And what were you doing there?"

Her smile evaporated at his question. "I was looking for a solution to a problem that I cannot quite put my finger on for the moment."

Anton realised that there would be no point in pressing for more information, for Hazel did not have it to give. "I have a theory, would you like to hear it?"

Hazel looked at Anton and her directness always made him believe that she was not afraid of anything – not his authority, or that of his granddaughter, the Lycaeon. Hazel was the epitome of impartiality and therefore perfect for the position she held, and he allowed her the time she wanted as she searched his eyes for guile or teasing. Satisfied, she nodded that she would. They continued walking along the pathway, deep in conversation.

"I think that there are more than coincidences at play here. You arrive from Europe to tutor my ward and before you have time to settle yourself into any kind of routine, the warehouse where you have taken to lodging is burned to the ground." He paused for a moment, waiting to see if Hazel would allow him to continue or would interrupt with comments of her

148

own. When she did not interject, he continued. "Yes, I know that you flit from place to place before you at last settle in one place when you arrive anywhere, but that is surely not common knowledge and therefore, the person that set that fire would not know that you were likely to no longer be where he had been watching for you."

"How do you know he had been watching me?"

"How do *you* know that it was a male?"

"Pah!" She huffed at his retort. He knew her so very well. "You may as well continue."

Anton smiled at her acknowledgement of him keeping a weather eye on her. "Since the day you arrived in London, I have been watching your every move."

"But, I can sense you, even when you are not close. I knew you were there that night on the dock side."

"Yes and it surprised me because you had not the skill to do that for the three weeks that I have been watching you. I was therefore amazed that you had suddenly acquired the skill."

She nodded for him to continue.

"Perhaps you did not sense the one that has followed you because he is not an Ancient, he is not even an Elder and he stays well into the background because, I believe, he knows who you are and more importantly, *what* you are."

"And why, do you think, would he have availed himself of that knowledge?"

"Because he has something in which you would be interested, in your capacity as Sentinel Exemplar."

"So the one I have noticed on occasion has had me under closer scrutiny than I have thought." She did not ask this as a question, she was mulling it over out loud. "Do you think he has been sent by someone, some Wolf, to keep an eye on my activities?"

149

"Perhaps, but who in their right mind would track a Sentinel and chance discovery, for payment? On the other hand, if you wanted a Sentinel followed, would you be able to trust someone to do it for you? They may just as easily inform the Sentinel that they had been sent and betray their employer. It makes no sense, so I believe that the one who wanted to know your whereabouts is the one doing the following. I have not heard of any questions being asked of you or your whereabouts but I suppose the grapevine is as good a source of information as any."

"But my only activity, as you put it, is that of tutor to Keme. There are fewer Throwbacks active than I recall – the last one was executed in Prussia, I believe, a long time ago. It was good counsel that advised allowing certain members of our clans to find out about the dangers of Throwbacks. I believe the knowledge was not always so widely discussed and it was left for Wolves to deal with the creatures themselves."

"You are right, Hazel, we did assume that First Laws would be obeyed unquestioningly by all. It would seem that not all Wolves could comprehend the danger of allowing a Wolf-Hume hybrid to exist and those in that situation needed to know exactly why they had to kill their offspring."

"Yes, the ruling elite cannot grasp the concept of being disobeyed and the lower castes don't always want to conform without demur."

Anton looked at Hazel with a frown.

"You know I am right in what I say, Anton, some Wolves are not just snobs about Humes, they are also snobs when it comes to Piaculum and Aeger Wolves too. *Some* are even snobs where the other bloodline is concerned, the alternative one to yours." She saw his expression and responded without need for pause. "I would beg you to not give me *that* look, Anton, you know as well as I do that I speak the truth. Amongst your family, there are those who think they are more elite than any of the other three lines and so are allowed concessions."

"Even if that were true…"

Hazel interrupted then. "Even if that were true?" her incredulity sounded in her voice and it was fast turning to anger. "You *know* it is true! Yes, I know that I am only a Sentinel and an Aeger to boot and therefore am not at liberty to criticise the royal line but I hope that you never forget how many Sentinels have given their lives to ensure that the royal line continues unbroken. How many have I personally called upon to fight, both for and with you, over the centuries and how many of those have proven disloyal and traitorous in comparison to some of your own offspring? I shall remind you, Anton, sir - none. Not one! Both of your sons betrayed you and your line and in all probability, your great-grandson followed suite. Phillipe, who happens to be one of the biggest snobs where your bloodline is concerned, is cause for concern for me, but I understand if you want to ignore the signs and would rather leave that decision to the Sentinels; after all, we're the ones charged with cleaning up such messes."

"Yes Hazel, I remember your quarrel with Phillipe and I also remember that he still bears a grudge. I do not expect to be spoken to in such a manner however, but I do understand your anger. I was not about to defend the snobbery, I know it happens, I also know that I am sometimes guilty of it."

Hazel held Anton's gaze but calmed herself down. "I lost my temper, I apologise."

"No harm done and I think it is quite understandable that you did lose your temper. It is an emotive subject and of course I do not underestimate the sacrifice made by your colleagues in defence of my family and bloodline but…" and again Anton was interrupted as Hazel's temper flared.

"Do not, for the love of the Lycaeon, utter the words 'they

151

knew what they had signed up for' or I swear to you, Anton, I shall drop the mantle of Sentinel Exemplar and you shall never hear from me again. I mean it, at this moment I have more respect for those Sentinels that have gone before me than I do for the entire so-called elite caste which hangs from your family tree."

"Sentinel," Anton's tone was chilled and Hazel knew that she had gone too far but she also knew that Anton realised that she did indeed, mean every word. "I was not going to say that, I was going to say that it is unfortunate that I cannot cut certain members of my family loose and relieve them of their elite status, and so your anger is unfounded, unwarranted and ill-conceived."

Instead of apologising again, Hazel turned on her heel and walked away.

Anton decided to allow her time to cool off before he spoke with her again. The problem with Hazel was that she was right; he *was* about to say what she had surmised but Anton valued his skin and her service far too much to push the envelope and see if she would carry out her threat. He knew from past experience that she probably would.

Later that evening, Anton and Keme were in the dining room of the hotel, enjoying a glass of brandy and talking. Hazel went past them and up to her rooms without a word of greeting.

Keme gave Anton a questioning look and Anton replied with a shrug of his shoulders. Hazel went past them in the other direction a few minutes later, wearing her shabby clothes once more. Keme stood and made to go to her but Anton placed a hand on his wrist and bade him stay.

Hazel had remembered what it was that had been bothering her. The Wolf at the meeting who had objected to the summoning of the Sentinels was neither an Elder, nor influential - as had been mentioned to him – and therefore, it was unlikely that the Sentinels would be interested in him, for he had not lived long enough to have gained any reputation or influence and had therefore, not had time to perform any deed worthy of the Sentinels' attention – or so Hazel had thought. Since her conversation with Anton earlier (before it had turned into a row) she had been mulling over what had been said and she remembered that Anton had made an observation about why Hazel had not noticed that she was being followed.

He had said: *"perhaps you did not sense the one who has followed you because he is not an Ancient, he is not even an Elder and he stays well into the background because, I believe, he knows who you are and more importantly, what you are."*

Whilst the role of Sentinel was shrouded in mystery, Wolfkind knew of them, their role in society and their powers to execute any Wolf except for Lycaeon herself without having to give reason or justification for the execution. The legend of the Sentinels was used in a Whelp's childhood to keep them in line and to make sure they grew up respecting authority; "you be a good student or the Sentinels will come and take you," was a common enough threat. To be taken where or for what reason was not elaborated upon, but it had to be a strong-minded and wilful Whelp to not take heed.

In a similar manner to the Hume police forces of the day, Sentinels were the keepers of the First Laws, laws that had been brought into existence before most living Wolves were born or bitten. They ensured that no Wolf murdered any other and went unpunished for the crime, and that none should endanger Wolf society by drawing the attention of Humes.

There the similarity to the Hume police force ended, for Sentinels were loyal to their Lycaeon – the King or Queen – and if necessary, would be prepared to give their life in defending the royal bloodline and as Hazel had reminded

153

Anton, not one had ever betrayed that trust.

They were called upon in times of war or revolution to fight for the Lycaeon against rivals for the throne, or packs that no longer wished to pay fealty to the throne or to fight the Humes – most usually in the service of other Humes – such as in the War of the Roses when Hazel was first Wolfed.

The task they most performed, however, was that of slayer of Throwbacks. The anomalies born to a Hume and Wolf mating pair or a mating pair of Wolves where one had bitten the other to make their own mate; both, without exception, produced Throwbacks as offspring.

The Throwback could grow undetected as such, especially in a Hume society – until of course, it became sensitive to the moon's influence. Some were more sensitive than others and a few were not affected to the detriment of their daily life. Those Throwbacks, the ones only slightly affected, were the most dangerous, for they were almost undetectable and yet could recognise a Wolf when they came in contact with it.

In olden times, those Throwbacks became Hunters of Wolf. They learned quickly or died young. If they were fortunate, they gravitated towards one that could teach the tricks of the trade and could therefore benefit from older knowledge – knowledge on how to detect a werewolf, how to prove that it was indeed a werewolf and perhaps even to have to go so far as to prove to others that a person was actually a werewolf. Then, the most important lesson – how to kill a werewolf without being killed, maimed or bitten in the process.

Back when Hazel was just starting on her long and arduous journey to become Sentinel, she was told of a prophecy that she might have been a part of. The prophecy had split and could have gone one of two ways. The first would have meant the destruction of Wolfkind and the other meant only hardship when the clans had to flee England's shores – losing almost half their numbers in the process. If Hazel had chosen a different path, she would have become the cause for their destruction. She would have betrayed Wolves with impunity – until the time came that she was alone in her species, and then she would have no help from any quarter.

As it was, she chose the correct path in a decision-making process that she had no way of knowing she had any part of. The outcome was that another she-Wolf betrayed her kind and was hunted to the ends of Cumbria to collect the dubious title of the 'Last Wolf in England' and Hazel was proven to become the most loyal and trusted of the Lycaeon's subjects.

After a few centuries, Wolfkind gathered itself together once more, some Ancients came back out of self-hibernation and the species rallied. New laws were added to the First Laws and it became forbidden to make another Wolf by biting or breeding without special dispensation. Never again would Wolf society allow humans to know that they existed. Wolves had to protect themselves by hiding in plain sight and not drawing any attention to their existence.

In ancient times, Wolf clans were valued members of any army; their strength and ruthlessness in battle was second to none and therefore was in demand for hand-to-hand combat. Legends of 'Berserkers' in ancient Celtic warfare have some basis in fact. Wolves enjoyed their battles and plundered the dead for added shock and awe tactics, but no more. With numbers depleted and kept low on purpose, Wolf society prospered in a different way; they kept their own counsel and infiltrated organisations where knowledge was power. Wolves hold high positions in the armed and police forces, intelligence and sometimes government and have done so for decades.

Chapter 4

A few nights on and Hazel was making her way to the docks again. She had a meeting.

Keme waited a while before making his own excuses to Anton and left for an assignation with Isabella, his new love. Had Keme known that he was stepping on the toes of some other paramour, he would not have cared, for Isabella had ensnared his heart. She was beautiful and amusing and she asked him questions of his old life in a way that did not make him homesick, but enabled him to relive his time – that other life - that once he lived. He had fallen fast and heavy for the petite young woman.

He told her of the hunting expeditions (though not of the one where so many of his tribesmen had been slaughtered by a Man-Wolf) and he told her of his grandfather, the shaman and what he had taught him.

Keme regaled Isabella with tales of his folklore and dismayed her when he recounted harsh winters when none but the strongest, wiliest or most fortunate had a chance of surviving.

Isabella most loved to hear of the long summer evenings

when he would lie awake and listen to his grandfather talking with the elders of the tribe and infrequent visitors or traders that came by. Then at last came the summer when Keme was allowed to sit in their circle and listen to the discussion of who was to be the shaman's next pupil. Keme hoped that it would be him but nothing was certain. Then the decision was made and Keme's heart leaped as a salmon and soared as an eagle – his future as shaman was assured. He knew that his grandfather had preferred to tutor Keme – he had been tutoring him since he was born, Keme knew – but the respect he had gained during his short adult life so far had swayed the decision in his favour. A near-unanimous decision in Keme's support was reached.

But Keme did not only talk of himself, he also asked many questions of Isabella's life. He knew that she did not enjoy her profession as 'seamstress' – the dangers were many and benefits few. He also knew that he handed over far too much money to her and she protested each time at the amount, but it meant that she did not have to ply her trade to the extent she once had and it also ensured that she and her room-mate, Mary, ate better than they had done for a long time.

Isabella's mother came from Hungary; her family had come over to England many, many years ago, when her mother was a babe in arms. They had worked hard and made a good living for themselves and all was well. Isabella was rebellious however and did not want to do as her mother told her. She did not want to go to lessons and eventually, she ran away from home. She was far too stubborn to think of going back, even though she regretted the hurt that she must have caused her family. Now, she was too ashamed to return. The career that she had fallen into had tainted her to the extent that she would not be able to show her face to her family again, they would turn their backs on her. She was, she admitted, dead to them by now.

Keme declared his love for Isabella and asked Anton how he should go about making Isabella his wife.

Anton was at first aghast at the notion, but Keme spoke with passion and eloquence of his fondness for the Hume and Anton advised that it was, indeed possible for a Wolf to marry a Hume, but there were many things to learn and Keme must promise that until he had been appraised of all the facts, he would leave things just as they were for now. Keme promised on the condition that he could continue to give Isabella the money she needed to live and so keep her as protected as he possibly could from the monster that was stalking 'seamstresses', without drawing undue attention to either her household, small as it was, or himself.

It was a joyful Keme that went again to visit Isabella. He was perhaps, therefore, not mindful of the one that followed him.

Jack watched as Keme made his way to Miller's Court and he did not wait around to see what time he left again. Jack was mindful of the vast police presence and he knew that he would stand out like a sore thumb, dressed even as he was – 'shabby genteel' was far too suspicious an outfit in these times.

Hazel stood in shadow, watching the boat crew unload the cargo. Crates, boxes and barrels were hefted from the bowels of the vessel and she saw men lift objects that they should not possibly have been able to move.

These were just some that she had arranged to meet, finishing their contract – working their passage over in secrecy and expedience.

She waited until the boat's cargo had dispersed along the dock and no trace was left before she emerged from the shadow of the warehouse. Then after making sure at least one of the crew had seen her, she melted back into the darkness and they followed.

They moved in silence, one by one. They spread out so that it was impossible to tell that they were a group. No human could have followed them for they flitted in and out of shadows and even up onto the rooftops. No Wolf would have dared to follow, for if it were discovered that one had been too curious, the Sentinels would have felt justified in eradicating them, such was the importance of secrecy.

Hazel had taken a gamble – she had invited far more Sentinels to London than had been imagined, far more than had ever been in one city without full scale war being the reason.

Hazel led and they followed in stealth and silence, never questioning where they were being led to, nor wondering why.

When at last they began to leave the city, their progress was swift and just as difficult to track. They spread out yet more and moved fast.

Arriving at open parkland most changed to Wolf, grasped clothing in their jaws and ran on ahead, joining with others of their kind as they went. The park was awash with Wolves that night. Hazel strolled with three who had remained in human form. She talked quietly to all and not a word was missed.

"I know that this is unprecedented but you all have my complete trust. Not even Anton knows of this arrangement."

"Anton? He is here?"

"Anton has made London his home for the past few decades. I have no need to remind you that knowledge of his whereabouts is sacrosanct."

She did not have to see their nods of acknowledgement, she knew these Wolves of old and would place her life in their hands without qualm – and for one such as her, paranoid to the nth degree, that was commendation indeed!

"We should have problems with just a quarter of our

number being here. There are already waves of protest reaching my ears. Do any of you know of David York? He is a younger Wolf, no more than two centuries old, a born Wolf, but not Pureblood. He has dark hair and grey eyes and no mate that I know of. He is also a meddler; he enjoys informing Wolves of their rights in our society and seems always on the verge of protesting some cause or other."

Hazel waited while they thought on the description she had given but none of her three colleagues thought they knew of David.

"No matter, I am certain that if he is involved in this, he will make himself known at some point. I think that he would like to be able to rub my nose in it if ever he were to put one over on me."

"Put what over on you?"

"Ahh, it is a phrase that I have picked up, Alex, it means to fool me. If he were able to trick me, he would like to boast about it."

The one called Alex nodded but still frowned in his puzzlement. "He cannot be so very clever if he would bring knowledge of the trickery to your attention."

"I would not say that he was not clever and he is certainly very sly about something, but he would *like* to show that he had fooled me, whether he would have the gall to follow it through is entirely another matter."

She stopped walking when she had led the group off the path and into a small copse where they could be reasonably sure of not being seen by passers-by – not that there were many people abroad given the hour.

"There is a Throwback here, I am almost certain that he is on the verge of either becoming a Hunter or worse."

"What is worse than a Hunter?"

"I do not know. I do not think that I have encountered

160

anything like this in four hundred years, since I began my training in Rome. There was one then. It rampaged through Rome and the surrounding hills, it killed indiscriminately and it could have brought Hume attention to our entire social order – which back then was great and powerful indeed. It killed Hume and Wolf alike and once left a part-transformed Wolf in the middle of the market place. It was a dangerous time for all and if we had not had the protection of the Pope, we would surely have been found out and hunted to extinction. In this, though, we have no protectorate to appeal to. We have no one in high places to watch out for our best interests. Indeed, if this 'Jack the Ripper' is found by Humes to be Throwback, then we shall be best advised to vacate London and perhaps even Northern Europe. We shall expect no mercy from the Humes."

"Why do you suspect Throwback and do you have anyone in mind, except for David York?"

"David York is not the Throwback, but I do think he knows the Throwback. I think it is trying to lure a Wolf to it. I also suspect that it had something to do with Almyra and Marcellus's disappearances. You knew Almyra, didn't you, Alex?"

Alex nodded that he did and his face was grim at the loss of her.

"So, the plan I have in mind is for separate groups, led by each of us four, but only my own group shall be made known to the Elders."

"What are the Elders?" Ralski asked.

"They are a group of Wolves, not quite Ancients, who have gained the trust of Anton. They have Anton's ear when it comes to Wolf politics and they seem to have the best interests of us all at heart. I do not know them as well as Anton does, but from what I have seen, they are loyal to him and give sound advice. They do not seem to be self-serving and nor does any have a hidden agenda that I have detected. For the most part, it would seem that they genuinely want the best for Wolfkind and are just as concerned about this as the rest of us."

"It seems odd to me." Ralski said.

"Yes and it did to me also at first, but I have spoken at great length with them all and they are supportive of Sentinels being brought in to find this Throwback."

"You have told them of your suspicions?"

"Yes. They held a meeting and invited me to speak to them and a number of their guests."

"You made this knowledge public and still they did not object to Sentinels arriving in their city?" Ralski was incredulous.

"I have and they welcomed my proposal, although I did not elaborate on the numbers of Sentinels available to me. Wolves in general believe that Sentinels are few and far between, that our role in our society is limited and that we have no need for large numbers. That belief soothes them and I saw no need to disabuse them of that notion."

"Hence the assumption that you have drafted in but a quarter of our actual number."

Hazel nodded. "Now, we need to make plans on how to capture the Throwback."

"You wish to capture it? Why not just execute it when we find it?"

"Because Anton wishes to experiment upon it."

"If I were that Throwback, I think that I should rather be executed." The last of their group spoke.

"As would I, Kirsty, as would I."

Jack hardly slept in the next two weeks. His work at the

hospital suffered, as did his volunteer work in the infirmaries. His studies were neglected completely. The only thing on his mind was the construction of his new work space and the experimentations that he could perform there.

It had cost a great deal of his cash in order to purchase, move and erect the equipment in the exact place of his choosing. He had to pay almost as much in bribery as the entire project cost. At last, he was satisfied that his new laboratory was complete and working as he wanted it.

All of a sudden, everything was going according to his plans and even his hopes. A young man had died under suspicious circumstances in the workhouse and Jack had been asked to autopsy the body on the quiet. He had been offered a bribe but had refused, whilst giving assurances to the workhouse Matron that her husband's heavy-handedness would not be brought up at any inquest. Jack 'found' that the young man had died when an old wound on his skull was aggravated after a fall where he hit his head. The collaboration between the three ensured that any inquest would find the death was caused by accident.

Jack did the autopsy and pocketed the adrenal glands from the young man's body. They seemed to be tender morsels and an unexplainable curiosity overcame him and he felt a compulsion to take them. Perhaps it was the full moon calling to his Wolf psyche, perhaps it was the smells and sounds whilst he was performing the autopsy, perhaps it was his own instincts striving for release or perhaps it was a madness overtaking his mind, driving him to perform unthinkable acts. Mayhap it was a combination of all those factors and Jack could not be blamed for being what he was – a forbidden product of an alliance, and one which should have been, if not prevented, then at least aborted.

The descent into insanity accelerated as the moon rose

163

above the rooftops. Jack made his way to his new laboratory and surveyed the equipment.

He seemed to have forgotten the morsels that he had procured during the afternoon, until he put his hand into his overcoat pocket and found the parcel.

He brought out the brown paper-wrapped meat and took it to a table where he carefully un-wrapped it, seeming to have forgotten what it was and how it had got into his pocket. He viewed the lumps of meat with suspicion until he recalled the circumstances.

Without thinking twice, he popped the first one into his mouth and moved it around with his tongue, savouring the taste and texture of the gland. He waited until it had acquired a similar temperature to his before biting down upon it. His teeth at first squashed the gland until at last, the pressure became too great and they ruptured the outer skin, allowing the blood and other juices to burst into his mouth. Jack's taste buds were swamped by the exquisite flavours and his eyes half-closed in apparent ecstasy. A dribble of juice and saliva oozed down his chin and, loath to lose any, he wiped it and sucked the drool from his finger.

Almost before he had chance to swallow, the other gland was popped into his mouth and bitten. Again, the eyelids drooped and his eyes rolled back to show their whites. Jack's body had ingested the secretions of the first gland and now he had given more to be ingested, his body made full use of the hormones.

A hit of pure adrenalin, swallowed in such a manner, would do nothing to a normal human as the hormone has to be delivered through the bloodstream. Jack, however, was no 'normal human'. His body leeched the adrenalin into his bloodstream and put it to work immediately.

Jack's body vibrated. He felt that he had boundless energy

and was aware of everything around him, even down to the rats peeping out from under the furthest table in the darkest shadows of his laboratory.

Jack forced himself to stand still and he concentrated.

He pushed the power he could feel coursing through his very blood vessels out along his veins and sinews, out to his extremities, his fingers and his toes. Then he allowed the power to flow back in the same way water would flow back and forth if in a test tube, tipped at one end, then tipped at the other.

The pure and savage energy he was in control of made Jack feel as though he were immortal. He felt invulnerable, untouchable!

Then he could feel something else, something that was beginning at his scalp, what he had begun to think of as his early warning system, which told if there was another Wolf close by. He began to prepare himself for confrontation until he realised that the Wolf he could sense was none other than his own Wolf-self.

He damned his oversight in neglecting to bring a mirror so that he could watch his transformation. He looked around but found nothing that could reflect his image to his satisfaction. Then he thought to go out to bathe in the Moon's luminescence but thought better of that notion. Instead, he went out through the back entrance to his laboratory, into the sewers.

He did not care about the smell. Though it was clearer somehow, he could ignore it easily. He was concentrating on the effect the adrenal glands were having on his body and his mind.

Jack emerged into the brightness of the moonlight and was stopped dead by the pureness of the scene before him. It was the ordinary streets in the ordinary town but his eyes took in far more than ordinary detail.

The moon's light bathed his eyes and made them able, somehow, to see these changes, the subtle alterations from ordinary to extraordinary.

It bathed his body and made it powerful, strong beyond measure and able to withstand exertions far beyond imagining.

The moon played with Jack's mind and made him think of atrocities he could commit without punishment or guilt. The moon sent Jack over the brink of madness and into that dark yet shiny abyss, deep into his own sense of self, tearing his sanity and any remnants of conscience apart, making him believe the things that he had previously only dared to dream of. Jack thought himself invulnerable and superior to those who had spawned him; his mother, the Hume; and his father, the Wolf were both inferior to what Jack was now, what he had become.

His first victim did not know he had been attacked, so swift did death arrive.

Jack saw the man staggering in a drunken gait; he gave the impression that he was pulling himself along the wall which ran alongside the footpath he was taking. He would stop and stand still for a moment, seeming to get his bearings, before moving off again. Jack could hear him singing to himself.

Jack hit him from behind, bashing the base of his skull, breaking the connection between life and body with one almighty blow.

Then the body was lifted with such ease that the tiny part of Jack that still remained was astounded at his own strength. Then the anomaly that Jack had become carried its prey high onto the rooftops to devour glands and flesh in a wanton spree of violence and gore. The dead man's throat was torn out and the thyroid gland was devoured. With that, the last vestiges of Jack's humanity became engulfed and the beast took over entirely.

The man's remains were taken high above the city and dropped without effort or remorse, into the River Thames to be washed up long after the soft flesh had decomposed beyond hope of the terrible injuries done to it being discovered.

Many hours later, when Jack's body had ridden itself of the effects of the glands he had consumed, he came to his senses. He thought nothing of where he had wandered to, his temporary madness giving justification to his whereabouts.

Keme did not seem to need or want to hunt on the first of the October full moons, he wished, instead, only to be with Isabella. They lay on her bed in each other's arms, murmuring their love to each other.

The door banged open, scaring them both and a drunken Mary staggered in, dragging a laughing man with her. They saw Keme and Isabella in bed and Mary's expression changed.

"You told me you'd be out tonight," she said, the quiet tone and even the slur in her voice did nothing to disguise the menace it held.

"Yes I did, I am sorry Mary. Come Keme, we should go."

Keme pulled back the flimsy sheets, but made sure that Isabella's body was still covered and then leaned to grasp his clothes. When he was dressed, he stood and made to herd Mary and her companion out of the door whilst Isabella dressed too.

Mary's companion did not want to move and Keme's herding technique became more forceful.

"Who are you shoving?" the man snarled at Keme, perhaps thinking that he was just a client.

"Would you like to watch as she dresses? Is that what you are about?" Keme asked, his voice sounded most calm but his eyes did not give the same impression.

The man was about to answer that he would indeed like to

watch when he realised what Keme was asking and he looked at his face. What he saw there gave him cause to change his mind and he removed his hat and backed out of the doorway.

Mary did not leave.

She stood in the open doorway, her fists on her hips, she was impatient for Isabella to get moving but Keme motioned for her to stay where she was.

"Mary, would you be kind enough to allow Isabella to dress with the door closed?" his voice was calm and his eyes were still furious but his learned manners stood him in good stead – for the moment.

"I've seen what she's got before. Let her get dressed."

Keme didn't ask again, he pushed her backwards into the arms of her waiting client, and he slammed the door on the pair.

He gave Isabella her dress and she took it as she clambered out of bed.

Mary began a barrage of hammering upon the door and when Isabella had slipped the dress over her head, Keme opened the door, taking Mary by surprise.

Isabella was slipping her shoes on and grabbing for a shawl as Mary and the man were re-entering the room. Keme reached for Isabella's hand and pulled her towards him, keeping his own body between Mary and Isabella. Then he allowed Isabella to leave in front of him and he closed the door behind them.

Keme did not speak as they left the house and Isabella did not push him to.

They went to Anton's hotel where Keme booked Isabella into an apartment and arranged for someone to collect the few meagre possessions she had left at her old room.

"I cannot stay here, Keme!"

"You can and you shall."

He brooked no argument, but left her to explore the rooms. Then he went to find Anton to tell him what he'd done.

Anton was nowhere to be found, however and Keme realised that he would most probably be out on the hunt.

Anton was not hunting, he was on his way to meet up with Hazel to see what she had been up to and if she had calmed down since their last discussion.

Anton used his instincts to try to locate Hazel but could not. He did, however, detect traces of large numbers of Wolves moving in the same direction, and so decided to follow that trace instead.

As he came to the more open parklands of Hackney Heath, he took great care to cloak his presence but was not overly surprised to be challenged as he reached the copse where the greatest accumulation of Wolves were gathered.

"My Lord, I realise that you have great authority over all Wolves, but please realise that this is a meeting of Sentinels and your authority does not extend here." A tall and powerful Wolf stood in human form before Anton and though both knew that Anton was the more experienced and powerful with far more battle experience, Anton also knew what he had been told was true. He had to respect the jurisdiction.

Anton nodded agreement and said: "Ralski is it?"

The other Wolf nodded.

"Yes, I remember you. Would you send for Sentinel Exemplar? I have a need to speak with her."

"Of course my Lord." Ralski said this but did not move. Anton was puzzled but patient. He saw a movement from the trees as another went to do his bidding. Anton smiled at the efficiency.

A short while later, a Wolf bounded up to Ralksi and nodded. Ralski then waved Anton past to follow the appointed guide.

Anton was stopped once more at another copse and waited. Hazel appeared. She nodded to him and said: "my Lord."

"Hazel, I would appreciate it if you could forget our argument. I said some things which may have seemed harsh at the time but I assure you, I value your Sentinels highly and you really should know this."

Hazel did not reply.

She turned to walk away, back to where she had been holding counsel. Anton followed and was not prevented from doing so.

When Anton saw the amassed Wolves in the clearing, he gasped at their number.

"I had no idea there were so many Sentinels that you could call upon."

"With due respect, my Lord, it is not your business to know."

"Hazel…" Anton began but paused when he saw her expression.

She waited for him to realise what he was doing wrong and when he did, the corners of her mouth twitched in the tiniest of smiles.

"Sentinel Exemplar," Anton said in a louder and more respectful voice. "I appreciate the fact that you allow me to observe your meeting. I assure you that I shall watch in silence and that nothing of this meeting shall pass beyond these trees."

Hazel nodded and the murmur that Anton had not noticed before, ceased.

"Sentinels, I thank you for answering my call in this dark time. You know, I hope, that I would never have summoned you without cause. There is a Throwback here. It has gone undetected for whatever reasons and for however long and it has grown cunning and clever in that time. I also suspect that there is a traitorous Wolf that helps it to prosper. We have to find both traitor and Throwback and execute one and capture the other, for my Lord Anton would experiment upon the Throwback to see what can be learned from the anomaly."

The group began murmuring once again and Hazel allowed it for a moment.

"Some, especially those amongst our more civilised brethren, may find that punishment cruel and unusual for so paltry a crime as being born a Throwback, but I know that I am preaching to the converted when I remind you all that we are here for the one purpose of ensuring our Lycaeon's perpetual safety. That would include keeping the knowledge of our existence from Humes. A Throwback holds no allegiance to our Lycaeon or to any bloodline and is therefore a loose cannon and a menace to all of us. At this moment, there are armies of Humes patrolling through the area of London called Whitechapel. I need not remind you that we have Wolves that are of an age where they cannot yet control their transformation at the full moon and would therefore risk being noticed by those Humes. It is then vital that we eradicate the reason for the Hume presence and we stop the murders. Tonight, it is essential that we are all on alert for this Throwback and as much on the watch for our younger Wolves – not for their safety alone, but because they can drop us all into full view of Humes just by altering their features at an inopportune moment. Hide yourselves well though, comrades, for if it is known that we have our own army on these shores, I should be accused of being traitor to Wolfkind – again." Hazel's wry smile gave a number of her companions cause to chuckle, for it was widely known that she cared little for such accusations because they had been proven times many to be unfounded and false.

"Now, you know what must be done. I have deliberately not given too many detailed instructions to your chosen commanders. I trust you all implicitly and I know that any decision you make over the next three nights – be the outcome for good or for bad - will be made for the right reason. With that in mind, go forth and take down the traitor and capture the Throwback.

The Wolves, instead of emerging from the copse en masse, took almost an hour to disperse. The mood was relaxed and even carefree as they waited to go.

Again, Anton was quite impressed at the organisation of the whole meeting.

"This seemed very well practiced, Hazel."

Hazel, who had been watching the others turn to Wolf and lope off, turned to Anton with a smile. "That is because it *is* very well practiced. We have had plenty of occasions in which to practice."

"You have?" Anton didn't mean to show his surprise.

Hazel ignored the question and instead asked one of her own. "The other day, were you going to say what I accused you of or was I, as you said, mistaken?"

Anton thought for a moment. He weighed up what he thought were his options and then dismissed them all. He decided instead to confess the truth. "You were right. I am arrogant; I am used to being so. I am not asking for your forgiveness for we both know that I do not require it. I tell you this because you were right and I know that is important to you."

"That is not fair or warranted. I do not expect an apology from you. I do not expect for you to respect Sentinels for our sacrifices past, present or future. I do not even expect explanations for your behaviour. What I do expect, Anton, and also what I believe I think I deserve after this time, is the absolute truth from you. Either that or nothing, it is all I have ever asked. If you cannot be truthful with me, then say nothing. I prefer no conversation to any containing lies. If I happen to be right on occasion and you do not wish to concede that fact then, as I have just said, say nothing." Hazel turned her back on Anton and resumed watching the others leave.

She pricked up her ears as she heard a squeal from outside the copse. Anton was right behind her, morphed to Wolf, their clothes in a pile as they exited the copse.

As the last batch of Wolves had left, they encountered a group of four young men. How they had got past the patrol was anyone's guess but it was obvious to the guards that they had seen far too much for them to be allowed to live – at least as Humes.

"What are you waiting for, Ralski? Kill them," Anton instructed.

Ralski did not move. His three guards also stood motionless, surrounding the four men.

The tension was palpable. Ralski and his three were aware that Anton had crossed a line and they were now waiting to see how Sentinel Exemplar would deal with the situation.

She was silent as she prowled around the group of terrified Humes. They were wise in the fact that they did not make a sound, even given the impossible situation – werewolves, *real* werewolves had them at their mercy and all four of them were very aware that such beasts possessed no mercy.

Hazel sat in front of the group and addressed one in particular.

"Why are you here, Paul? Were you not given sufficient warnings not to come?"

"I…" he began, but gave up on the attempt and was silent.

"I shall tell you then, if he will not," one of their number stepped forward but was persuaded by the guards growling their displeasure that it was not a good idea to be moving towards Hazel.

"Yes, you are brave enough? Edward, is it?"

"I am Jeffrey my Lady; Edward is my brother, here," he nodded to the one standing to his left.

Hazel nodded to indicate that he should continue.

"We want to join you."

Before Hazel could answer, Anton voiced his derision. "Impossible! You foolish boys have gone and got yourselves killed for no good cause."

"Sir, I beg of you…" Jeffrey began, but Anton would have no discussion, he leaped for the boy and would have killed him in a trice if Hazel had not pre-empted his move and made a leap to deflect the boy from Anton's trajectory.

"How dare you, Hazel?" Anton rounded on her.

"With all due respect, my Lord," Hazel mirrored Anton's movements and they circled each other, heads down and level with their shoulders, teeth bared and jaws set and slavering. "It is I that should ask the question. You are interfering and encroaching upon my authority. You have no weight here, the Sentinels are not mine to *command* and so they are certainly not yours. We work together to the benefit of the Lycaeon and if by those actions the rest of Wolf society also reap rewards, then all well and good, but you are no longer Lycaeon and so we cannot and do not owe you any allegiance, save for the respect of your Ancient status. Do not trespass in Sentinel affairs my Lord, it is not advisable."

The four Humes had gone way past frightened but they were, to their credit, still and calm.

"You dare threaten me with the Sentinels?"

"I turn that about my Lord, and ask if you dare question the Sentinels authority?"

The pair of Wolves continued to circle as Anton thought about this. He took but a few moments and then altered

174

direction and loped for the trees. It was only moments later that he re-emerged fully dressed. He bought Hazel's dress with him and she slipped it over her head as she transformed back to her human shape.

"I concede," Anton said. "If I may continue as an observer, I should be interested to see how you deal with this incident."

"Of course you may stay as an observer, but please remember this; you have no say in the ways of Sentinel, you handed me over to them – us – when I was a Whelp and I was taught well. I was an excellent pupil and I was *asked* to become Sentinel Exemplar. I did not think that I should become one so high in our ranks after so short a time, relatively speaking. I wear the title with humility and with a vast amount of pride. I feel that I have now earned the title, as do all other Sentinels so far as I am aware. I do not command the Sentinels; it is more that they wish to do what I ask of them. I do not ask anything that I would not do myself and that is why they follow me with such unerring devotion. We are growing in number for a reason, Anton. That reason is that Wolves wish to join our number – a precedent that has been set under my regime. We accept only those who have shown years of devotion to our cause – such as these boys."

"What? What have these boys done?"

"These particular boys have done much. They have followed me to Europe and back again. They have studied our ways and our laws and have shown respect for everything Wolf. They have, on more than one occasion, killed a Throwback. They have been warned off and told of the dangers, they risk death from Wolves that do not know of their devotion – or do not care for it - and here they are, in the midst of our summit, having got past some of the best guards I have in my squad. They have proven themselves loyal and ask only one thing as reward."

"To be made Wolf? I am afraid that you have been duped, Hazel. These boys want what every Hume wants; they want immortality and eternal youth. They want power and a reason to commit murder without fear of punishment." Anton's tone was derisory but Hazel waited for him to finish his tirade.

"No Anton, the thing they all want is to talk with us, to be friends, comrades. They have asked for nothing, especially not to be bitten by one of these beasts."

The Humes were watching and listening in awe. They knew that their lives were being argued for and they held their nerve, almost as though this had happened before.

"Of course they have not asked for it, for surely that is the only way they will get their heart's desire."

"It has been offered, on one other occasion. But only one of their number took us up on the offer. Ralski, who was that boy, can you recall?"

Ralski stepped forward, he had not changed to Wolf and Anton took more notice of him then. He too was a young man, younger than these boys.

"I recall a boy who dared to accept your offer, I recall that he was bitten and that he suffered agonies from the wound but I also recall that you ensured that he was comfortable and that he did not die and when the full moon rose that night, you took me and showed me what I could do. It is my fault that these Humes found their way to our meeting. The have followed us from the docks and they had got very close by the time they were discovered, and they remembered me and instantly trusted me. I had forgotten them for a while, but I remember my friends, my childhood friends and they want to join us."

"And have you promised that they can join us?" Hazel asked.

"No."

"And have you promised that if they are refused, that they may still return to their lives in safety?"

"No, I have said that if they are refused, they will die here. The only thing I have promised is that if they are to die, then it will be quick."

Hazel nodded and took a moment before she continued.

"What do you offer us?" she asked.

"We offer loyalty to the Lycaeon, to our comrades and to Wolfkind. If necessary, we offer our lives if needs be." Paul had found his voice once more.

"All of you promise this?"

"Yes." They chorused, though not in voices that were loud and fearless.

Hazel smiled and whispered to Anton. "Well? Do you think we could have room for four loyal Sentinels amongst our ranks? Four more that would defend your granddaughter to the end? Well Anton, you wondered at the numbers of Sentinels, you have part of the answer here." They began moving away from the group as they talked, their voices growing a little louder as they did.

"You do, of course, realise that you violate the new law that prevents Wolves making others without permission from the Council?"

"I most certainly do, and who, do you think, has been set to enforce that new law, and with what resources? A law is not worth the paper it is written on if it is unenforceable. That is the reasoning behind the few First Laws that we have, if there are too many and they are too complex, there is too much room for question. We need rules set in black and white, not shaded in greys. My Sentinels are loyal to the Lycaeon first and Sentinel Exemplar and all the other Sentinels second. It is dinned into them constantly throughout their training. Most have never seen the Lycaeon, nor would they expect to, but all would lay down their lives in order to protect hers. Wolfkind in general sneer at Sentinels, they think that we are traitors to our kind, for we execute the judgement that is there for our protection. You know full well that Wolves are conceited creatures, they think that the First Laws are there for their benefit only when they need it and when they are the ones on the other side of that fence, they think the First Laws are a nonsense, made for no good reason and they should be permitted to bend that Law if they so choose."

"Yes, but that also includes you now."

"It does and it is left to me to deal with any consequences arising from the decision I made."

"It could also look, to others, that you have amassed your own army. Be very careful, for if your enemies found this, you would be held up to the same judgements as you are bound to hold others to."

"Do you assume that I have not already thought of that? Do you think that I went into this decision without due care or attention? And then, do you assume that I am the only Sentinel to have commanded such an army? The only difference between me and the others that have gone before is that I am the first Sentinel Exemplar. I should not have to preach our history to you Anton. It was prophesised that I should be the one to carry the mantle of first Sentinel Exemplar and that during the time that I do so, Wolfkind shall have the chance to prosper alongside Humes. We have yet to come to that part in the prophecy and who knows if it shall ever happen? Who knows if that chance has been and gone or if, when the time does come, we are willing to accept it? You know as well as I do that there are some who would overthrow the Lycaeon and put another in her place. We are here, for now, to ensure that that does not happen until Victoria is ready to allow a challenge to her reign. Even then it is a decision that is not yours to make."

"You challenge me, Hazel. At each turn you challenge my authority…" But Hazel interrupted him.

"You are mistaken. I do not challenge your authority, for as I have to constantly remind you, until you take back Lycaeonship, you have no authority over me." She walked away from him, back to where the Humes were waiting.

"Ralski, do you trust these Humes?" Hazel asked.

"Yes, with my life."

"Good, then that is what would be forfeit if they betray the Lycaeon." she said this in a tone that was even and sombre. "I charge you with their care, with their welfare and with their training. If you are unsure, then ask your mentor for help or advice. Who is your mentor?"

"Kirsty."

Hazel nodded and turned to walk away. She had her back to the group as she gave the command. "Make the bite deep; for it shall be the last scar they bear from their human life, it shall be a reminder of what they once had and relinquished to serve the Lycaeon."

"That is it? That is all?" Anton was incredulous and angry.

"That is all that is necessary for now. Their training will begin this evening on the rising of the full moon." She had to raise her voice a little to be heard above the cries of fear from the Humes. They knew what was coming, for they had asked for it, but the human body is a wonderful thing and instinct to protect itself overrides any thought – rational or otherwise.

"You can afford to have four newly Wolfed Humes roaming the streets of London? Not to mention the loss from your ranks, of the ones that are to train them." Anton asked.

"I am sure we shall manage."

"You are exasperating, Hazel."

She turned to look at him as he spoke.

"If I were acting just as your once-protégé, then yes, I agree, I would probably be most exasperating to you, but you forget I am no longer the same Wolf that you handed over to the Sentinels. I am now a product of their teachings as well as your own, and therefore, I am, as you seem to insist on forgetting tonight, Sentinel Exemplar and I am a different Wolf entirely. You must try to learn how to separate the two sides of me. On the one, there is Hazel who will always respect and love you and will put up with your arrogance and demands without question and with only a little rebellion and on the other is Sentinel Exemplar who will always respect and love you, but who also commands equal respect in her own right. You overstepped the mark here this evening. My Sentinels noticed it and were waiting for me to put you in your place. I did not, because I respect you but I also respect myself and here is fair warning Anton, as one Wolf to another, do not do that to me again. It is not necessary, there are ways of disagreeing with me, but trying to take command and then being belligerent about it is not the way. I will not stand for it again."

She faced Anton as she said this and she did not waver once.

"We shall speak of this back at the hotel," Anton said, only controlling his anger with some difficulty.

"No, we shall not. If you do not accept that this is how it has to be, then I will not be going back to the hotel and we shall have nothing more to say to one another." After a few moments pause, Hazel then said: "I understand if you need to think on this, Anton. I have work to do. Let me know of your decision."

She ran out of the copse and as she went, others followed her in human form, not wolf. They did not slow until they reached the more populated area of the city and there they split up into ones and twos, Hazel going on alone.

Hazel knew that her presence on the deserted streets was conspicuous and would look to be a trap but she waited and watched anyway.

It did not take long before she was approached by a lone man. He walked slowly and with great care. She assumed that perhaps he did not wish to alarm her but soon realised that the reason for his deliberate gait was because he was drunk. The whole populace seemed to survive on a diet consisting only of gin, she thought.

The man arrived and smiled at Hazel. She smiled back, unworried.

"'Ere love, you wanna escort 'ome?" he slurred. He was even more drunk than he had at first seemed. "It's dangerous round 'ere nowadays an' a pretty little thing like you didn't oughta be on 'er own. C'mon, I'll take yer 'ome."

He pronounced it 'dannerus' rather than dangerous but Hazel knew what he meant. She smiled and allowed him to take her arm. He led her down a street and then stopped, perplexed.

"Where do yer live then?"

"Not too far from here, I believe I live close to where you live, don't I?"

He looked at her again and his perplexity deepened. "Oh? Not far from 'ere then?"

"That's right. I'll be fine getting home from here. You look tired though, you go in." she smiled at him again and removed her arm from his grip. He nodded and slurred a fond goodnight and staggered off down a narrow alley between two houses.

Hazel heard a chuckle from the shadows and for a horrible moment was transported back four centuries to when she was first made Wolf.

She shook off the memory and fixed the smile back in

181

place as she turned to see Ralski.

"You're rather tender-hearted for a blood-thirsty killer, aren't you?" he asked with a wry smile on his lips and genuine humour reflected in his eyes.

"I have my moments." Hazel said, returning his smile.

"I was waiting for you to rip out his throat and feed. I think I would have relished watching you at work."

"I don't need to feed anywhere near as much as you do and so I cannot be bothered with all the mess and having to clean up after my kill."

"Yes, I've been wondering about that too. It is very inconvenient and interrupts the flow of my killing spree if I am in that sort of mood."

"Yet it is a necessity. No Wolf these days should be too engulfed by bloodlust as to have to kill in the wanton manner which was the norm back before I was made. I have heard reminiscences of such times and those that recounted the tales did so with such wistfulness that it makes me yearn for the days when we were not governed so strictly. But it is a necessity, we must hide our presence, Humes must not know of our existence. Before you ask why," she stopped Ralski's question before he uttered it. "I shall tell you. Humes are our food source. We must protect them from our over-feeding because if once we outnumbered them, what would we feed on? Also, if we made our presence known, Humes would react in the same way as we see them react against each other: They would declare war. We would lose the war, but it was not always so. At one time in our past, we would have held our own against Hume armies – indeed, we did so – but those times are also past. Our attributes are our ruthless blood thirst and physical strength, but now Humes have surpassed us. Yes we could utilise the same weaponry that Humes do but the playing field is now levelled. You do not need superior strength to wield a rifle; you do not need a hunger for blood to kill in vast numbers. Hand-to-hand battle was our forte but that time is gone. We have adapted to the new ways and made changes to our modus operandi – the way we do things. We have had to make new rules to preserve our ways and traditions and to ensure that our Lycaeon and her bloodline is able to continue."

"I understand why we must cover our tracks and make sure that any kills are undiscovered or disguised as a different means of death. I also understand that our Lycaeon is the most important member of our society. What I do not understand is why we are not allowed to make more Wolves. If we had the vast numbers that we are capable of, we should surely overrun the Humes and take control."

"And they would bow to our superiority, our strength and almost immortality," Hazel said. "And they would pay tribute to us and worship us."

"Yes, and now you speak my thoughts out loud, I realise that I sound like a dictator. I suppose then, that there would be in-fighting for control and our society would be torn asunder."

"Much as it was before the First Laws were founded and enforced. Much as we were before our society became regimented and structured. We are superior to Humes in strength and life-span but we are much the same as they when it comes to love of power. If we did not have our First Laws then our society would crumble and we would be so busy fighting each other that the Humes could wait until we were weakened and kill the last one standing."

Hazel watched as Ralski pored over her explanation in his head. He came to a conclusion and nodded to her. "I agree, it would be far too easy for a species such as ours to become megalomaniacal and I think that I prefer life as it is, not as it was."

"A good decision," Hazel nodded. "You do worry me

sometimes, you know. I often wonder how you would have turned out if you had not had a patient mentor. I think that perhaps you would have been wilful and opinionated to the extent that you would have become disillusioned with how things must be and you could have turned rogue."

"Is that so very worrying? There have been Wolves that have gone rogue before."

"And I am certain they will again but none have come from the ranks of Sentinel. I recruited you personally and therefore my reputation rested upon your shoulders, it still rests there. If you had gone rogue after I had recruited you and persuaded the other Sentinels and the Lycaeon that you were indeed made of the right stuff, I would have been disgraced – and your demise would have been swift and brutal. It would not have satisfied me in light of my disappointment."

"You spoke for me?"

"Of course I did. You were the youngest Wolf to have graced the ranks of Sentinel and had the shortest training. You showed most promise and more loyalty than some Wolves I have known and yes, I had great faith in your ability. I took a chance that your questioning mind would be patient enough to wait for the answers you asked for and I am pleased to have been proven correct in my assumption. As I said though, credit for that does not lie at your door alone. Your tutor was perfect for you; I know that she still is."

The hint did not go unnoticed but it did go unverified. Ralski kept quiet whilst Hazel fished for more information. Hazel gave up the quest for more information after a few moments and laughed with genuine humour.

"Kirsty has already asked if your relationship is appropriate. I have assured her that it should cause no problems."

Ralski made no comment but the quiet was enough for Hazel.

"Go now, we have work to do. I will not be able to lure any predator with a guard present."

As he turned to leave, Hazel became serious again and she asked: "what of the boys? Who is caring for them?"

"The boys are wounded and are back at your warehouse. There is a guard and someone with medical knowledge, just in case. I do not have that knowledge and it was thought prudent for me to take his place out on the hunt."

"Very good," Hazel said and she smiled again as Ralski left her. His exit was both swift and silent.

She walked back to where she had been 'escorted' from a few minutes before and loitered there for a while. No one showed her any interest and she saw no women making any attempts to ply their trade and so she moved on. The few men she saw were not interested in her or her apparent trade as she walked and until she came to a more populated street, she was not approached. The glares of distrust she drew from the women also hoping for custom from the passers-by made it obvious to her that strangers of either gender were looked on with wariness. Hazel decided to give it up as a bad job and move on yet again. She was beginning to wonder if the mode of entrapment was worth the effort and she began looking to move on up into the rooftops to evaluate the surroundings from a better vantage point when someone took her arm.

Hazel looked down at the hand which was gripping her arm and pinching the skin. The hand was large and dirty with broken and dirty fingernails but female for all that.

"Whachoo want?" the woman's voice was gravely and slurred and held a thinly veiled threat in the undertones.

"What do you mean?" Hazel asked in a bland tone which came out as 'whadder yer mean?' Anton and Victoria would have blanched at the accent and dialect she slipped so readily into.

185

"Don't give me that, I knows what you're up to. Gerroff my pitch! Things is slow enough round 'ere without more competition. We don't needs no fresh faces round 'ere."

"Yer, alright then. I'm off. No needs ter rip me bleedin' arm off, is there?" Hazel tugged her arm from the woman's grasp and tottered away as though in fear for her safety. She heard the giggles and cat-calls from the woman's colleagues and thought that those few ladies of the night would probably be all right if they kept their feisty attitude and kept close together. The danger lay where the women worked alone – or were caught unawares.

Hazel realised that she was going against the centuries of slaughtering and feeding on Humes that she had so readily and eagerly participated in as she ensured these women were working in relative safety, but she felt a little responsible for the danger they were in at this time. It was down to her and her Sentinels to prevent this type of anomaly from preying on the fragile Humes – they were, after all, the food source for her kind.

As she pretended to flee from the threat of violence, Hazel smiled. The women had no inkling that they had 'chased away' one that could protect them from the real and ever-present danger of the Throwback that potentially hunted them all.

Hazel walked along the cobbled street, past other ladies of the night plying their trade. It seemed that they either sensed Hazel's previous 'defeat' at the hands of the territorial woman or they had heard of it through some grapevine, but the jeers greeting Hazel as she moved on were encouraging. The women still had their instinct to fight and whilst they had that, they had a chance.

Hazel did not judge these women on the morality of their work, she knew what she had done in order to survive and some of the things were far, far worse than partaking in sex for money.

Her head was bowed and she appeared defeated. As she made her way out of the area where the largest concentration of 'seamstresses' held court, she was aware of someone following her. Her senses and her instincts pricked up in an instant. She searched with her mind but found no trace of anomaly, no trace of Wolfness. This predator was purely Hume.

She stopped and leaned her forehead on a wall as though in despair.

The ruse worked and he didn't take long to approach her. He took her arm in a gentle manner and pulled her close to him in an embrace. He stroked her hair and his touch was gentle too.

"I saw you, my sweet." His accent was not local, perhaps a Northern one? "I saw you being moved on. The woman was nasty and rough and she should have been more tolerant. These are dangerous times for women in your trade. You need to stay close together, not be moved on to separate. Divide and conquer is what I believe this murderer is trying to do, setting people against one another, making them wary of strangers."

"And what are you proposing? That I should go back and assert my right to stand on the corner, where they have always worked? I cannot imagine that those women would take that proposal kindly," Hazel replied, keeping her eyes cast down.

"No, of course not." e crooked his forefinger and placed it under her chin, lifting her head so that he could look into her eyes. Hazel wondered what on earth he was up to.

He gazed into her eyes for a long moment and then began speaking again. Hazel noticed the subtle changes in his breathing, his manner and his speech. The man was becoming excited.

"You are beautiful, my dear. Beneath the grime and filth,

your beauty shines. You should not be working these streets, you should be married to some rich gentleman who would cosset and pamper you and who would take such care of you that you would never be cold or dirty again."

Hazel was used to eccentric behaviour, but this one took the whole bakery. Was he making a marriage proposal? It certainly seemed as though he was about to make a proposal of some sort. Hazel waited.

"But instead, you lower yourself to the behaviour of an animal – nay, worse than an animal! Beasts of the field rut in order to procreate, whereas you and your kind take payment for such behaviour! The love of money is the root of all evil!"

Could she have been wrong in thinking that the murderer was a Throwback? It hadn't seemed possible that it could have been anything other than a Throwback, given the evidence of her own eyes and senses but this man seemed to be intent on berating her for her chosen 'trade'. She allowed her eyes to grow wide as though in fear and the man carried on in his tirade.

"That chap, Jack the Ripper has started a crusade that I wanted to join. He has the courage of his convictions and I will join him in his crusade when I can find him! Until I do, I shall continue in his work, mimicking his actions and help him to rid first London and then England of the blight upon our fair country. Those that infect decent and god-fearing men with their diseases, syphilis and gonorrhoea will be cleared out – permanently! God cannot do it; it has been left to man to clear up his own mess. The first woman, Eve, tempted Adam with her wickedness, the apple being a symbol for her wantonness and since then, man has been repeating his behaviour, destroying families and the decent working man and now it shall be stopped, one filthy, disease-ridden whore at a time!"

Oh good, a man with a mission, ridding London of prostitution single-handed. Hazel realised that she had stumbled upon – or rather, had been stumbled upon by - a fanatic. Her own instincts began to take hold, self-preservation first and foremost. Then her perverse sense of danger made an appearance and she decided to goad him more.

"I see," she said. "You caught the clap and your wife threw you out, is that how it went?"

"My wife died," he seemed to sag as he admitted it. "She died during childbirth, our son died with her, but it was then that the doctors discovered that she had caught the disease. I was disgraced; her father threw me out of my job and out of my home."

Then he rallied again and became furious at Hazel.

"It is whores such as you that tempted me. I would never have strayed if I had not been made the offer!"

"Yes you would."

That was enough for the enraged and embittered widower. He slapped Hazel with the hand that had lifted her chin so tenderly. With his other hand he drew a blade from his coat and made to slash her face.

"I wrote of my last victim. I sent a piece of her to Mr. George Lusk. With you, I shall send not just a piece of kidney; I shall send him your heart!"

Hazel's reactions were far swifter than his and she dodged the blade's arc with ease. She punched him full on the nose and it erupted in a spray of blood and snot. Far from stopping him, however, the blow infuriated him more and he again lunged at Hazel with the blade in his fist, pointing towards her.

She could tell that he was not proficient at knife fighting by the way he held the weapon and she dodged him again and again, throwing the odd punch and slap at his face as she did so. He was beginning to tire when she decided enough was enough and moved forward, past the extended arm, into his embrace almost. She reached up to grasp his head in both of her hands and gave a sharp twist of his head; the ensuing crack announced that his neck had been broken. His death was instantaneous and Hazel was not even out of breath.

She made the judgement that she could leave this particular kill as it had fallen. The cause of death would be deemed the result of a fight – which it was. She had no reason to disguise the cause of death and even if someone had seen her kill the man, there were no witnesses that could identify her as the killer without reasonable doubt. She would don a different dress and coat and then the only recognisable feature would be her long red hair. She was satisfied that she would not be brought to the attention of any authority.

Hazel walked away from the dead man, she never looked back. She did not see the Wolf watching her from the shadows, but she knew he was there and she had a good idea of who he was.

Chapter 5

David had been watching his estranged son and was now becoming worried for the safety of everyone in the vicinity. It had been all very well when he had thought Jack to be a benign type of Throwback but after watching his progression through discovery and acceptance of his new psyche, on past insanity and into absolute psychosis, David realised that not only were Humes in great danger, but so were Wolves and therefore, so was he.

Perhaps the time had come to intervene.

David went to Jack's house but found it empty. There were obvious signs of desertion as he peered through the windows at the back of the house. Furniture had a thin veneer of dust and doors were closed. The kitchen was the only room that showed any signs of habitation, there was crockery piled in the sink – by the looks of things, the maid had been either dismissed or given a leave of absence.

David did not know where to look next for his son.

As he left the back yard, he saw a familiar figure. The man saw him and did not pause; he did not seem pleased to see David, but was neither frightened nor angry either.

"Hello father," Jack said, as he came up alongside, surprising David by keeping his tone flat and unemotional.

"Hello Jack. I wondered how long it would take for you to figure out your birthright."

"Won't you come in? I think we have a lot of talking to do."

David nodded and followed Jack into the back yard and through the back door into the unkempt kitchen.

"I shall not offer you any refreshments, father, for I would not wish you to think that you are a welcome guest here," Jack said as he walked into the kitchen and removed his hat and then his coat.

David removed his own hat and stood with it in his hands, playing the rim through his fingers in a nervous manner, it seemed to Jack.

"You seem perturbed, father." Jack mentioned his observation in order to perhaps make David even more uneasy.

"Yes, Jack, I suppose that I am. I have some worrying news for you and information that could perhaps save your life. You are bringing yourself into the greatest danger imaginable."

"Danger? From whom?"

"From the Sentinels of course…" David paused mid-sentence, he realised that his son knew nothing of Sentinels and therefore, he realised his own mistake in allowing Jack loose in the world.

"Sentinels? I have nothing to fear from Wolves."

"Oh, you think not? Jack, you are in mortal danger! I do not know how they track you, but know this; they can and will find you and destroy you!"

"I think not, father," and the disdain in which Jack held his father was apparent and clear to David. He realised then that Jack was so far past eccentric that he might not be redeemable. But David had to try; he owed the love of his life, Amelia, that much at least.

192

"Son," David tried another tactic. "Explain to me what has happened these last years."

Jack looked at his father, deciding whether he was worth the effort or whether he should eject him from the house and go on with his plans for the full moon, which would rise in a few short hours.

He decided to eject him, forcefully if necessary. After all, Jack was superior to all beings – or so he assumed.

"No father, I do not have time for this. I am preparing for the evening and the full moon and all it promises. I shall weigh up my options and choose whether the time is right to change or not. I assume that you are compelled to change under the light of such a moon. I have supposed, therefore, that I have the edge over you and that I am more powerful in intellect and possibly strength."

David stared at his son. His eyes were wide in surprise at his haughty speech and eventually, David could hold his mirth no longer and he laughed.

"Why, you pompous ass! You think that because you are neither Wolf nor Hume that you are better? You are worse! Humes are food for Wolf yet only a comparative few shall become prey. Throwbacks, like you," David caught hold of his son's jacket and pulled him up close, "are a half-breed - neither one nor the other - and are fair game for the Sentinels. One in a million Humes may die by Wolf, but every single one of the Throwbacks shall be killed, either by Sentinel or Wolf, and no consequence shall befall the executioner for the kill."

"Is that why you are here, to take my life?" Jack was very frightened but David had to give him credit, he stood his ground, he did not try to break from David's grip.

David lost his temper then. He threw his son from him with the force borne of that anger.

Then David was upon Jack in an instant, his face a visage

193

of death and destruction, his words barely distinguishable. "Foolish human, you idiot boy! I have no wish to kill you, I never had a wish to cause you harm. I wanted to prevent any harm befalling you, you are my son! Even if I had not made a promise to your mother, I would never want harm to befall you. Had I realised that you would come to this, I would have made you full Wolf long ago. As it is, I hope it is not too late." David snapped his jaws on empty air as Jack understood what it was that his father meant to do and pushed hard with his feet to throw the surprised Wolf off him. He scrambled to his feet and grabbed a small bottle from the table.

Looking down at the bottle to make certain of what he had, Jack opened the top and fended off his father's attack with his free hand, holding it in a 'stop' position. "Father, do not attack me again. I can kill you with the contents of this bottle. Get out of my house or I shall use it, I swear to you."

David changed his features back to human again and took great stock of his son and his words.

He saw the bottle but did not quite understand what it contained but decided to take no chances.

"Very well Jack, I shall go."

"I suggest that you never return and that you never approach me again. I can kill you, father for what you did to my mother, the misery you caused her and the pain she suffered, not only in her illness, but in missing you. For that agony alone, I would have no regrets in causing you as much pain as I possibly could."

Jack held the bottle in front, as though it was a deadly weapon and David believed the threat and left with only a snarl in response to the warning.

Jack knew then that his time at his house was finished. This could be the very last time he was here and he took steps to remove all equipment and resources from the building – or at least the necessities that he would utilise in his new and secret workshop.

Jack planned to spend the rest of the day taking everything that he could to his new laboratory. He had not intended to spend the day thus but needs must go when the devil drives.

He moved a rudimentary camp to his workshop and made it as comfortable as the basic conditions would allow. He had a pallet for a bed so that he was not lying directly on the cold, hard floor and a wood-burning stove for basic cooking and warmth – although he did notice that for at least a few days of the month, cooking and heating would be the last of his priorities. If his clothing became dirty or dishevelled, he did not care, for he had in effect cut himself off from his work, his Club and his colleagues and associates. He was determined to continue his experiments and see them through to their conclusion.

Jack had left some of his belongings at his house, such as his journal, the Grimoire and his notebooks for he did not want them to become damp.

Once he had removed most of the items necessary for his continued experiments to the laboratory, he closed up his house and ensured that everything was cleared away – including the crockery in the kitchen – Jack left and didn't look back.

That evening, though he was hidden from the moon's glow in his laboratory, he felt its pull on his wolf psyche and he could not resist, though he tried.

Without the adrenal glands to give him the boost on changing, Jack found that he was not performing as he had the previous evening and, frustrated beyond measure, he followed a young woman along a darkened street.

Jack was about to make his move when she saw him and stopped under a street light.

"'Ere, who are you following?" she shouted to him, her voice quavering with fear.

Jack didn't answer her but continued towards her. She saw the gleam in his eye and became more frightened, looking around her but unwilling to move from the relative safety of the street light's meagre glow.

"Don't come closer mister, please. You're frightening me." She was at least honest.

Jack was close enough that he could smell the stale sweat on her clothes but he paused before he got close enough to touch her; he could hear someone approaching at a run. He turned to see two men sprinting towards them. The woman did not recognise the men, he saw that by her expression and so, not needing any encouragement other than fear of capture, Jack turned and fled.

He did not see the woman clinging to the arms of one of the men, relief on her face and in her manner. Jack did not see the other man continue for only a few steps in pursuit of him and then turn back towards the woman that had so nearly become his next victim. He heard their conversation but not the words and he realised that she had indeed known the men, they had come to her rescue but Jack was furious with himself. He felt that he could have dispatched all three of them, had he only known that they were not Wolves, but Humes.

Discretion is the better part of valour and if he had to play the same scenario again, he would behave in much the same way. By the same philosophy, he could do no more than believe his father when he had told him that Wolves were so much more powerful than he. He had felt the sheer strength of his father's arm as he shoved him backwards and he had seen for himself that his father's visage could alter at will and so for the time being at least, Jack must behave accordingly and not take chances when it came to other Wolves. If he had to make a choice between an encounter or escape, he must always choose escape. He made a mental note to re-evaluate the theory that he, as the sum of his parents, was an improved version of both species.

Jack had stopped once he realised that he was no longer being chased and he looked back to ensure he was safe. His anger erupted then; he had missed a chance of acquiring more glands to enable him to change to full Wolf.

Jack stalked through the almost deserted streets in search of a lone woman to take advantage of.

Instead, he found a boy. Jack saw the boy standing with his back to Jack, his head bowed and his attention on the ground; he was poking something with a stick. The something was lying in the gutter and seemed to be quite bulky, half as big as the boy. Jack could smell a foul stench and realised that the boy had discovered a dead something and, curious, was examining it in his own way.

The boy had found a dead and decomposing dog. Its guts were exposed, stretched beyond their endurance and split, spilling out the remains of the animal's last meal. Rats had begun to remove bits of the fleshier parts of the remains and in places, bones were also exposed.

Jack was able to draw near to the boy before he became aware of anyone close. Instead of being afraid, the boy seemed protective of his prize and stood between the carcass and the newcomer as though unwilling to share even the sight of it.

"What do you have there, my boy?" Jack asked.

"It's a dog, mister. I didn't kill it, I just found it."

"That is certainly interesting. Do you see how it died?"

"No mister, I thought it 'ad just dropped dead. What did it die of then?"

"Well, I think that perhaps it has been beaten or knocked down by a cart or a carriage. Do you see the front leg? It

197

is broken and so are some of the ribs. Do you see? They protrude... I mean, poke through the fur and skin. I think that the dog was old anyway because its fur is grey and its coat is in poor condition. It has mange and most likely fleas, but they will have gone now." The boy hung on Jack's every word, taking the information in and nodding as he did so.

"Would you like to know more? I have some animals at my work place and I would be most happy to show you the differences from this poor mangy animal to the ones I have been studying."

The boy had probably never been shown any attention of the kinder sort before and after only a fleeting moment of hesitation, eagerly nodded and said that he would like to come and see Jack's animals.

Jack lifted his hand to place it upon the boy's head in a show of affection for the benefit of any that may have noticed a boy walking away with a gentleman and the boy flinched out of his reach, surprising Jack into withdrawing his hand with a jerk.

Once the boy had realised that Jack was not meaning to hit him, he relaxed again and allowed the hand to rest on his head for a moment. Jack cringed at the dirty hair under his palm and it took a great deal of self control not to jerk back his hand again.

Jack managed to keep the revulsion from his voice as he continued to speak to the boy. Not once did Jack ask for his name and the boy didn't offer it.

The unlikely looking pair strolled along the dark streets chattering away like old friends and soon they were close to Jack's hidden work place. He dodged behind a large pile of rubbish, debris, wood and rubble and beckoned the boy to follow him. The lad did not move for a moment or two, weighing up the appearance of the secret entrance but Jack called from the shadows, "come on lad, it's this way."

As the boy caught him up again, Jack explained the need for secret entrances. "My work needs to be kept secret but I also need to be close to the place where I procure…" Jack saw the puzzled look at the unusual word, and he changed his manner to the one he most used in the workhouse infirmaries. "The place where I get my experiments from."

The boy seemed to accept the explanation and continued walking, following Jack.

They came to the entrance to a darker alley and Jack went on into the gloom without hesitation. The boy followed with caution. He got halfway along the alley before he stopped and pressed his slight body to the brickwork of the wall, trying to make himself part of his surroundings almost. He was aware, all of a sudden that there might be something not right. Without a word, the boy turned back the way he had come and began to hurry back to safety.

Jack saw and realised his escape attempt and caught hold of him. Jack plucked the boy off his feet and swung him around to catch hold of his head, pressing it to his own body by way of his hand being forced over his lower face, pulling the boy to him. The boy could neither escape nor shout for help.

The urchin was dragged, struggling both for release and for breath, into the darkness that hid the entrance to Jack's lair.

The boy struggled less as Jack bundled him into a large box in a dark corner of the room. He was part-suffocated and dazed, beginning to lose consciousness. Jack began to prepare the operation with a thoroughness that bordered on obsession for detail.

The operating table was cleared, the objects that had been placed on it in a convenient and temporary position were put away and the surface was wiped over. The boy, by now terrified and silent in that terror, was dragged from the box and given a glass of gin. He sipped it and looked up to Jack's face, and tried to smile at his captor. Jack smiled back but the smile did not seem to give the boy any reassurance. He continued to sip at the gin and Jack grew impatient. He gestured that the boy should finish the glass and when he had, Jack re-filled it. The boy was already reeling and would have been unconscious in next to no time. Jack put his arm under the boy's chin from behind and exerted a slight pressure, pulling the boy's head back to rest on his hip. After a few moments of the gentle pressure, the boy lost consciousness and Jack felt certain that he would not wake because of the gin in his bloodstream. He stripped the boy and laid him first on his front. Jack cleaned and examined the boy's body from a clinical point of view, noticing that he had a slight curvature of the spine and a few broken and healed bones in his arms and legs. The boy had had a hard life, short though it may have been. Jack noticed bruises and lacerations, both old and new, the he lived close to abusive people, that was certain and Jack thought to himself that the boy's pain was now at an end.

He turned the boy over and examined him again. Once the dirt was removed, he saw scars on his face that he had not noticed before. The boy's cheekbone had once been broken and had set not quite evenly, it gave an odd cast to his left eye. He had a scar across his collarbone, a broken rib and his hips were not aligned correctly, giving the boy one leg higher set than the other, making it seem as though he had one leg longer than the other. There were many injuries and damage to the boy's form and Jack surmised that he would have been enough of an oddity to give the other street urchins excuse to ostracise him. The boy would have been lonely.

Jack did not realise, (though Hazel would have been able to explain) that his humanity was trying to justify his actions, perhaps in order to relieve the guilt that his sub-conscious anticipated.

Once his rudimentary examination was complete and Jack was happy with his findings, he took his tool roll of scalpels, scissors and the like and opened it out within easy access. He took a scalpel and began the operation.

Jack was just about to make the first incision when he heard a noise, the sound of a stone hitting the metal outer door and he paused to listen. He put down his scalpel and moved to the inner door to listen closer.

The sound came again, a tiny noise that he would have missed had his hearing not been accentuated by his Wolfness.

Jack froze in place, wondering why he was being given a warning that someone was close. Then he heard a voice. He recognised his father's voice and he gave a contemptuous snort and went back to his work on the boy. The boy was still out cold and Jack smiled. As an indulgence, he bent his head to the boy's chest, just to hear the heartbeat and the air as it was pulled into his lungs to inflate them. Jack also imagined that he could hear the flow of the life-blood as it was pushed through veins and arteries. Jack was salivating as he straightened up.

After he had butchered the boy, piled all the bones to be disposed of and had tasted the meat (and been disappointed that it was not as delicious as he had anticipated), Jack looked to the glands he had removed. He knew the adrenal glands had an effect on him and he had become curious as to whether the other glands would also have an effect – perhaps in a different manner or to a stronger or lesser effect.

He cursed his forgetfulness as he realised that he had again forgotten to bring with him a looking-glass in order to see the effects the consuming of the glands would have – if any.

Jack pocketed the glands after wrapping them in a piece of brown paper he had brought to the laboratory for the purpose of the transporting of meat.

As he let himself out of the back entrance to his lair, he imagined that he had avoided the Wolf that had trailed him to tap on his front door.

He thought wrong.

His father was waiting for him.

"Hello Jack," he said and sniffed the air. "Oh Jack, you insist on making mistakes at every turn. Why on earth would you want to carry glands on your person? Do you not know how tasty they smell to Wolves? Let me help you, son, you are in grave danger. Wolves that are searching for you will abandon that search in order to find the source of the delicious smell – the glands that you have in your pocket. Then they will have you!"

"Is that right?" Jack asked, a plan forming even as he spoke.

"Jack, I came to plead with you once more. Allow me to bite you, to make you full Wolf. It may yet save your life."

"I shall think on it father, that is all I can promise."

Jack left his father behind, in the dank passageway between his secret laboratory and the streets of Whitechapel and continued out into the open. Taking heed of his father's warning, using the greatest caution, he made his way back to his house to locate a mirror. Jack wanted to see what he turned into when he consumed the glands. Then he would catalogue his findings in his journal so that he may study that as he had the Grimoire years before.

Jack prepared himself; he laid out the glands before him in the kitchen. He had carried the large mirror from his bedroom and leaned it against the table, and then he placed a chair before it so that he might study his face once he had noted the changes to his body. He had drawn the kitchen curtains so that no one could see, even were they in his back yard. He undressed and stood before the mirror, entirely naked. Then, thus prepared, he took one of the glands, the adrenal gland,

and placed it into his mouth. He watched his face as his teeth burst through the flesh that encased the gland and watched as his whole body began to vibrate.

Nothing seemed to be happening at first and he attributed that to the fact that the boy's glands were not as large as the man's glands that he had consumed before, so he popped the other one into his mouth and, impatient to see the results, bit down hard and swallowed.

He was dismayed at the transformation. He did not resemble a Wolf at all. He looked, instead, like a man possessed of a disease such as leprosy, one which disfigures and makes grotesque that which was once normal.

Fur sprouted all over his face and body in sporadic places and his features seemed to alter as he watched, even after he assumed that the transformation had finished.

As he watched, more fur grew and disappeared. His nose elongated and then, a moment later, flattened – both alterations disturbing and uneven. He realised that his father had spoken truthfully, he was not a full Wolf and his powers were greatly reduced in comparison to others which he sought to compete against.

In desperation, he consumed all the glands and noted that the transformation was still unsatisfactory. When his mouth came to resemble a misshapen leer, so twisted that he found it impossible to close, he could watch no more. He turned the mirror from him in disgust. It fell to the floor and shattered.

He knew then that he must become full Wolf as his father had offered.

He realised a moment later that if that one fact was true, then others must be true also. He was in grave danger from those of his father's species. They were hunting him and now he knew they could kill him and hide the fact of his disappearance – they could murder him and dispose of his

203

body with total impunity.

Jack realised that he must take up his father's offer to bite him and make him full Wolf before he was captured and executed by those who hunted him.

As he thought on it, he came to one last conclusion – Jack was not consumed by the bloodlust that he had been overtaken by the previous time he had consumed the glands. Either the effects had been imaginary or they were minimised by the pre-pubescent glands. One other option occurred to him; perhaps he did not change every time he consumed glands? He had to find his father!

Jack made haste to dress and return to his lair, where he hoped his father would be waiting for him. If David was not waiting, then at least he knew where to find him and because of his precautions, Jack knew that he was at least safe there. Jack had to keep to the shadows; he could not risk taking a hackney carriage because of the way he still appeared – a misshapen and even deformed man, much in the way that Dr Jekyll and Mr Hyde were portrayed in the novel – surely, anyone seeing him as such would have no misgivings in denouncing him as a monster, perhaps even as Jack The Ripper! The irony that he should be captured because of his appearance after the care he had taken to disguise and hide his actions was not lost on him.

David was not there when Jack arrived.

He had not expected him to be but he had hoped. Jack waited for only a few minutes and left. He did not know where to begin his search and wandering aimlessly through the city would only bring more chances of the other Wolves catching sight or sense of him and therefore chances of his capture – what had David called them? Sentinels?

What Jack could not have known was that David was already captured.

After Jack had left to go home, David had made sure that he was safe before going his own way. It was on his way back from Jack's property and to his own that Hazel had appeared in front of him, so silent was she that for once, David was startled.

The element of surprise played by Hazel worked well and David was thrown mentally off-balance and she knew it.

"So this is the reason that you were so opposed to the Sentinels presence in your city, David? You have spawned a Throwback and you were trying to protect it from us. You have done very well so far in the fact that we have not yet captured and executed it but our time is drawing near, there are enough of us now to find and execute it and we shall."

"You are mistaken, Sentinel Exemplar." David gave a small bow in greeting in an attempt to cover his shock at being confronted. "That is not the reason that I am opposed to your presence."

"Oh? Then why?"

David realised that she was enticing him into her trap and his mouth snapped shut on his reply.

"Oh no, David, refusing to answer will not save you. I know your guilt and you are being arrested. The sentence will not be proclaimed until we see how co-operative you are in the capture of the Throwback."

"I will not co-operate in his capture."

Hazel smiled but said nothing. Her smile was enough for David to realise that even though he knew she was trapping him, he still walked into that trap.

"How did you know?" he asked at last.

Hazel looked at him, her eyes blazed with a gold light. "I am Sentinel Exemplar; it is my job to know."

"But you did not know at the meeting, you allowed me to stay and listen to your plans."

"Why do you think I allowed you, a relative whelp in terms of age and experience, to stay and listen? To hear the pain and anguish of those families that lost their loved ones to this anomaly. The very anomaly that you created and for whatever reasons, did not follow the First Laws and you suffered it to live. The Throwback that is even now, playing a part in the destruction of our very society, for if it is captured, then the Humes will finally have proof positive that we exist. Not for more than three hundred years have we faced such a danger and if you do not know our history, it was the time when a bitch betrayed our kind – *her own kind* – and wolves were hunted to extinction and when I say 'wolves' I also mean 'Wolves'. If it comes to the worst, David," she spat his name with such hatred that he flinched, "we shall be hunted and eradicated and it shall fall to you. That is the reason that I am holding back on your sentence, for if you do not help us and we have to find this Throwback ourselves, it will take longer and therefore, the danger to us as a whole is magnified. If one Wolf is killed because of this, I shall hold you directly responsible for his death. Now, will you help us or no?"

If David had not realised the implication of his actions before, then he certainly had an awakening in those words. It took only moments of thought for him to nod his head and he was rewarded by a look of pure contempt from Hazel. Not only had he betrayed his species by allowing the Throwback to live but then he had betrayed his son in an instant. Damned if he did and damned if he didn't perhaps, but Hazel had expected a far greater show of loyalty for his son. Perhaps even negotiations for his son's life, but to give him up without any plea for help was, to Hazel, cowardice.

"Take him away." Hazel gave the instruction to Kirsty; though small in stature, she had curves that made both Hume and Wolf take more than a second glance. She used her voluptuous body and her apparent lack of guile to lethal effect, ensnaring men and Wolves to her bidding – one for the purpose of food and both for whatever her heart desired. Without guile? No, not Kirsty.

She took David in a grip that ensured he knew that she could snap his arm with no effort and less conscience and of course, he went with her.

Ralski was right behind them as they left, unseen and unnoticed but Kirsty's back-up should she need or want it.

Hazel followed after, making certain that they had left no trace of the capture or of their presence.

Hazel had read David well. He was a natural coward and the touch of silver on his bare and tender flesh, accompanied by the threat of more to be laid on more tender areas, had him giving chapter and verse on his relationship with Amelia, the birth of their son and the history of Jack and his eminent career.

David did not realise, but Anton had also made enquiries after learning of Jack's presence at the summer camp of Keme's tribe.

The coincidence was too great and Anton had left England's shores in search of the source of Jack's knowledge. Hazel did not anticipate that Anton would be returning soon. She had an idea that Jack had acquired extensive knowledge and that would have taken months, if not years, to gather.

Instead, she worked on the knowledge that David was giving up to them. She soon had Jack's address and so sent a squad over there to search the place. She knew that Jack also had a lair somewhere close to where they had apprehended David, but as yet, he was keeping the location close to his chest.

The squad had finished a quick search and were almost ready to leave when Jack arrived at his street. He was fortunate that the street was straight and that his house was halfway along it, for if he had been closer, the one left outside to guard the front of the house would have sensed his presence before Jack saw him.

Jack realised at once what had happened to David and he fled.

The guard gave the alert to the squad exiting the house but again, fortune smiled upon Jack and they realised a chase would not be advisable in such a well-to-do area. They took their findings – meagre though they were – to Hazel.

She accepted that they had not pursued him, but she sent them back out to scour the area once more for traces of the Throwback.

Jack was in a quandary. The Sentinels now knew of his home so he certainly could never return. He was unsure if they knew of the laboratory and it was with extreme and paranoid caution that he returned to it.

The last chance of becoming a full Werewolf had escaped him – or had it?

Once in his laboratory, Jack took a notebook and wrote everything that he could remember from the Grimoire which was still at his house. He realised that writing his journal may have been an error and leaving it at his house was one error too many.

With his diabolical mind set on his actions, Jack set to work. He pulled the small cage closer to the large cage and made enquiries of his more nefarious contacts so as to procure the items he thought he would need.

Hazel was becoming frustrated with the lack of progress in finding the Throwback and even with David's information, its whereabouts remained unknown. Hazel realised that David had finally grown a spine and had resisted more torture but

Hazel could not bring herself to bother too much about its capture – it would happen eventually and at least while it was in hiding, it was not committing any more murders. That meant that at last, attention of the police and other agencies were being diverted from Whitechapel to more pressing and current occurrences in the capitol.

She suspected that the Throwback was leading her into a false sense of security but for the moment, she was willing to follow where it led.

Perhaps, if she had any idea of what Jack was planning, she would have redoubled her efforts to flush out the Throwback.

Hazel entered the room at the back of the warehouse. She had chosen this building because she knew from living in the area that this was in the process of having a change of use in its contract. The lawyer holding up the process was a good contact of Anton's and was happy to keep the building tied up in legalities for the time being.

That meant that she was free to use the building as she wished and at this moment, she wished to cause damage to a particular Wolf.

"David, I know that you are relatively young in the great scheme of things, but you have a great knowledge. You know something and I would like to know it," her voice was quiet and calm but her hands were wringing the riding crop that she held. "I hesitate to use threats or violence, but rest assured, if I need to, I surely would. Do you believe me?"

David sat up on his makeshift bed and looked at her as she spoke. His eyes were full of new-found bravado – a much altered expression from the one that she had seen last on his face, when she had given the order for him to be taken away.

Since that order, she had not visited and had been pleased with the reports from his interrogation.

Under her express orders, no torture was to be used. David seemed to have now realised that she was loath to use this method but he was mistaken in the reason for it. He imagined that Hazel was abiding by the First Laws. He was about to be educated on that subject.

"No Hazel, I don't quite believe you. I think that if you were allowed to torture another Wolf in order to gain information for the greater good, then you would have used it by now. I think that you have to abide by the same law that we do – First Law. I also believe that you, above all others, have to keep to the letter of that law and that you would be in far greater trouble if you were to bend even one aspect." He sat back on the cot, leaning against the damp and filthy wall, a look comprised of contempt and nonchalance on his face.

"That is what you believe?" Hazel asked.

He nodded his answer, not bothering to speak his reply.

"Then you are a bigger fool than I first took you for."

He was astounded by the speed with which she covered the empty space between them both. She grabbed him by his coat collar and drew his face up close to hers, holding him up off his bed, as she whispered to him. "I did not allow my Sentinels to use torture on you because I want to see your reaction when the silver is passed over your testicles." She held his face close to hers for a moment and then threw him back down on his bedding.

He was shocked at her use of the word 'testicles'. He had never heard a lady use the word in his presence before and Hazel knew that his genteel upbringing would be his downfall.

"You will tell me where the Throwback is hiding, David, because if you do not, as I believe I told you when we arrested you, then you will be held as liable as the Throwback is for any death or injury to any of my Sentinels. Believe me when I say this, for it may be the most important thing that you will hear.

If any one of my Sentinels – or indeed, any Wolf – is killed, then I shall invoke an ancient punishment, a Pack Judgement. At the end of that, if you are found guilty – and of course, you will be – then the pack rends you limb from limb and you are left to writhe on the ground, just a torso and a head, until one of the relatives of the dead feels that you have suffered enough and ends your life for you. It is not pleasant. I have seen it only a few times but it is effective in the fact that it deters Wolves that hear of the judgement from straying from the boundaries set in First Law. If, on the other hand, no-one is killed, only injured, then I shall invoke a Pack Kill. You know what that is, I suppose?"

David's eyes were wide as he imagined how the Pack Judgement would go for him but he managed a feeble nod in acknowledgement of the question.

"Good, then I have no need to explain; only that the hunt would wait until the injured Wolf was recovered enough to join in and he or she would be the one to make the kill. Now, this is your very last chance. Do you wish to tell me where your son is?"

"Are you open for negotiations, Sentinel?" The timbre of the younger Wolf's voice was respectful and tinged with fear which made his voice shaky but he continued after clearing his throat. "I ask that because my son has killed only Humes, I would like to fulfil my dead wife's wish that I bite him and make him Full Wolf. It is for her sake that I ask this, not mine. I always hoped for her to be bitten and made Piaculum for me so that we could both enjoy the benefits of being Wolf together. Though she was only Hume, I did love her and I was trying to gain permission to bring her over to us when she became pregnant and we fled." For the first time, David raised his eyes to Hazel's and held her gaze. Hazel could see the emotion in his eyes and the desolation at the loss of his wife

211

and the potential loss of their son. "I realise that my son has succumbed to a kind of madness but I believe that he could be brought over to us and would, in time, make a fine addition to our pack. His knowledge of medicine and surgery would be invaluable to our kind if only you would consider the trade? I propose his life in exchange for his service to Wolfkind."

Hazel watched David make his proposal. The Wolf was desperate, that was true and quite understandable under the circumstances. It was a desperate plea for his son's life, but he would be an asset to Wolfkind into the bargain. Hazel did not have to consider long.

She nodded and said: "Very well. If we can capture him quickly, with no damage done to any of my Sentinels, I agree in principle. This is, of course, subject to the Lycaeon's final judgement. I would present his case favourably if it came to it, I give my word."

"Then that is good enough for me. I shall lead you to his laboratory so that he knows that you have not trapped him."

In the meantime, Jack had been very busy.

Jack walked through the streets of Whitechapel as though he belonged there. Just a few months prior, he had felt uncomfortable and out of place if he walked on his way to see a patient – one of the 'gratis' patients, of course – but now, after the atrocities he had committed and the misery he had caused, he felt almost at home. No one gave him a second glance, there were few people on the streets anyway, but those went about their own business as though he too was a lifelong resident.

Jack did not yet realise that he had caused pain to any left to mourn his victims, he assumed that he had had no effect on the lives left in his wake – only to those that he had slain.

He had a reason for being in the area – revenge - and to tie

212

up one last loose end before he gave up his new hobby.

He had given a task to Mary to get Keme to the lodging house on the pretext of picking up a few of Isabelle's belongings that she had found. Of course, she had told Keme that he could have the necklace back, as long as he was willing to pay for its return. Keme did not consult with Isabelle about the necklace and other items as he thought to take possession of them in secret and present her with them as a surprise.

Jack waited for Keme behind Mary's door as the time that they had agreed upon approached. Mary assumed that she would be getting cash for this bogus transaction, either from Jack or Keme (or perhaps both) and Jack waited with a hood soaked in chloroform.

A light tapping on the door set Jack and Mary on edge – for different reasons.

Keme entered the room as Mary invited him in and Jack hooked the hood over Keme's head. The struggle was violent but short-lived. Keme was unconscious upon the floor before anyone was injured.

Then, Jack dealt with Mary Kelly, the disloyal friend of his love.

"Have you got my money then?" the woman asked as Jack laid the unconscious body of Keme on the dirty floor of the room that Isabella and Mary had once shared. He noticed how much the room had changed in the short time since Isabella had moved out.

"Yes, I have your money. In fact, I have more money for you than we agreed upon, if you are willing?" Jack left the details unsaid and Mary's eyes gleamed with greed.

"What, you want to make the beast with two backs with him lyin' there, do yer?" She feigned reluctance, perhaps in an attempt to eke more money from him for the inconvenience he was causing her. "But I need the money; I'm weeks behind in my rent now that Izzy's not here anymore." Her tone had altered to one of a wheedling nature – one that irritated Jack and set his teeth on edge.

He hid his irritation very well as he pretended excitement and began to paw at her upper body. "Yes, I think that I should like very much to make the beast with two backs with you."

"Let's see yer money then." Mary imagined that she now had the upper hand in the transaction and pressed forth her advantage. Jack removed his wallet from his jacket and showed Mary more folding cash than she had ever seen in her life. Her eyes grew wider yet and her fingers twitched to get hold of even a part of that cash.

Jack took it all from the leather wallet and held it out to her. Mary didn't need to be offered twice; she snatched the money and turned her back as she hid it somewhere about her person. When she turned back around, Jack was almost naked. He had been removing his clothes and folding them onto a chair close to the window. When she turned around, he was just laying the last of his garments on top of the pile of clothes and unusually, his shoes were also on the chair. Mary imagined that it was a quirk of his and hoped that he had no other oddities connected with his sexual habits – such as laying on a beating, before, during or after sex.

"Oh, sir, you are ready aren't you?" she made reference to Jack's obvious excitement but unfortunately for her, got the reason wrong.

Mary began to undress and emulated Jack in the fact that she folded her dress and shawl as she laid them on the chair closest to the bed.

Jack made to kiss the woman and she welcomed it. He traced his fingers across her neck and followed the fingertips with his lips, ignoring the stale smell of sweat rising from her filthy body. He also ignored the gritty texture of the skin on her throat from not having washed in a number of weeks. Jack realised that though this was a grown woman, she had needed Isabella's guidance in everything – from paying rent down to when to wash. Without Isabella's influence, the money Mary had earned had gone on gin first, food second and little else after.

The pressure he exerted on her throat with his fingers increased suddenly and she put up a bit of a struggle when she realised that he was no longer intent on sex.

Mary had blacked out long before Jack began to play. Her neck was beginning to discolour where the fingers had pressed hard and had bruised the skin and he touched it with a tenderness that would seem peculiar if he managed to remember the fact later.

He turned her head to face him as he began to work.

The knife that he used on this occasion was not his usual preference of surgical quality. He had chosen this blade for its weight, not its finesse.

Once he had hacked through her throat and put an end to her life, Jack began his game.

He tied Keme's elbows together behind his back and secured the wrists in a similar fashion – tight and very secure. Then he tied the knees together and pulled the still unconscious form up into a sitting position and made sure that Keme was held steady by tying his ankles together and bending the legs at the knee in order to prop him in the sitting position.

Then Jack went back to the task of reviving Keme by means of bloodletting on Mary Kelly.

First, Jack arranged the legs so as to give him room for the operations that he was planning.

Jack sliced through the tender flesh of Mary's breasts, talking all the while as he did so.

"I'll cut this bit off here and place it up here," almost in

215

a sing-song voice, he removed a breast, cutting deep to take muscle as well as tissue in one circular incision and placed it under the head. He was careful not to move the head too much in case he pulled it right off. "Then I'll take this other piece and put it out of the way, over here," Jack removed the other breast in much the same way, cutting deep down to the ribcage, and placed that at the bottom of the bed. "Now - I'll – make – sure – that - nobody – sees – you – in – the - same – way – ever – again!" He punctuated each word with a series of slashes to the face. Once he had made sure that Mary Kelly was as unrecognisable as he could, he checked on Keme to see if he was awakening and on finding the young man still unconscious, Jack resumed his game.

He began a parody of an autopsy. The abdomen was sliced crossways in three large swathes from breastbone to pubis but not in a smooth and practiced manner of an eminent surgeon, Jack was far removed from that particular part of his mind. He performed with the random jerkiness of a madman conducting the orchestra of the damned.

He pulled back the flaps of the abdomen and as an afterthought, sliced down to remove all three pieces from the body. He laid those pieces of flesh on the table, out of his way. Then he cut at the thighs of the woman. Taking the flesh almost down to the knee on one leg he then leaned across the body to hack flesh from the upper leg, and then the genitalia and the buttock on the other leg. He again laid out the pieces on the table in what would seem to be the butcher's table of *Sawney Bean* – "Only the most tender cuts of meat on the front to draw in the custom! Ha ha!" he cried as he waved the bloody knife about his head. As he brought down the knife, he cut down the leg of the corpse almost to the ankle and was amazed at how deep the cut had gone with so little effort. He opened up the cut with his fingers and tried to peer inside.

216

Jack continued the knife waving exercise he had started at the table and sliced and slashed at the upper arms and face once more, seeming to be dissatisfied with the previous mutilations he had inflicted. On more than one occasion, he forgot that he was naked and wiped blood from his hands down his front as he would have done had he been wearing his apron. His belly and upper legs were decorated with vivid red streaks, fingermarks slashed across his own flesh in a parody of the wounds he was inflicting on Mary Kelly's remains.

He removed pieces of the internal organs and put the uterus and kidneys along with the breast, under the head, again being careful not to remove the head from the body.

He took the liver and threw it up into the air and left it where it landed, between the feet of the corpse.

Jack took the spleen and dropped it on the side of the bed closest to him and then removed the intestines and tossed the slippery morass over to the other side of the bed.

Then he took another glimpse at his captive and dissatisfied that he was still not awakening, aimed a kick at the man's thigh. The kick would have been ineffective even had Keme been conscious for Jack had not got his shoes on.

By this time, blood had soaked through the thin mattress and was dripping onto the floor. Jack held onto the side of the bed and tilted his head under to watch as the gore dripped through. He began giggling at the sight of it and at the sound of it drip-splashing. His hearing was acute at that moment and he felt that he could hear the blood as it oozed from the corpse, down through the mattress to form a droplet and fall from the underside to merge with the pool that was already spreading on the floor.

Then Jack, humming a tune that he remembered from church perhaps, went on his last spree. He hacked at the face of the woman, holding the knife in a very light grip so that the movement was as flexible and as fluid as possible and took slicing cuts at the face and arms, flicking his wrist to almost scoop at the cheeks and nose, glancing off the bone on the cheeks and forehead and on one cut, removing part of the nose. He saw the effect of that cut and attempted it again on the cheeks and forehead just to see what effect it produced.

Before Jack was finished, he was in the throes of utter insanity and he took out the heart and held it above his head, lifting his face to bathe in the blood that he squeezed from the ventricles.

Then he took the piece of flesh that had, only hours before, been the mainstay of the living, breathing woman that lay destroyed and mutilated before him and he took a bite from it, relishing the dense muscle as his sharpened teeth sliced through the flesh and he chewed in something akin to ecstasy.

At last he had finished his pantomime and found that a discarded bed sheet made for a convenient towel to remove the majority of the gore from his body. He threw the sheet onto the fire in the hearth where it caught light almost immediately.

When Jack left Mary Kelly, she was no longer concerned with the money she had been promised - he left her eviscerated remains for the police to deal with.

Jack dressed and before he hefted Keme onto his shoulder, he made one last gesture, perhaps to draw attention away from his escape – "Murder!" Jack yelled out of the front door and scurried back to lock the door. Then he took up the body of his captive and left by the back door. He had to put down Keme's form for a moment as he reached through the broken window and locked that door too. His escape to his laboratory, where everything was prepared for his final experiment was unhindered and uneventful.

As it happened, no one came to investigate the shout of alarm and he made his way to his lair. He dumped the still unconscious Keme in the largest cage and then busied himself with preparations as he waited for Keme to awaken.

Keme did not take much longer to regain his senses. He came to and looked about him before moving about. He did not try to grasp the bars – a fact that disappointed Jack who was observing from the shadows of one corner. Jack thought that he was invisible in the gloom, but Keme took but a few moments to lock onto his position and glare at him in silence. The two men regarded each other for a time, Keme reclined upon the dirt floor of the cage and Jack standing, still swathed in darkness. Then Jack left the gloomy corner and walked around the cage with an obvious thirst for knowledge about his captive.

"You must be wondering why you are here." Jack said at last. Keme remained silent, only his eyes moving, following Jack's movements around the cage.

"Did you hear me?" Jack tried again to engage Keme in conversation but Keme only watched the other as he paced around his prison.

After more than thirty minutes, Jack tried once more. "Are you ready to talk with me? I know that you understand my language, I have heard you converse with others."

But Keme remained mute and, with anger growing, Jack left the building. He made certain that everywhere was secured and then made for home. He avoided the direct route back home, and therefore, his latest work area, but the buzz had already spread. His latest victim had already been discovered and he took great care to avoid drawing attention.

His heart almost stopped when he saw a policeman in his path. Should he avoid or ignore?

As he was distracted, concentrating on this dilemma, his arm was taken hold of. He was pulled with firm and insistent gentleness, into a doorway.

219

"I would not go past that policeman if I were you. Your hair is dark and stiffened with blood and you stink like a slaughterhouse."

Jack did not dare turn to see who his advisor could be, yet he dare not ignore the advice.

"What is it to you?" he asked, trying to cover his surprise with a belligerence that he had noticed other East End residents use with frightening regularity.

"Nothing whatsoever to me, son."

Jack recognised David's voice at last and turned around with caution.

"What on earth have you been up to, Jack? The whole of the East End is again up in arms about the latest atrocity you have committed – it was you that killed that woman this morning, wasn't it?"

"Atrocity? Me? I have not the slightest idea of what you mean."

"Jack, I have something to tell you, something that can help…"

But David did not get to finish what he was about to tell Jack, for Jack saw the look in his father's eye and he realised that he was about to be trapped. Jack pulled his arm from David's grip and moved backwards. He glanced to the side, in the direction that he had seen the policeman and with relief, saw that the policeman had gone. Then Jack ducked down, below his father's attempt to grab him again and as he dodged backwards, he fished something from his pocket. He waved the bag at David and said: "Do not follow me!" then ran in the direction that he had seen the policeman.

Hazel gave the command to follow Jack and also advised caution for she saw David's expression. She delayed her pursuit to question David.

"What was in the bag?" but before David could answer

with his opinion, they heard a terrible screech as three Wolves voiced their distress almost as one being. Hazel and David caught up with the Wolves that had chased Jack and were dumbfounded at their agonies. The Wolves – all of those that set off to chase Jack – were writhing on the ground in anguish. Their flesh was sizzling; the stench was terrible, their hands clawed at their eyes and as Hazel and David watched, unable to do anything, two of her comrades died of their injuries. The one remaining managed to grunt the warning "Silver particles... breathing impossible... eyes..." before she too expired.

David was in shock at the sight of the dead Wolves. These Wolves had been his captors and his wardens, but for all that, had not been cruel or unreasonable toward him. He felt a genuine sorrow for their deaths and an absolute horror for having been witness to them.

Hazel felt different emotions. She turned to David with a look in her eyes that had him backing off in terror. She reached forward with a hand that had begun transformation and grasped him by the throat. As his eyes bulged with the pressure she was exerting, he saw her eyes change colour first to the usual preternatural yellow and through to a bright and sparking golden colour, flashed through with deepest black flecks. As her other clawed hand reached forward to tear his head from his body, he imagined that he saw those flecks radiating from the inner pupil to shoot out from her head in a dazzling display. He could still see the sparks as his decapitated head hit the ground and then, as it rolled, he saw his body crumple and fall to the ground and then nothing. Perhaps his son could have explained that the illusion was probably due to his brain being starved of oxygen, causing hallucinations, but then again, perhaps they were not hallucinations.

Hazel lifted her face to the sky and though it was still

221

daylight, she howled her wrath, knowing that any Wolf within earshot would understand that the chase was on in earnest.

She waited until two Wolves had located her and once she had given the instruction for three bodies to be disposed of with respect and honour and one to be given to pigs, she set off to find her quarry.

Hazel went forward with great vigilance; she had seen what the Throwback was capable of and did not wish to suffer a similar fate to her three companions. The scent of the Throwback was dwindling but she realised then that the silver would have had chance to dissipate if she left it long enough.

Jack heard the screeches behind him and knew that he had bought himself some time. He had to work quickly, and to do what he needed to would take perhaps more time than he had.

He made his way back to his laboratory, passing through more than one slaughter yard in order to confuse any pursuing Wolf and with any luck, throw them off his scent.

Keme had to be forced into his Wolf form somehow and because it was no longer the full moon, Jack's vast knowledge of the Werewolf legend, lore and attributes would be tested to the extreme.

Jack knew that Keme was but a young Wolf and therefore should be susceptible to outside influences that could force a change but even these could take time – which was the commodity that was in shortest supply.

At first, Jack tried disembowelling one of the animals he had purchased just the day before, for this purpose. Keme watched with a mild curiosity, but nothing more. Then Jack tried the ancient methods, the ones that Hunters had used for generations to hunt Werewolves. Blood was sprayed in Keme's direction, stale and almost congealed blood and also fresh gore from the body of the dog he had just killed. Keme sneered in response to Jack's attempts. Keme realised what

Jack was trying to do and so he was concentrating on not changing his form.

When Jack picked up a flask of liquid and removed the lid, Keme could not help but sniff at the scent coming from the container. When Jack put back the stopper and then threw the flask at the cage bars for the container to smash and spray the liquid onto the captive, Keme could never have expected the change in his body that was forced upon him. Almost in an instant he was Wolfen, full Wolf, snarling his displeasure at Jack and before he could concentrate once more and change his form back to humanoid, Jack doused the animal with another bottle-full of strange smelling liquid.

Keme collapsed onto the dirt floor within moments of the second dousing. Jack watched and smiled.

"The first bottle contained urine from a female wolf – that in itself would not have been enough to force your change, but the wolf in question was in season, ready to mate. Added to the liquid was also Mary Kelly's heart and pituitary gland, I took them when I had killed her; I pulverised them and only added the pulp on a whim. You see, I had to have you in your Wolf form because I need your strength."

After a few moments, Jack noticed that Keme had stopped moving, he was barely breathing and Jack opened the cage door; he was full of impatience but not so eager as to chance that the Wolf was playing 'possum'. Armed with a staff of silver, Jack poked Keme's body and when he did not move, he touched the silver cane to one of Keme's front paws, on the tender area between the pads. The flesh sizzled but the animal did not flinch, but he did grunt his pain.

"Ah, paralysis," Jack mused, half to himself.

He dragged the Wolf from the cage and set about his next task.

He took exquisite care in the operation and, ignoring

the moans of pain and performing with uncommon skill; he flayed the pelt from Keme's form all in one single piece, leaving the skinned body intact and perfect – and deceased. Keme expired during the operation; Jack had heard the death-rattle and checked for vital signs, of which there were none. He assumed that shock had worked with the distilled aconite to send Keme's body into deep shock which slowed his heart to such a rate that the body could not survive the strain.

On one more whim, Jack sliced the scalpel across the base of the palm on his left hand and pulling the tongue through the dead Wolf's teeth, wiped saliva along the self-inflicted wound. Jack thought it best to cover all eventualities, in case the ceremony did not work as he hoped. Then, after binding his wound, Jack set forth to begin the ceremony that would turn him from a despicable abnormality to a powerful creature that he knew as 'Werewolf'. Jack did not give a moment's thought to the welfare of his father, nor of Keme's family – blood or adopted – he concentrated on his own desire to become Wolf.

He did not, therefore, hear or sense Hazel's approach and the first he knew of her arrival was that the fortified and bolted door was smashed from its hinges, sending splinters of wood and pieces of metalwork flying through the air in his direction. A massive splinter of wood gouged its way into the flesh in the back of Jack's thigh and he screamed in pain as he turned to first grasp at his wounded thigh and as a secondary consideration, to watch Hazel stride through the wreckage she had made of his door.

She raised her hand to strike him dead where he stood but as he cowered in front of the flayed corpse of Keme, she sensed something about him and she paused.

Jack noticed her pause and wondered why. He thought that perhaps even she had realised that he was a more powerful being than she had yet encountered but when she began to laugh, a harsh and humourless sound, he changed his mind and began to stand up – until the pain from the sliver of wood cut through from his thigh to his brain and he again clutched at it.

Hazel saw the sliver of wood protruding from his leg and grasped it and whilst he was still only beginning to protest, she pulled it out of the flesh. Then she did a surprising thing, she smelled the sliver, scented the blood that it was soaked with and smiled. Jack thought that the smile was far worse than the expression she had been wearing when she burst through the door - that was terrifying enough, but the smile, the malevolence held in it such promises of searing agony and torture that Jack was intelligent enough to quake in his boots at what the smile meant for him.

Hazel began to look around at her surroundings. She saw the cages and the tethered animals, the laboratory equipment, ingredients in jars, and the desk with books strewn across it, one notebook being the only object that was placed deliberately and neatly. Then she saw the large glass jar with the head immersed in liquid and her eyes paused in their roving. She frowned for a moment and then her gaze moved on.

Jack wondered for a fleeting moment if he could possibly escape whilst she was occupied with scanning his work but he froze as she shook her head and gave a silent warning for him not to try. He was shaking with fear as well as shock from his still-bleeding wound as she continued her visual tour.

When at last, her eyes came back to the operating table which held the corpse of Keme in Wolf form, one tear escaped and dripped onto her cheek to drop once more to her coat where it was lost in the fibres of the fabric. If she noticed, she did not give any indication. She looked at Keme – or what was left of her pupil and shook her head. She moved Jack with a hand to his shoulder and saw what he was obscuring – Keme's

225

pelt. She scooped it up and smelled the pelt and two more tears dripped onto the silky fur.

"You have no idea how much trouble you are in. You have no idea of how much pain you have caused, not only to me, and you have no idea of how much I want to kill you right now, but I shall not, for I know that there is someone who will make some kind of amends for your actions. There is someone for whom vengeance is not just one act against another being, it is a series of acts against the other, designed to bring forth screams of such perfect pitch that the one screaming was not aware he was capable of such a sound. I am going to give you over to Anton, the one who was charged with this one's safety." Hazel indicated Keme's body lying before her. "He will be delightfully vengeful, unforgivingly vicious and perfectly, ultimately skilful in your torture. I suppose that I would have felt a little sorry for you before you killed my protégé, but now, I shall delight in watching as Anton tortures you day after day."

"You were about to kill me, why did you stay your hand?"

"Ah, you noticed, did you? I was indeed about to slay you, I would have if you were still Throwback but now, something has changed. You are not Throwback, or at least not wholly so. What did you do? Did Keme manage to bite you?"

"No, I opened my hand and wiped his saliva in the wound."

"Oh, the infection takes so little time to take hold, does it? Anton will be interested."

"Infection? Please explain."

"I think not. You deserve nothing but a swift end to your miserable existence from me but that is no longer necessary. You shall be rewarded for your experiments, you will be helping with more experiments than you could ever have imagined."

Hazel had the larger of the two cages sent to the same warehouse that had recently held Jack's father and so, in the same building, but in far less comfortable conditions, Jack was

226

imprisoned. He was bundled into the cage with more force than was necessary and he stumbled and reached out to grab the bars to stop his fall. His hiss of pain was satisfying to all watching, but especially to Hazel. She made a silent promise that she would not inflict unnecessary harm upon his person whilst they awaited Anton's return but that did not mean she would act to prevent harm befalling her 'guest' in the meantime.

Chapter 6

In the days that they spent waiting for Anton, Hazel read the Grimoire that her search party had discovered when they searched Jack's house. Then she read the journal that her search party had found in the house and it helped her to understand many things. It was unfortunate that she had not taken the time to read the journal before making a deal with the Throwback's father, David, but she decided that it would have made no difference to the outcome, except that perhaps she may have executed David before he had led them close enough to its laboratory.

Hazel read of experiments that the Throwback had made - his experiences and the murders he had committed in the name of 'research'. She was aghast at the range of scenarios he had thought up in order to get close enough to a Wolf and give them cause to change. She was also worried at some of the situations Jack had got himself in to. By rights, bringing himself to the attention of Wolves should have brought nothing but a similar fate to the curious cat. However it had not and he had appeared to have witnessed many Wolves going about their usual business – that of slaughter and feeding on defenceless Humes.

Hazel read through the daily journal and a few entries caught her eye and she thought to find out more of the events described.

February 26th

I had a notion (in retrospect, not a very wise one) to go out to see if I could find and observe any night creatures. I chose an evening completely at random and I must remember that mistake and learn from it, for I fear that I may have gone abroad far too near to the Full Moon and therefore, placed myself in unnecessary peril.

I met with a streetwalker. I saw her and went across to talk with her. She was very stand-offish and I did not take to her. Her voice was irritating and I did not speak with her for more than a few sentences. I did notice that her gaze was shifting towards something to my rear and I bade her farewell and left her. She began arguing with another man and I stayed to listen for a moment.

Well! It seems that they were partners in crime for he accused her of alerting me to his presence (she had not) and therefore denying him a means of income.

When the argument escalated into near-violence he seemed to come to his senses and instead of beating her (as I and she thought he was about to) he lowered his walking stick and departed.

As I also turned to leave, I heard her once more begin her patter. She had been approached by yet another man and she was asking if he wanted company (or words to that effect). I did not listen to the whole conversation for I was on my way but then I felt very odd. I turned around and she was being assaulted by the man. He punched her in the stomach a number of times and I must have given a gasp of shock for he turned in my direction and then, realising that he was discovered, made off at a run.

I went to the woman's aid and found that she was unconscious. I realised that she had been attacked more severely than I had first thought when I saw blood on her skirts. I lifted her skirts and saw that she had been stabbed, not punched! The fortune of the woman was that she was wearing her heavier winter garments and that must have saved her worse injury.

I inspected her to the best that I could under the circumstances and as

230

she was coming back around, I began to make my exit once more.

To my horror, I heard someone in an alley close by. I looked but could not see anyone, the shadows were so dense, but at once, I did see twin orbs of amber light. They flashed as bright as a sunburst and I became frightened for my safety.

I did not wait around to see if the woman was dead or dying, I fled!

I did find out that there was a widow, a 'seamstress' by the name of Annie Millwood admitted to Whitechapel Infirmary (the closest to where the incident took place and the one that I happened to call in at on Monday morning on one of my volunteer visits). She had a number of stab wounds in the legs and lower abdomen.

The admission report states:

'... stabs to the legs and lower torso with a knife.'

I did not see the woman but she was kept in for almost four weeks and so I can assume that her injuries were as serious as I had thought.

April 7th

I noted that the assault I saw had

been recorded in 'The Eastern Post' today.

The woman, named Annie Millwood was admitted with stabs to her legs and torso and had been attacked by person or persons unknown. There were no witnesses to the attack but it is in some doubt whether she was telling the truth, if the wording in the article is to be believed.

I make this note because it is less than a fortnight after her release from the Infirmary. She was sent from the infirmary to the workhouse at Mile End Road on making a complete recovery but only ten days later, she has collapsed and died. The Coroner's Report states that she collapsed while 'engaged in some occupation'.

The Inquest just two days prior to this entry gives the cause of death as: 'sudden effusion into the pericardium from the rupture of the left pulmonary artery through ulceration'.

I did not have an opportunity to see the body and I feel that I cannot ask specifically to see that particular corpse for fear of arousing suspicion. My thoughts, however are that the rupture could have been caused by a blow to the chest if it were of sufficient violence and I wonder therefore, if the would-be assassin

232

returned to finish the job he had started on that night.

Again, I have no means of investigating why someone would wish to murder the woman and whether she had knowledge of the creature that observed from the shadows that night. I wonder, if I too am in danger. I must take heed of this unforeseen warning and keep a very low profile, lest someone should wish to remove me from this mortal plane.

It would appear that the Throwback was more savvy than Hazel at first thought, she did not realise that it had done so very much research or watched so many Wolves and therefore, unlike others of its kind, did know to some extent, what it was and what its potential could be – moreover, it would seem that it embraced its potential and would like to know still more. The enquiring mind can be a dangerous thing – especially to those of whom it is enquiring.

Another nagging query in the back of her mind refused to surface and so she allowed her mind to wander for a moment, not concentrating on the journal or the problem at hand and at last, her mind made sense of it. The one that had attempted to kill Annie Millwood had been Hume by the evidence of the first report, yet when she was eventually killed, if the Throwback was right in its theory, a great deal of strength – perhaps even superhuman strength – would have been necessary to cause the woman's death.

Which Wolf that Hazel knew would want a Hume killed without harvesting the glands? It was ingrained that Wolves disguise their kills but to kill a Hume and not benefit from that kill by way of feeding was unusual enough to take notice of.

May 25th

The feel of the approaching summer months seem to have awakened more than a curiosity in me. I also feel quite invulnerable!

As I begin my experiments in earnest, so I must continue to record my findings.

I realise now, that the phenomena I witnessed at my mother's graveside was personal only to me. David could not have known that his features altered.

The Werewolves are not guided by their bloodlust alone. They take into account a wide and varied amount of other factors.

Yesterday afternoon I was asked to autopsy a woman that had been brought in. She had seemed to be strong and healthy but had been attacked by a wild animal it would seem. I weighed and measured the organs as is my norm and I noticed that there were no signs of disease or even illness about her. I was careless however and I slipped with my scalpel and I have a very deep cut on my left palm, I do not think that it requires stitching but I shall keep an eye on it.

Then, last evening, I encountered yet another of the creatures. I saw him as I went into the theatre and his visage altered as did my father's and I was so shocked that I had an attack of some sort. I came home immediately and then I went out into the slums to watch the moon.

I met a delightfully provocative young woman who led me away to her bed. I do believe that was my first experience of a 'seamstress'. I am not best-pleased with my behaviour and feel utterly ashamed this morning.

May 26th

I have spent one of the very worst nights of my entire life! I had the most horrendous visage as I pondered and daydreamed up in the attic (heaven knows how I found myself up there) I 'awoke' to find myself moongazing and was shaken from my reverie by a terrifying visage peering at me through my attic window.

I was terrified to the point that I spent a good deal of the night cowering under my bed!

235

I am beginning to think that tracking the creatures may not be a good idea after all.

May 27th

Last evening I went out once more. I conducted an experiment and endangered myself greatly. I have had a horrible fright but it is all in the name of science and so I record my findings here.

It would seem that I am not exact in my theories. I cannot control a creature, a werewolf by appeasing it with a sacrifice, it is not enough.

The next test subject of mine was that of a crone. I propositioned her in error (I realise this in hindsight). As I was casting about for sense of a werewolf subject, one found me and the crone became alerted to my shock and decided that she must escape the situation. She was sliced along her spine and expired in front of both my subject and myself.

It bade me finish off the kill and promised that it would not steal it from me. How odd that it should reassure me in that way, did it believe me to be of the same species? It thanked me and then warned me that my sword would be no match for her own weaponry and I believed her! Her voice, however, was enchanting, it washed over me and cajoled my inner being, perhaps the beast could communicate with the part of me that is beast - that part of my own psyche which can sense them and it was leading me into danger! I must be extremely wary in future. I shall be on my guard.

Later that night, I was approached by an unseen werewolf and, in great fear for my own safety, fled to my house. I was exceptionally unwell the next day and I can only assume it was delayed shock that incapacitated me.

Although, now that I read back on my writing, I realise that I have put a gender to the beast. Yes, it was definitely female.

Hazel was curious, it was perhaps two Wolves that the Throwback had encountered yet no one had reported the anomaly. Also, the autopsied female seemed to have been significant. If the Throwback had mentioned it in its journal, then it had not been a usual occurrence.

She read on.

May 28th

How extraordinary! The corpse of the

237

woman that I was autopsying on Thursday has been stolen. It would seem that one of my assistants has absconded with the body of the woman that I instructed him to finish. I am well aware of the irony in this situation - a man of scientific study stealing a body (perhaps for material gain) but who would he sell such a body to, surely not the resurrectionists?

Oh dear, I must remember to not allow such irreverence to creep into my work at the hospital for I should surely be reprimanded for such a joke!

June 17th

I have had the most fortunate of escapes! I have encountered two werewolves - or 'Wolves' as they prefer to be known - and they were both delightful company for the evening. Almyra and Marcellus as they were known approached me in a most cunning fashion and I felt compelled to invite them in to my home. I gave them a tour of my house and laboratory and I was permitted to interview them - though I was not allowed to write down their conversation.

Hazel was reading through the mundane witterings of the

238

Throwback and almost missed the significance of this entry.

She took better notice of the passage and re-read the beginning.

August *(early)*

I return to this, my Journal after an absence in my studies. I am afraid that some of the events mentioned here scared me badly and I did indeed keep a low profile.

I recall that the Wolf I encountered when I decided upon another experiment was curious but not inflamed by the smell of blood. I did not get a clear look at his face as I stabbed the woman and so I am totally ignorant of the identity of that particular werewolf.

I had gone out with the intention of discovering a werewolf and perhaps forcing it to change to its wolf form. I followed a streetwalker and her companions on a whim and used her in an impromptu experiment. I had detected a werewolf and thought to inflame it beyond its control. The experiment failed. I did not see clearly enough, the Werewolf's features and so I cannot identify it. It was two weeks after the Full Moon and I assumed then that the werewolf would be at its weakest and therefore more inclined to change under duress. I am ashamed to tell that it was not the other that became out of control, but me. As I attacked the streetwalker, I found that the non-reaction from the werewolf enraged me and I stabbed countless times.

As he watched, I must admit that I grew angry and stabbed the woman repeatedly. She was of course, dead long before I had finished. I stabbed her heart quite early in the attack. I am not a sadist you see.

I have vowed to not become as frantic as I did then; I shall make every attempt to remain under control at all times during my experiments.

The murder has been reported in the newspapers. Martha Tabran had 39 stab wounds upon her person.

August *(late)*

The late Almyra and her companion visited me in my dreams - I am so glad that she grew back her hair - and we relived the interview and she explained at length her thoughts and opinions of the events of that night, which leads me to other conclusions:

The stage of the moon plays a part, of that I am certain, but it is also combined with the age of the subject. If the subject is old or even 'Ancient', then they are less susceptible to the moon's influence and more able to change at other times of the lunar cycle too, it would seem.

Also, blood alone is not necessarily the only catalyst for a werewolf becoming excited or enraged. Other bodily fluids can also contribute, but it seems, only with the much younger members of their species.

It would also seem that they have their own means of disposal of corpses, for the old woman that I sliced open in front of Almyra that evening has never been reported as found or murdered. I do not even know if there has been a search for the missing woman. Perhaps then, she had no one to miss her. That surely is the saddest part of this particular story, not that she was brutally murdered and then devoured, but that she had none to mourn her passing. It is, of course, a shame that I did not think to ask that question whilst I had a captive audience, so to speak and I forgot to ask the question again last night, but I suppose that that is how dreams go sometimes.

It is surely unfortunate that I had cause to dispatch the youngest two that I have yet encountered. Almyra and Marcellus confronted me and took me very much by surprise. I was not prepared for them. Would that I could relive that evening, I would know better then.

I autopsied Marcellus's body and I am so very disappointed that I cannot publish my report for the perusal of my colleagues. They would, I fear, believe me to be either insane or a liar - neither of which would be acceptable to me.

I neglected to autopsy Almyra but instead, I dismembered the corpse and soaked the body parts in a solution of diluted arsenic. Then I made parcels of the parts from her clothing and placed them in a trunk. I first removed the uterus for further study. The head, I also kept.

The trunk will be disposed of at my convenience. Marcellus has already been buried.

This evening, I decided that I must further my studies. I have the advantage that I seem to be able to sense these creatures and I am astounded at their number!

Whilst there are not thousands of

the creatures in this area, I have sensed
perhaps a dozen or so. There may yet be
more.

In the interview with Marcellus and
Almyra, they both alluded to a society
and I can assume from that that there are
more yet for me to encounter.

She read the whole entry and understood at last, what had become of the lovers. She also realised that it cleared up perhaps more than one case on the police's books – that of 'The Body in the Trunk' and perhaps even of the dismembered arm which was discovered floating in the Thames.

Hazel knew then that she had recognised the severed head in the jar they had found. That was Almyra's final remains.

Hazel could see from the rambling fashion that the journal had begun to be written in, that the author of this journal was beginning to show signs of the kind of madness that can overtake those known as Throwback.

His writing was becoming disjointed and the style was changing from one date to the next and even skewing backwards in the time-line to relive events that he had already experienced. Toward the end of the journal's entries, the style was changing even on the same line. It would appear that if Jack had still been practising at the hospital at the times of these entries, he would have been noticed and admitted to one of the insane asylums.

Although werewolves consider
humans - or 'Humes' - to be a lesser species,
I believe the opposite to be true.

243

We 'Humes' are not governed by our bloodlust, neither are we enslaved by the phases of the moon. Granted, we are less powerful in strength but we are less strong than many other species. We are unable to change form, but we are not forced to do so either.

We cannot use our senses as well as them, but are they any more adept than - for example - dogs?

I, on the other hand, am both human and I am also able to use my senses to discover the creatures.

My conclusion, therefore, is that if I am a hybrid of Hume and Werewolf, then it is I that is the more powerful of all three species and if there is one of me, then I think it safe to presume that there may be more.

I am a super-species and so perhaps, the best way forward for humankind?

I cannot recall suffering any illness, not a cold nor any of the childhood diseases. Perhaps, therefore, I am immune to disease.

I must study these creatures better. The way I can see to do this best is to capture a youngster (for an Ancient would be too strong and not susceptible to the experiments I intend performing upon it).

Perhaps I can use my previous studies from Europe and the New World in order to change my own form. A Wolf Belt allegedly alters one to wolf and I think that I have enough knowledge on werewolf lore to manufacture some similar device. I must make some experiments. If I can lure one young enough, I can perhaps manipulate it so that I can harvest a pelt. This would mean that I must kill it whilst it is in wolf form but I have contacts that can be discreet and a cage would not be such an unusual purchase.

I have made up my mind! I shall, therefore, capture one!

September 1st

Last evening, marks my first success! I am elated, even euphoric! I made a plan to find and observe a werewolf and I went out into the slums again. I had the sense that there were a few about as I wandered. I saw one woman. She paused as I tried to hone my senses. I am able to sense these creatures better now and the confirmation is the visible alteration of their faces. I became wary of the woman - she seemed

245

different somehow. As I probed with my
mind, she paused and looked about her.
I saw her doing so and stopped what I
was doing for fear of alerting her to my
presence. That encounter made my heart
beat faster!

With that passage from the journal, Hazel knew exactly what it was that had bothered her. She had known that the Throwback was searching her mind but she could not recognise the sensation. She also realised that when in the laboratory, she had known that it was going to attempt an escape and she had shaken her head 'no' to advise against such an action.

Was she then in tune with Throwbacks? Is that what the prophecy had foretold? Was that the reason behind her rise to Sentinel Exemplar?

Hazel became contemplative then. She stopped reading for a while and went off deep into her own thoughts, trying to recall more on the prophecy.

There were 'forks' in each chain of foretold events and she had made a choice in a number of the events which were directly linked to the future of all Wolfkind.

The first 'fork' that she knew of had happened before she was Wolfed properly but it was manipulated in order to fulfil the prophecy. Did that make the prophecy weaker or stronger?

There were so very many questions without answers. Hazel determined to sit Anton down for a week if necessary and grill him on what he knew; it was time for her to know all about her own birthright, her own prophecy. It was time that she was given all the information on exactly how she was to "lead Wolfkind to a new and bloody era" – as the then Lycaeon had said.

246

The decision made to see this through to the end and then question Anton gave her a resolution to that particular problem and she continued with the journal.

A few minutes later, I saw a younger man. He was also a werewolf and it was far easier to recognise him as such. Perhaps she is able to conceal herself? I shall be much more careful next time. I hastily worked out where the man was going and intercepted his route.

Fortunately for me, a streetwalker was loitering along Bucks Row in Whitechapel and I did not even have to waste time communicating with the wretched woman. I approached her and hit her hard with the handle of my cane. She stumbled to her knees and I felt the tingle begin in my scalp and before I knew what I was about, I had sliced her throat from behind. Taking a firm hold of her chin, I lifted it and ran my blade across her neck. I must remember to retain control of my excitement for I cut far too deeply, I fear. Her head was very nearly off! (Had I tapped in to an inner strength, one that is entirely bestial in origin? I must remember to watch for that on the next time).

I had allowed the prostitute to fall to the ground in the gateway to one of the slaughter yards; she fell onto her back, and I lost no time in pulling up her skirts and I then opened up her belly. Perhaps she was still hanging onto life by a thread as I sliced her abdomen for my incision was very sloppy and jagged, not the work of a skilled and practiced surgeon at all, I am afraid. I had to work fast; I could hear the young man's approach... or did I sense him? Was the tingling sensation part of sensing or part of the excitement? The young man that approached stopped dead in his tracks before he saw the body - of that, I am certain. He was young and swarthy - bearing a resemblance to a native of the American shore if I am not mistaken. He was young and healthy to the eye, his dress was impeccable - not the Native Indian traditional dress at all and he was shocked when he discovered the newly dispatched corpse.

I saw him as he discovered my work. Though I had almost thrown myself into my hiding place, it was, by great fortune, a good vantage point. I could see both my subject and the body clearly through the slats in the gate of the slaughter yard where I was concealed.

His expression was delightful! I almost gasped out loud at it.

He could smell the aromas from a way off and he approached the body slowly and with a great deal of caution.

I watched as he seemed to shudder - in revulsion, I first thought, but I soon realised that it was raw excitement. I could only see his back at this time and I assumed he was about to vomit. He did not bend to the corpse but he did turn around. It was at this point that my pulse rate leaped! I saw his eyes - they glowed with an amber luminescence and his visage altered - just as others have before him. His face turned to wolfen and back in less than an instant! I no longer believe that this phenomenon is a physical occurrence. I now believe that the change is my own inner beast recognising the beast within others.

Again, that is an exciting revelation indeed!

Once I had gathered my senses once more, I continued to note exactly how the young man was reacting. He was barely able to control himself. He was still shuddering visibly and I could see that his

249

face had altered.

It became wild and feral. His eyes glowed yellow for longer than an instant. It was a glow rather than a bright flash that I usually experience when I 'see' the inner beast. His teeth became sharp and grew longer and unless he hails from a tribe that practices cannibalism, I see no need for an Indian to file his teeth.

But wait! This is too coincidental, surely? Could this young man be the same that I tracked almost to the Canadian border to find? I cannot believe my excellent good fortune! It must be him!

I digress.

The young man's teeth were longer and sharper than they had been. He was standing less than three yards from me and he did not see or sense me, so great was his distress. And yes, I saw that he was indeed distressed. He was still shuddering violently. His eyes were a different hue to any I have seen - either human or werewolf - they had a circle of yellow around the iris - although this could of course, be my inner beast seeing the different colouration.

His face had become very hirsute - not only along the usual traces - beard, moustache and sideburns; the growth continued down to his shirt collar (and beyond, I presume) and up across his brow and the bridge of his nose - which also looked oddly elongated - muzzle-like I suppose.

I was thrilled that I was able to witness the transformation into werewolf at last. But I was thwarted! Although the changes that had already taken place were not reversed, they did not continue.

He was visibly fighting with his inner self, I could see that most clearly and after a few moments of struggle, he ceased his shuddering, took a number of deep breaths, looked closely at his hands, rubbed them together and then seemed to concentrate. He at last set off, away from the trap I had laid for one such as he, without ever touching it and not once that I saw, did he look back.

As he left the scene, I felt, rather than saw, another werewolf also close by. I believe it to have been yet another, but I do not believe that it was a threat to my subject.

I was free of the tingling sensation on my scalp once more and after a few minutes, I began to think of leaving my

251

hiding place. I am once again, thankful of my great fortune for before I vacated my position, the young man reappeared (preceded momentarily by the tingling scalp). This time he was not alone. His companion was a woman. She seemed to be dressed only a little better than my victim and it struck me as very odd that the young man had brought a prostitute along with him - for what purpose? Then I observed that she was the one who led this little group. He had brought her to this place but then she took control of the situation.

They both startled at something and a few moments later, I too heard someone approach. How they heard the man from such a great distance is beyond me - for now at least - perhaps they have superior hearing too? It would indeed make sense.

The pair also had to hide and I heard them murmuring to one another for a moment or so but then I heard nothing. Either they fell silent or had dropped their voices too low for me to hear.

The newcomer saw the corpse and approached but unlike the first, he became alarmed and called to a companion. Both men inspected the corpse and one claimed to be able to feel the woman breathing.

The two men left abruptly after the cursory examination. I almost gave myself away, for I slipped on something underfoot and I believe one of the workmen may have heard me. No harm done, he fled.

Then a policeman arrived, and he also examined the body and he called to another for assistance.

A Doctor Llewellyn (whom I vaguely recognise) arrived and declared her dead and an ambulance was used to take the corpse to the mortuary.

My study and his companion waited a short while and then left also. I am glad that I am patient for I waited even longer and saw one other depart. I had not seen him arrive so I cannot be certain that he did not witness my experiment but if he had, then surely he would have intervened once I had sliced her throat - or confronted me once everyone else had left?

I believe that the young man - werewolf - is staying locally, for I seem to think that he knows the area, for he found his way back easily enough, unless of course, he is able to track using his senses.

I have much to think on!

I was delighted this morning by seeing my work (or at least part of it) immortalised in the Daily Telegraph. It reads well, designed to shock the reader.

September 8th

I am not quite right in myself. I am ashamed to confess that this morning, on my way in to the hospital early to finish the work I had left the previous evening; I was overtaken by the melancholy that has been plaguing me of late (and the reason for not completing my work). I was in a state of distress and I cannot explain it, but upon suddenly being confronted by a low and base streetwalker, I had an overwhelming desire to take her and see exactly what lay on the inside of her. I felt a need to dissect her and discover the secrets that her innards held.

At the moment of realisation, I seemed to be captured within a bell jar. I was watching my body, my outer self talk quietly to the woman, whilst inside my head, I raged, unheard, clawing at the glass jar encasing my inner mind. I was, at that moment, divided in two - one part physical and the other mental and the separate parts could not or would not communicate!

I saw myself, dressed in my apron, which I use when performing autopsies. I do not recall putting it on and I cannot explain as to why I would have put it on. I also know that I was not wearing it when I finally came to my senses, a few streets from the hospital back entrance, and I do not recall where I put it. I cannot find it and I thank the mistress of good fortune that I did not ever feel the need to inscribe my name upon it.

The uterus and partial bladder that I had in my possession is also inexplicable and both went into the incinerator once I had made certain that I was not observed. I am fortunate in the fact that members of my staff are well used to seeing me covered in gore in the early hours of the morning, for that is when I usually perform the autopsies.

Now, as I stare up into the moonless sky this evening, staring out of my attic window, I may have found the explanation for my melancholy. There is an empty space where the moon should be, but as I stare up, I can feel that it will not be so very long before it begins its return to full once more.

September 19th

I make note that an arm has been discovered, floating in the Thames. It is being passed off as a student's prank and I wonder if it is so or if one of my chickens has come home to roost?

It is with great trepidation that I prepare to venture out tonight. It is the first of the three September full moons and I am especially aware of the extreme danger in which I am about to place myself.

The danger is threefold.

First, if the Police discover me, then I am, of course, undone. My career, my liberty and my recent studies, not to mention my very life is at stake. Even were I able to escape conviction, I would be forever tainted and would surely lose the respect of my peers.

If I did not escape conviction, then, at best, I would face the rest of my natural life incarcerated at Her Majesty's pleasure. At worst, I would be executed.

Second, if the public at large discovers me, I would probably be done to death in a melee of vigilante fervour. At

256

least that end would be quick.

Third, and by far the most terrifying. If I were to be discovered by the Society of Werewolves, I doubt they would be too concerned regarding the murdered prostitutes but if they were to suspect why I was murdering them and further to discover Marcellus and Almyra's deaths were by my hand, then I am certain that my prospects would be limited. I am equally certain that my demise at the hands of these creatures would be a painful process.

I ask myself for the umpteenth time, then: Why am I hell-bent on venturing out this evening?

The answer is simple: It is the only way that I can alleviate the exquisite agonies, both physical and mental, that I suffer under the light of the full moon.

The sensation has been building for almost a week now. My whole being is vibrating as though my every sinew were as taut as a violin string and was being tortured by the Devil's own bow, slowly drawn across, back and forth, at a constant rate, with the tension increasing, creating a higher and higher pitch until I feel that my very blood vessels are

257

attempting to vacate my body!

I can feel every vein straining under the pressure, even the thread-like veins in my eyeballs feel as though they shall explode at any moment, leaving me blinded and only temporarily relieved.

I am ashamed to admit that the only way I have found to relieve these sensations is by stripping off all of my clothing and bathing in the cold luminescence of the moon's merciless glow. I cannot even bear the lightest of chiffon upon my skin. I have to undress. So far, I have managed this in the privacy of my attic, but the sensation has progressed so that even with the window thrown as wide as possible, it is not enough. The glass between the moon and my skin is also too much to bear. I need to go out tonight; I need to find a place where I can strip and moon-bathe in secluded safety so that I retain, if not my dignity, then at least my sanity.

September 20th

Last night, I did not know what to expect and therefore, I was exceptionally cautious - too cautious to enjoy the evening, I suppose, but I shall know differently for this coming evening!

I went out of town and onto Hackney Downs. It is not an ideal place to be 'as one' with the moonlight but it sufficed. I found my senses accentuated and my hearing gave warning of anything close.

I wandered in the darkness until I found a suitable copse, which gave enough cover for my activities. There I stripped almost naked and felt the moon upon my skin, washing it with the cold and soothing rays. I had become used to the discomfort, I suppose, but when the moonlight touched my bare skin, I immediately felt the relief from the irritation I was plagued with.

At last, I felt comfortable enough to divest the remainder of my clothing and I lay on the grass in the midst of the trees, with the moon shining its light upon me. I may have dozed, or slept, I cannot recall but if I did then it was for minutes, not hours. I watched the moon dip and make its way down to the horizon and at last, I felt the cold seeping into my body. I dressed and made my way home.

I am amazed at how energetic I am, I ran almost all the way home and I am not exhausted from running, or from the lack of sleep. Although I have taken the precaution of giving Lizzie the three days off and I have informed the hospital that I shall not be at work. I shall sleep during the day (if I can, I am so excited) and prepare for the evening.

September 21st

I am invigorated! I return from my second evening under the light of the full moon with such a feeling of well-being that I can hardly stand it! I want to dance and shout and sing but decorum and propriety prevent me from doing so.

I went out to dinner at my club as usual and then took a stroll rather than the cab that was offered. I aroused no suspicions, I am certain, though I did explain that I had received some good news in the mail and that would account for the smile that I could not remove from my face. I have spent the entire day in this state of excitement and the evening topped it off to perfection!

I again visited the young woman who had so expertly taken care of me on that first episode, an age ago.

I saw her talking to a dirty and rough-looking chap and I beckoned to her. I had no shame! I was still dressed in my good clothes and I noticed the looks I got from everyone who saw me! (They must think that I am the Whitechapel murderer and I do not care!) But she dismissed the man with a brief argument and came over to me willingly enough. Her smile was bright in the moonlight and her eyes sparkled, as did mine, I can assume. She chattered and prattled on as she led me again to her room in Millers Court, I believe, (the window is not yet mended and the cold air is beginning to blow through, past whatever it is that she has blocked the hole with).

I notice so many minuscule details when the moon is full, I am sure that my brain must be full to bursting with them by now. Her eyes are a muddy-blue colour, not quite perfectly clear, but everything else about her is utter perfection! I feel that maybe I could be falling in love, but I must also be thoroughly realistic and accept that I could not possibly take her as a wife... although, I could, I suppose, take her as a mistress. Perhaps find her a job so that she can keep only to me? Ah! Day-dreaming about her now, I must pull myself together.

261

We made love for the whole evening. That horrid little bed is barely adequate, but the sheets appear to be reasonably clean and I enjoyed my time with her immensely.

I retired back to my Club (just as I vowed I would, should I ever repeat my first experience with her). I reclined on clean sheets and a good sized bed and drifted into a dreamless sleep, the moonlight streaming through the open window onto my naked body, repeating the relief of the night I spent on Hackney Downs.

Evening:

I anticipate this evening with such a growing excitement that I cannot wait for darkness to fall and the moon to appear! Tonight I shall take another victim but not for the purpose of research, this time I shall indulge in my own pleasure for the sheer sake of it! I want to taste the flesh of a 'Hume' for myself. For once I have done so, I am convinced that the way shall be clear for me to change into a Wolf if I should desire it. I know the rituals that I need to perform and it is the optimum

262

time (I suppose that I should have done this last night rather than indulging in other 'pleasures of the flesh' but I doubt that one evening will make much difference).

After I sacrifice a human and partake of their flesh, I shall visit my concubine (I do not yet know her name, tonight I shall ask it).

September 22nd

I am beside myself in anger! I have been betrayed and I shall seek retribution. Last night I had planned to take a sacrifice so as to enable me to become full werewolf. As I hunted for a suitable subject, I happened upon a werewolf male - the very one that I saw on the first night that I experimented in luring one and encouraging it to change. It was too good an opportunity to miss and so I followed him.

He went directly to the rooms in Millers Court where I have spent many a pleasurable hour in the arms of my love. I flitted around the back of the building, fearful that I knew where he was heading. He was brazen and blatant in his mission. He did not knock upon her door, but opened it and went in. She was expecting him; I saw them through the broken window!

As they embraced, I could not watch further, I fled.

I spent the rest of the night I know not where, distraught and desolate under the full moon. I went home before dawn and went straight to the attic and watched the last of the moon's glow as sunlight enveloped it and it was gone for another month. I have wasted the moon's power and shall become maudlin and depressed again soon.

October 2nd

I am in a state of utter confusion! I seem to have been suffering blackouts for I cannot recall my actions for minutes and sometimes hours at a time. I read one of the tabloids yesterday which told of a letter written by the perpetrator of the heinous crimes which hold Whitechapel and London in thrall. It is signed "Good luck, Yours Truly, Jack the Ripper". This must surely be my subconscious making itself heard, drawing attention to me in order to stop my experiments.

Perhaps though, it could be the

wolfen psyche trying to protect its brethren by condemning me. If this is so, then I must be on my guard for if the part of me that is not human were to conquer, then it would be to my end. I must hurry to find a way to lure a young werewolf to me so that I may harvest its pelt and become master of this body and of this traitorous psyche.

Of course, it could well be a hoax for I have not had chance to see the letter to find if the hand writing matches my own. The spelling (if it is written verbatim), the grammar and the use of street slang does not match my usual eloquent style and I can hope against hope that it is indeed the work of some malicious trickster. Though I cannot conceive of the reasoning behind the jape, it is in the poorest of tastes. The threat to remove the next victim's ears is quite atrocious and not at all 'jolly' as was written. I do not think that I care for the other side of me, rather in the same way that Dr Jekyll loathes Mr Hyde in the novel of the same name.

Although I do confess to taking a liking to the name that has been bestowed upon me, I find it feeds my vanity.

On another front, I have heard tell of the discovery of a headless torso in the

basement of the new police headquarters
being built in Whitechapel. I had thought
that it would take far less time than this to
discover, I admit it. The gossips are having
a field-day with this news. It has not
even been released to the press as yet and
the information has come directly from
the brother of one of the workmen who
discovered it. The details are almost exact.
The corpse was discovered wrapped in her
black petticoat, tied with string in a neat
parcel. The solution of arsenic worked well
too, it would seem, for the odour should
surely have made the parcel noticeable
long ago if not for the preservative of it.

Dear Almyra, I do hope that they
never discover your head for I would be
undone, seeing as it is still in a specimen
jar in my basement. I wonder if the other
limbs will now be uncovered or did I hide
them well enough?

October 9th

There is mischief afoot! I have been
out and about watching and listening.
There is much fear and speculation about
the murderer and the police have been
drafted in en-masse! I dare not enact my
fury upon the traitorous strumpet that

266

betrayed my affection - not yet.

I have taken to discovering more of the youngster by the name of Keme. He is indeed of American Indian extraction but the circumstances of his Wolfing are still a mystery to me - yet. Mary is most generous in her affections and information for she is jealous of her friend's good fortune in snaring such a sponsor as Keme and is more than willing to share her bed and her knowledge with me - for a price, of course.

He visited Miller's Court almost every night and it would seem that my absence was not noticed. How she could lay with that savage in favour of a gentleman is beyond my comprehension, although it is not beyond Mary's, for she has noticed that he is kind to Isabella (I have, at last, discovered her name) and he gives her so much money that Isabella can afford to pay for the lodging and food and still not have to go out to ply her trade. Does she not realise that I too, would have shared everything with her?

I shall not visit Mary again for she is beginning to become curious as to my interest in Keme. I could, at first, pass it off as interest in Isabella, but I have gone beyond that in my questioning now. I must take great care.

I shall also begin to put in place the means by which I shall capture the one named Keme. I have decided that he too, should suffer my rage. I shall harvest his pelt and flaunt his demise to his lover.

October 21st

How the time passes! I have been occupied to the detriment of this journal but it is with a great satisfaction that I write tonight.

Last evening was the first of the October Full Moons and I am, again, euphoric! I went out into the bright moonlight and I became almost full-wolf!

My experimentation has led to a discovery. I find that I am able to begin a transformation if I concentrate hard enough and if I utilise the adrenal gland from a fresh corpse.

My new work-space is ready and completed. I have installed a large cage with a small holding cage attached in order that I can manipulate the wolf easily when I do capture him.

There is a fully-equipped laboratory and I have been busy distilling *wolfsbane (aconite), deadly nightshade (belladonna) and foxglove (digitalis).*

I am certain of the properties of aconite and of their effects upon werewolves. I intend to discover what the effects of the other two are and record my findings. I have an inkling of what should happen from my tutor in the Black Forest many years ago but as yet, I have not had the chance to perform these experiments for myself.

I anticipate that I shall have plenty of time in which to perform the experiments for I also have the knowledge of the Grimoire and the preventative measures that I have taken to ensure the werewolf pack cannot possibly find my lair.

That was the last entry in the journal and Hazel closed the book and put it to one side so that when Anton returned, he could read of the madness and discoveries that lay within a Throwback's psyche.

Chapter 7

In the days that they spent waiting for Anton, Hazel invited Amelia and Marcellus's families to the hotel. There, she explained about the murders and the evidence in the glass jar. Amelia's father wanted to see his daughter's head and though it was against her better judgement, Hazel agreed to it.

At first glance he did not recognise the face in the jar, the head was shaven and bloated from the fluid it was submerged in, but once recognition took hold, he became tearful and could do nothing but sob quietly for a few minutes, leaning heavily upon Hazel as he did so. She was uncomfortable with his display of grief and had to force herself to remain in the room as he pulled himself together and lifted the jar level with his face in order to look into his darling daughter's eyes for one last time.

When he asked, pleaded and at last, demanded to be allowed to see the brute that had murdered his daughter, Hazel could only refuse. No chance could be taken that Jack would be dispatched from his miserable existence before Anton had been given chance to experiment on the Throwback-made-Wolf. Such opportunities were few and far between and this

270

one came with a guarantee that no remorse would be felt by the experimenters.

Anton's arrival at Southampton was neither heralded nor broadcast. His journey to London was swift and uneventful, with no stops along the way. Anton arrived at the warehouse and sent his baggage on to the hotel ahead of him. He also sent word that if Hazel was there, that she should join him immediately.

The message was unnecessary; Hazel was already waiting for Anton's arrival. She had assumed that he would not bother going to the hotel first.

Anton strode into the building, removing his gloves as he approached Hazel.

"We did not part on good terms, I regret that," Anton said and Hazel nodded. "Although I did not anticipate coming back to this tragedy."

"I know. I too said some things that perhaps should have been worded better but what has been said cannot be unsaid and we have to live with those words now. However, it is our choice how we move forward after this."

Anton nodded and said, "Friends then?"

Hazel broke into a smile and she nodded too. "Friends."

Anton needed to be brought up to speed on the events that had happened while he was abroad. He was not displeased with Hazel for executing David but he did have a few misgivings on why he was killed. "You lost your temper and allowed your anger to make a decision?"

"Yes. I had agreed with him that if none of my Sentinels were harmed then things would go as he wanted in that I would bite the Throwback to make him full Wolf."

"You agreed to that? It is without precedent!"

"Yes, I know and subject to the Lycaeon's agreement, it would have been done but as it happened, three of my

271

Sentinels were killed – including Brynn whom I believe you knew well and Edward, one of Ralski's friends, and they died in the most horrible and painful manner and yes, I was angry."

Anton lowered his eyes in contemplation. "I see and I understand."

"I have a good team of Sentinels, Anton. They are all loyal to our Lycaeon but they are also loyal to me and one of the reasons for their loyalty, even unto death is that they see that I am not an officer that only gives commands, I lead by example and I mourn the loss of every Sentinel killed in battle – even those that are yet training as Edward was. I inform the Lycaeon of every loss and the Sentinels know this and appreciate it, it means that their death will not go unnoticed and therefore is not a waste. I also do not send in my Sentinels as 'cannon fodder' under any circumstances."

"Yes, I agree, you have brought together the Sentinels in a way that no other commander did before. Even when they are solo they are still a collective, they answer to you and do communicate with the others in their geographical area which can only be a benefit to your organisation." Anton waited for Hazel to say something more and when she did not, he prompted her. "There is something that is playing on your mind, what is it?"

"The Throwback killed Amelia and Marcellus. He noted the details in his journal and he kept her head as a souvenir."

"Good grief! Have their families been told?"

"Yes, I told them most of the details, I left out the journal because it is too graphic. Perhaps I should have also left out the detail about Amelia's head being preserved in a jar; it may have saved some upset."

"Her father saw it?"

Hazel nodded.

"What details do you wish to keep from the families?"

272

"He writes in great detail of his herbology and other experiments. He writes of how he paralysed the couple and how they died of wolfsbane poisoning. I did not want those details known. But there is one other thing that I have not yet told you."

Anton again waited.

"The Throwback is now, or is at least on the way to becoming full Wolf. I suspect that in the next day or so, as the full moon approaches, his wound will begin to heal at a miraculous speed and come the full moon, he will be as he wanted. He assumes that I cannot touch him now. He does not realise that I hold sway on his execution because you have other plans for him."

"Indeed I do, I plan to keep him indefinitely and experiment on his body in all manner of ways. At the end I shall ask you how you would like his end to come to him."

"I can tell you now. I would like him flayed alive before an audience of my Sentinels so they can see the final justice being done for the three that he killed with silver particles. Also, I would ask that if any of my Sentinels wish to observe the experiments before his end is dealt to him, that you will give them free rein, for nothing will bind them closer to me than to watch cruel and unusual punishment being carried out upon one who dared to injure one of my Sentinels. The crueller the better and I shall enjoy the thought of his imprisonment."

"You ask a great favour of me, Hazel; I prefer my work to be kept secret."

"And it shall be secret still, for none of my Sentinels will break your confidence, I shall make that understood. We are of one mind; the one that killed our comrades seems to be getting away with the crime because he has managed to make of himself full Wolf. They neither know nor care how he managed it, but the fact that I have held off on his execution

273

is giving them cause for doubt and I wish to scotch that as soon as possible. Will you make the announcement?"

"No, it is better to come from you - that you negotiated it on their behalf – which, of course, you just did."

Hazel smiled, it was not a pleasant smile, it was grim and determined and also sad. The loss of her three comrades had hit her harder than it should have and Anton knew that a change was on its way. Hazel needed to protect herself and if she was being affected in such a way, then she had to draw back – at least for a while. The Sentinels had proven their worth yet again under the Exemplar's guidance and Anton knew that Wolfkind owed a massive debt to the Sentinels – again – as did the Hume society.

Then Anton had a revelation. He went after Hazel who was making her way toward the meeting place where the Sentinels awaited an announcement from her.

"Hazel, you need a sabbatical."

"A what? Why?"

"Listen to me, you have become far too close to the Humes that you protect."

"My remit is not to protect Humes…" and she stopped in mid-sentence. It took but a moment for her to think on it. "So then, why have I been protecting their society? Why have I tried to ensure no Humes were killed if I could possibly prevent it? Why did I *care*?"

"Because, perhaps, as prophesised one, you are different. You seem to absorb the psyches around you and if you are constantly surrounded by Humes, then you take on more of their attributes and the Wolf in you fades."

"You forget I was once Hume, so perhaps it is that my inner self that absorbs Wolf?"

"I think not. You recall that when we began your tutoring, you embraced the Sentinel within you almost without prompting? After but a short while you were far more advanced at becoming Wolf than even those that were born Wolf, surpassing your peers – the others that were still learning how to control their change?"

Hazel looked Anton in the eye and held his gaze. "Are you implying that I am a sponge?"

Anton laughed with genuine delight. "Yes, exactly so! You take on the psyche of those that you surround yourself with. If you were to spend a year with my father and his pack, you would become more pure Wolf than even I am."

"Your father? Is that possible Anton? Is he still alive?"

"Oh yes, he is still alive and still runs with his pack, though it is diminished from the force it once was."

"So if I were to leave these shores and take my pack out to the wilderness and live alongside them, I would become more *Sentinel-like*?"

"I do not know, I could guess that you would not, for you have taught these Wolves to be Sentinel in your own way. If you were to find your tutors and live amongst them for a time, then perhaps you would once again be the Sentinel you were – tough, relentless, cold."

Hazel raised her eyebrows at Anton then. "I was once tough, relentless and cold?" she asked but her expression told Anton that she was being sardonic and he smiled.

"Perhaps you have a point," Hazel continued. "Maybe I should get away from these Humes; I am not here for their benefit. I protect Wolf from discovery, not Humes from Wolf."

"Still, you did a good thing, you stopped a Throwback and prevented it from being captured and therefore discovered for what it is – was – and you have provided me with a new pastime to keep me occupied for a while. The experiments can only benefit Wolfkind; I do not perform them purely for pleasure."

"I know this, I recall the knowledge that you passed on to me as we travelled across Italy and without your experimentations, I should not be as able to understand Throwbacks and I should not be as able to sense them, I am certain of it." Hazel turned to continue on her way towards the waiting Sentinels.

"One thing more, Sentinel Exemplar,"

Hazel froze as she realised he had used her official title for a reason.

"You must evacuate all Sentinels from England by tomorrow evening."

"I assume that is a directive from our Lycaeon herself?"

"Yes and no. I have spoken with her and she has allowed me to make the decision."

"Very well, we shall be gone by nightfall tomorrow."

"I did not mean you…"

"Nevertheless." Hazel cut him short and continued towards her meeting.

The waiting Wolves were silent as she approached. None were speculating on what they were to be told. They waited and Hazel sensed their mourning and their anger. Most had known one of the proven Sentinels that had died but only a few had known Brynn for he had kept himself very much to himself and was very much the lone Wolf but they all knew of him, his reputation was impressive. It was hard for all to accept that a Throwback had not only killed two of their most respected colleagues, but that it had since escaped justice by making itself Wolf by some sort of necromancy.

Hazel did not have to wait for silence in order to speak and so she got right to it.

"The Throwback has been captured, it is true, and it is also true that it has managed to make itself full Wolf. It is not true that it will now escape justice." Hazel waited while the buzz of excited questioning began, but she held up her hands to ask for quiet and the assembled Wolves complied. "I have asked Anton – and for those of you that did not meet him the other night, he is the Ancient that was with us as we made plans to capture the Throwback. I have asked Anton to take the Throwback to his home." Again she was interrupted by a buzz of voices from the Wolves, but this time it was not a questioning, it was an angry buzz which reminded her of a wasps' nest disturbed. "Allow me to finish before you become angry if you please!" She had to raise her voice to be heard over the angry murmur.

"You have always trusted my judgement in these matters; at least allow me to explain." An uneasy silence descended and the atmosphere was charged with resentment boiling beneath the apparent calm. "I have negotiated with Anton that he shall keep the Throwback indefinitely to use in experimentation to further our knowledge of our species. The experimentation, I am assured, will be extensive and excessively painful for the *victim...* I mean *subject*." She again waited while the truth of the statement sank in and the murmur changed from anger to curiosity.

"Anton has always been curious as to how and why Throwbacks are different from full Wolf and this is the perfect opportunity to *dissect* the question further. He assures me that the experiments will be excruciating and prolonged. He has also agreed that when the time comes that he is either bored of his subject or the subject has no further knowledge to be gleaned from it, then he will execute it in the same way that it executed one of our own – by skinning it alive." At that statement the amassed Wolves took great stock of what she had told them, they were aghast at the notion of Keme having been skinned and were better appeased that the punishment fitted the crime.

But one had doubts.

"How shall we know that Anton will keep his promise to you?" the Wolf asking the question was one that Hazel recognised as long-term Sentinel and one that had hunted with her many times. His question was validated by other Wolves nodding and agreeing with him.

"Mark, how can you ask such a question? You have been with me for decades now and have you known me to be persuaded so easily?" she looked him in the eyes and he held her gaze without wavering.

"No, but the circumstances are not usual. In this case, the atrocities are extreme and the very fact that it made itself full Wolf are enough to make me wonder if Anton will not merely question it on how it managed the feat."

Hazel nodded in understanding and answered: "Anton already knows how it made itself full Wolf so he has no need to ask it. What Anton is trying to find out is how a Throwback differs in more physical ways. In other words, he will be cutting open the Throwback and searching inside, then it will be stitched together, allowed to heal and operated upon again… and again… and again. The operations will be performed under no anaesthetic and with only muscle paralysis, so it will feel every cut, every movement of internal organs and every stitch. It will live its life in agony – either physical pain or the anguish of knowing that it will happen again… and again. I have also negotiated that any of you may go and observe the experiments at minimal notice and then, once it has been decided that it is to be finally released, Anton will invite us all to watch the execution."

"And if it should die on the operating table?"

"It will not, but if it did, then it would have been in agony and to assure me, the corpse will be kept for me to examine."

"Are we to be allowed to question Anton on what he will

be doing?"

Hazel was about to answer but was interrupted by Anton's voice. "I shall always be available for any Sentinel to ask questions. I only ask that this is a matter for those here present right now and that it never is spoken of amongst other Sentinels, or other Wolves, not even Ancients."

The answering buzz from the Sentinels had altered in tone; it was now that of scorn, for Anton's question had not needed to be asked.

Hazel smiled and folded her arms. Anton caught her gesture and understood that her command was not one born of fear but born from ultimate respect and it was because she allowed her Sentinels leave to question her that she held that respect utterly.

"One more thing, Anton," Hazel said. "There are no other Sentinels to be told of this matter. This is every active Sentinel that we have. I called for their help and all answered that call."

"Oh," Anton said and was at a loss for words for a moment. "That is unprecedented."

"Yes, but it was important that we catch this Throwback, it needed to be caught alive and I could not have done that with minimal forces."

"All Sentinels answered your call? But how did you contact them?"

"We have a network now. The days of Sentinels working in isolation are long outdated and long gone. There have been drastic changes to our structure; I doubt that you would recognise it now. We have evolved, which is the reason that I am not worried about adding to our numbers without permission from the Council of Elders."

"You are on dangerous ground there, assuming that you are above the Council's warrant for your summons to answer to them."

"Yes, I know and I also know that none of my Sentinels will let that information find its way to the Council's ears."

"You are *that* sure of their loyalty?"

Hazel held Anton's gaze for a moment and nodded. "Unto death."

Anton realised that she was issuing a challenge to his own loyalty but he did not rise to it. "I understand."

"So, we make arrangements for travel," Hazel changed the subject. "To where?"

"I shall take the Throwback to Rome. I should prefer at least some of your Sentinels to accompany me, for their peace of mind as well as yours."

Hazel nodded again and realised the concession that Anton made – as a peace-offering perhaps, or as assurance that he would not betray her work ethic to the Council of Elders? "May I ask a question?"

"Of course you may my dear."

"Will you please introduce me to your father?"

Anton was shocked into silence for a moment. "My father, what for?"

"Curiosity." Hazel smiled at the reaction she had induced.

Anton snorted in an amused manner. "You know what happened to that cat…"

It was Hazel's turn to laugh then. "I would still like to take my chances, Anton."

The following evening saw a private charter ship being loaded with a covered cage – the smallest of the pair that had been purchased by Jack. Inside was a smaller crate with the Throwback inside it. He knew that the wooden crate was the only protection he had from the silver-coated bars of the cage and if he had any sense, he would not attempt to break out. If he did manage to break out of the cage, the only thing that awaited him was a painful and lingering death, for Hazel had instructed the Sentinels guarding the cage that if the Throwback escaped, they were to have free rein on removing limbs before calling for any intervention from her. She announced the instruction within full hearing of Jack and he quaked in the crate, long into the voyage.

On arrival at Ostia de Lido on the Italian coast, the cage was loaded onto a carriage and transported to Rome. By that time it was beginning to stink for limited care was given to the occupant's comfort, the only consideration was that he did not die from hunger or thirst.

Close to Rome, after an uncomfortable journey, they arrived at Anton's home. Hazel had been before, but not for decades and she marvelled at how little it had changed.

The dungeon below the property was cool in comparison to the warmth of the day above ground and was furnished both with laboratory equipment and with paraphernalia of a more diabolical kind – for the purpose of torture and coercion – Anton would get his answers, she knew for certain.

The Sentinels that had accompanied them – Mark included – were satisfied with the laboratory and the dungeon and after witnessing the Throwback's emergence from the cage and crate and his interment in one of the cells, they accepted Anton's offer of hospitality for as long as they wished to remain in Rome. Hazel and Anton both knew that the Sentinels would send word through the network that everything was as had been promised - so ensuring their continued loyalty to their Exemplar.

'Jack the Ripper' as he had come to be known and would be known in legend and horror stories for longer than anyone could foretell had come to his final resting place, far from human justice and a world away from misguided human mercy. There he would languish in the untold and immeasurable agonies that could be inflicted upon his body and mind for as long as he survived – unable to escape either physically or mentally – to be tortured and experimented on not as punishment for the untold horrors he had wrought upon human prostitutes, but for the killing and brutalising of at least six of the Wolf number – one of which was unique and therefore invaluable. Until Hazel received the message calling her to the execution of the Throwback-turned-Wolf, he remained there still, observed by as many or as few as wanted to see.

Hazel was the first of the group to leave Anton's home. She left one late spring morning just after the full moon had disappeared from the horizon.

She had mentioned that she was growing restless to be off and that they were not to be surprised if she was there one day and gone the next.

Hazel wandered through the Italian countryside, a pack on her back, her hair pulled into a tight ponytail and her face hidden in the shadow of a large, and rather masculine hat. The worn shirt and trousers she wore as she travelled gave the impression that she was perhaps a young man out to seek his adventure and fortune and she was not approached or accosted. She slept in fields - or barns if the night was too cold, and she had money for food if she could not or would not hunt.

She travelled at her own pace, as slow as she liked and for the first time in decades – perhaps even centuries – she was at peace. There were no others to speak to, none to ask questions of and none to answer to. She sometimes talked to herself and reminisced of times long ago.

On one morning when she had been alone for almost two months and was just deciding that it was perhaps time to get back in contact with her network, she sensed another Wolf presence. It was not close and she knew that it did not know where she was, but she also knew that she was being searched for, perhaps even tracked.

She could not tell if it was Sentinel Exemplar that was being searched for or just a Wolf that had crossed the tracks of another, but she was aware and on alert.

Any other that was being tracked that way would have lost their nerve and become anxious, especially after being tracked for a week or more, but not Hazel. She continued as she had been, travelling in a northerly direction, or thereabouts, meandering through villages sometimes, but never anything larger than that. The tracker was keeping pace with her wanderings and perhaps thought himself to be unnoticed because of the distance.

When Hazel tired of the game of cat-and-mouse, she turned the tables and the hunter became the hunted and in no time at all, became the captured.

Hazel was not surprised to see who the erstwhile hunter was.

Marcellus's brother confronted her and he realised that his game had been cut short before he was ready.

"So, Marcus, what do you have to tell me?" Hazel asked. She put down her back-pack, removed her hat and looked up at the moon which was once again a good way towards being full.

"My father tells me that you caught the Throwback that slaughtered my little brother." His demeanour belied the pent-up fury, yet his tone was calm, almost serene and as he spoke his voice was gentle and sophisticated, like a patient tutor indulging his favourite pupil in the lesson which both loved and excelled at.

"I did," she nodded the confirmation. "And because of the journal that I discovered, we found his remains and your father and sister were able to lay him to rest properly. I take it that you have not sought me out all across Italy to thank me for my efforts."

"No Hazel, I have not. I have come to ask for answers."

"I understand. If I can answer your questions, I will."

Both Wolves were standing facing the other, both relaxed and smiling under the moon's glow. To an outside observer, this would perhaps seem as though two friends had met in an unlikely happenstance – another Wolf would be very wary.

"You did not kill the Throwback."

"That was not a question, it was a statement," Hazel pointed out. "But no, I did not kill it, nor did I give the order to kill it."

"Will it be killed?"

"Yes."

"When?"

"Ah, that is a question to which I do not know the answer."

"So it is true, you have allowed it to kill Wolves and will not complete your obligation to the First Laws."

"What obligation is that?" she asked, for the moment playing dumb until she knew the full reason for the confrontation.

"Suffer not a Throwback to live - that obligation." Marcus was showing that he was indeed the elder of the brothers; he played the patience game very well indeed. She had not managed to rile him yet, but he was close, she could feel his mind raging.

"I did not suffer a Throwback to live. It was no longer a Throwback when I found it."

Marcus was puzzled for the moment. She saw the emotions fighting in his mind – rage that she was so very calm and unrepentant, bewilderment because he had always been brought up to believe that justice would prevail and sorrow because of the loss of his youngest brother.

"Marcus, you should not be here, you should not have tracked me this way – you should have told your father of your plans, he would have stopped you. What of your sister? She will have lost two brothers if you continue on this path. Your father could not bear another one of his sons killed."

His eyes narrowed, he seemed to be considering this statement.

"The murderer of my brother and his fiancée has escaped punishment because he was Throwback when he killed them, but Wolf when you found him?"

"Yes, that has summed it up adequately I think."

"And it was you that made that decision?"

"I held off on his immediate execution when I realised that he was – or was soon to be – full Wolf, yes."

"And you felt no remorse; you *feel* no remorse for that decision?" Marcus's anger was building.

Hazel's own anger was climbing too, soon it would tower above her and take her into it as easily as a tornado whisks up everything in its path, she would be almost helpless in the eye of that storm and she would annihilate whatever stood before her and threatened her.

Marcus was a loyal brother and son but he was pushing too hard for revenge and in his eyes, Hazel was the only one he could take that need for revenge out on. The murderer was beyond his reach in a prison cell and the only other Wolf that had anything to do with the decision to keep him alive was out of reach because of his bloodline. Marcus could not challenge Anton on the judgement because first, Marcus would not survive. Second, the challenge itself could be deemed at an act of traitorous intent and in theory, could place the rest of his siblings and his parents in mortal danger. Anton was legendary for the fact that he had put to death his sons and their sons for making an attempt upon his leadership. If Anton was willing to put to death his own male heirs, he would have no compunction in decimating a minor Wolf from a bloodline that was not even pure. The third point in this equation was that the only Wolf that stood before Marcus at the moment was Hazel and though she was an Ancient Wolf – close to five hundred in years - Marcus was the oldest of his brothers, and he was almost Hazel's age.

Marcus believed that he was able to take revenge and even if he were not, the added weight of his father would be enough. Surely they could both take her on.

Marcus's father, Marden, stayed behind the hedgerow, hoping that his Ancient status was enough to be able to cloak his presence from her. He had not thought it wise to go searching for revenge on Hazel but in his grief-stricken mind, he was easily persuaded by his eldest son. Now that Marcus was confronting her, Marden was again having second thoughts and was hoping that his son would return to his senses very soon.

Marden heard his son begin talking again and he listened closely.

"I repeat madam, do you feel no remorse for making the decision to keep my brother's murderer alive?"

"I did not answer because I was hoping that you would come to your senses and leave me to continue my journey in peace. The answer, if you insist on having one, is no. I did not feel remorse for the decision and no, I do not feel remorse for keeping the Wolf alive. It will prove beneficial to our kind through experimentation. I regret that your brother died and that I could not save him, but from the journal that the Throwback wrote, it was partly due to Almyra and Marcellus's arrogance that they died. If they had not decided to play with their food, they would not have been in that position and would therefore, still have been alive. No, Marcus, I feel no remorse."

"I thought that you would not."

Marcus sprang at Hazel and he had sounded so calm and

collected that she was taken by surprise for a split second.

Marcus hit Hazel low under her ribs and took her down to the ground.

With some Wolves, Hazel's gender played a part in her advantage, because males assume that females did not fight dirty. Of course males and females hunted together and were as adept as each other, almost as strong as each other and equally vicious but the use of dubious tactics seemed beyond them, somehow – perhaps even Wolves had an inherent sense of protection for the fairer sex – perhaps some did, but not all and certainly not Marcus. Marcus was under no such illusion. From the very outset, he knew that Hazel was capable of great trickery and was wary of every possibility for deception. He thought he was relatively safe as he bore her beneath him and pinned her arms under his weight. His face contorted and altered to the shape of the Wolf within and he tried to snap his jaws on her face but he reckoned without her legs. She bent her knees and braced one foot to the floor, bringing the other knee up to one side of Marcus's spine with such force that she heard ribs break.

His breath was forced from his lungs with the blow and his grip loosened enough for her to push him over and off her. He lay in the dust gasping for breath.

She stood above the injured Wolf. "Normally, I would give you the benefit of the doubt for the attack on me, Marcus but because of a few factors in the attack, I deem your life forfeit." She bent to pull him to his feet and realised that the reason he had not recovered and renewed his attack was because one of his lungs appeared to be punctured by a rib that she had broken. With no effort at all, she lifted the part-Wolfed man by his jacket collar and held him - wheezing instead of screaming – before her. She spoke loud enough for the Wolf watching the battle to hear her: "Now, Marden, it is too late

287

for you to launch an attack upon me. Your eldest son is all but dead but if you would prefer, I can leave him in agony whilst I deal with you."

"Please. Let him go, allow him to live, show some mercy." Marden's voice rose in pitch as he spoke. He emerged from his place of concealment as a man broken and distressed.

"Your voice sounds your desperation Marden. I believe that Marcus is your last surviving son is he?"

"Yes, he is and if for no other reason than that, let him live." Marden had clasped his hands in front of his body in an unconscious gesture, pleading for his son's life.

Hazel looked direct into Marden's eyes and said, "No." Then she severed the younger Wolf's head from his body, ending the struggle for breath.

Marden flung himself at her. He was the elder Wolf by a good many decades, perhaps even by a century and his residual strength was far greater than Marcus's had been and yet Hazel had no trouble in defending herself from his rage-fuelled attack. In short order, Marden too lay dead in the dust, his eviscerated corpse bleeding out even as his eyes fluttered the last of the body's reflexes.

Anton had been wrong, she did not need to be surrounded by other Wolves to regain her Wolfness; she just needed to be alone with herself. She was more Wolf than she appeared. It would seem that there was another side of her and that was the one that more resembled the chameleon; her inner being was secure and purely and utterly lethal.

Hazel continued on her way after digging a hole to bury the corpses she had made.

Today...

The audience in Anton's drawing room was silent as he finished his tale. Red looked at Anton for a moment and before anyone else decided to speak, she did.

"Very clever Anton, how did you know of that part?"

"Ah, I did not, as you think, send out a minder for you." Anton smiled.

Red was amused at Anton's use of such modern terminology – or at least, modern for him. "Then how did you know?"

"When you left my home on that spring morning, I knew that you were off on the sabbatical that I had advised you to take and I also knew that you would make your way towards home, you always do. When, a few months after you had gone, I was told of two bodies discovered buried in a ditch, one decapitated and the other eviscerated, I thought it to be your trademark. You do like the gore to wash over your hands, my dear, you always have. Of course, the Scribe confirmed it for me, but I had to ask in a specific manner. He is almost as cagey as you are."

Red shook her head and curled her lips in a wry smile but said nothing more.

"Do you know why your colleagues took to calling you 'Red'?" Anton continued.

"No, I assumed that it was because of my hair colour." The question had puzzled her and Anton saw it in her expression and laughed.

"No, my dear, it is because of your method of execution!" he was laughing by that time. "You are called 'Red' not for the colour of your hair, but for the colour of your hands!"

The entourage in the room had by that time, joined with him in his laughter, amused because she had accepted the name willingly, without knowing the reason for it.

Anton held up his hands after a short time, and the room became quiet once more, almost sombre even.

"Now I think it is time that we go to the dungeon to continue with the reason for you all being here this night."

They followed as Anton led them down through the house and to a large and imposing door. It was closed and Anton unlocked it and led the way down the stairs to his laboratory.

There was another door as they reached the bottom of the stairs and Red guessed that it had been put there as a form of soundproofing for she remembered how the howls used to reverberate up the stairwell when Anton experimented upon his subject.

Though it had been ten years since she was last at the laboratory, nothing seemed to have changed. There may have been some newer and more modern equipment but the layout was the same as when she had first brought the Throwback-turned-Wolf down to be locked away for the rest of his days.

"Did you get your answers, Anton?" Red asked.

"All in good time, my dear, all in good time," came his reply.

When all had assembled inside the room, there was little space left for anything else. Red wondered where the operation was to take place.

"I have one question to ask of you all." Anton said. "If I were to ask for leniency in this matter, that we execute the subject in a more conventional manner, rather than the barbaric method prescribed by your Sentinel Exemplar all those years ago, what would your consensus be?"

The question was met with a stunned silence. This was not what had been expected – not by any of the assembly.

"What are you asking, Anton?" Red was the first to voice her question.

"I am asking what the answer would be if I were to plea for mercy on Jack's behalf."

"On *Jack's* behalf?" Red asked – her voice held more than that one question in its tone. "Anton, at the risk of presuming to speak for my Sentinels and at the further risk of sounding disrespectful, but have you gone soft, or mad or both? Do you remember what that Throwback did to your protégé? Do you remember what it did to my Sentinels? Do you remember your promise, your solemn vow? I hope this is a speculative question, Anton because if it is not, I believe that you will have a riot on your hands."

Anton looked about him and the amassed Sentinels glowered as one.

"Yes, it was a speculative question; I wanted to see if your resolve and that of your Sentinels was as strong as it was on the day he was delivered here."

Red seemed sceptical but a movement to one side of the room caught her eye and she glanced to where an old man was sat, camouflaged in part by the clutter piled on the table in front of him.

"It is true, the one known to my tribe as 'Pahana' which means 'Lost White Brother' told me of his plans and he wanted to show that my grandfather's spirit lived on in great warriors such as these," the man stood as he spoke and he

291

gestured around the room, smiling as he looked about him.

Red saw the great resemblance that the old man bore to her once-pupil Keme and her eyes prickled and she was amazed that after all these decades, Keme lived on in his own grandson.

Anton gestured that Red come forward to meet the old man and she went, not wiping her eyes because she did not want to show those behind her that she was affected and she did not want to show disrespect to Keme's memory by hiding the tears from his grandson.

Anton said: "Mingan, this is 'Misko' - Red, but your grandfather knew her as Hazel." Anton waited whilst Red showed her respect by bowing to the old man and he smiled. "Hazel, 'Mingan's father was known as 'Ma'iingan'. Before you ask it, Keme was married and his wife was pregnant at the time of his change."

"He left his home and family and even his wife and unborn son and he knew that he may never see them again?" Red was incredulous.

"He did leave them, but for the safety of the tribe. He could not have taken them with him and he could not have stayed. They mourned his loss when Pahana came to tell of his death at the hands of that one." Mingan pointed to the back of the room where a cell was swathed in darkness. As Mingan pointed, he snorted and huffed in derision. Hazel remembered the same gestures as Keme had used and she again saw the strong resemblance.

"I think that you are not telling me the whole story, Anton. I think you have an ulterior motive. What are you up to now?"

"You are right of course. I have brought Mingan here to not only witness the punishment, but to partake in it. With your leave I shall ask him when he deems the Throwback to have suffered enough. It shall be his decision. Do you agree to that, Sentinel Exemplar?"

292

Red nodded her agreement. She could think of nothing more fitting than Keme's grandson partaking in the revenge for his ancestor's death.

The atmosphere was tense and hushed as the gurney was wheeled from the cell, its occupant covered from head to foot by a sheet. The body was breathing but not moving otherwise. The once-Throwback known as Jack had been prepared either before the meeting had started upstairs a number of hours earlier or other Wolves had been working as they were listening to the story.

"I will tell you now Mingan, the pelt from this creature will not be given to your tribe. It will be burned for I will not allow any tragedy to come about from this night." Anton worked as he spoke; he prepared his tools and washed his hands. He donned a gown and an apron to prevent his clothes from being bloodied.

Mingan said nothing; he watched and waited – as did the rest of the audience. Most had waited more than a century to witness this and all were grim as they watched the preparations and listened for Anton's explanations.

"It has never made a kill or fed upon human flesh. That is the only experiment that I did not perform upon it. If you would like me to allow it to make its first kill, then I shall and then it shall have its one desire, to become full Wolf before it dies. I know that it is its heart's desire because it has told me on numerous occasions." Anton faced Red as he said this because he knew that she and Keme had both had the experience of not being allowed to make a kill and to therefore be trapped in Wolf form.

"Does that mean the Wolf that you have been experimenting on all these years, it is still in the form of a wolf?"

"No, it is human. One of the questions that I have been trying to find the answer to is why it has never changed to

293

Wolf. I thought that I should never find that answer and that I would be experimenting upon it for decades to come."

"I take it then, that you have found the answer?"

"Yes, I studied the notebooks until I could quote vast passages of them verbatim, and yet I had missed the one spark of knowledge and I had to ask for the answer, for it was not written down."

Anton continued to busy himself in his preparations. He was so used to having an audience for his experiments that he was able to ignore the crowd even though they were close enough to almost assist in the operation he was about to perform.

Red was not the most patient of Wolves and she could wait no longer. As she began to form her question, Anton smiled to himself, his back was facing her so that she could not see his smile begin and therefore would not get angry with him for teasing her this way.

"Are you going to tell us what you discovered? Is it something that we should be wary of for the future? Is it something that could affect others? Anton, you are teasing me, I can tell!"

"Yes I am, please forgive me. The information took so long for me to discover that I wanted to keep it to myself for a little while longer. You see, when it went across to Europe to make a great study of werewolves, it encountered a witch." Anton paused to await Red's reaction. She frowned at him and thought for a moment.

"I don't believe in witches," she said, but her tone was not confident because she could see by Anton's expression that he was expecting her to say that exact phrase.

"I know you don't, but I have always told you that there are stranger things on earth than can be imagined by us mere immortals." Anton smiled at his own joke. "Jack found a witch and it asked her to tutor it. She must have sensed something in it for she agreed and for many months Jack studied. It asked that she teach about herbs first because she claimed not to know about shape-shifting. Then she taught it all manner of things concerning Wolves and how to detect one that is like us – a 'werewolf'. If you remember the lessons that I taught you on our own way through France and Italy centuries since, those lessons were very similar to the ones that Jack learned.

Anton and Red were so intent as they were talking that they could ignore their audience and because their audience wanted to hear more of their leader's beginnings, all were silent and rapt in the conversation they were eavesdropping upon.

Even Mingan could not help but listen. He had been hearing tales of his grandfather and his great-great grandfather's battle with the giant and evil wolf-spirit for decades. He was now the tribe's shaman - although he was more of a spiritual leader these days – and was the one who perpetuated the story of how Keme (Falcon) had killed the great and evil wolf-spirit but had made a mistake and skinned the pelt and wore it at the ceremony of the Wolf Moon. It was a story that he would delight in the retelling to his host, Anton and the others if they should wish to hear it, but for now, he was listening to another tale – one that he would retell to his tribe on his return.

As Anton finished reminiscing on the lessons that a young protégé named Hazel and her study partner named Nichasin had been taught, Anton at last came to the point of the tale.

"The woman was indeed a witch and she did know of Wolves and how we change, hunt, survive and develop and when Jack was told that she did not know the secrets of shape-shifting and did not know how to help him become Wolf, it grew angry and it killed her. Before it took her life, for she was a tough old woman, she cursed Jack and because it was a curse born of anger and desperation, it worked. It may also have

295

something to do with the mixture of herbs and potions that she threw at it in the battle for her survival; for it confessed that she was desperate to stay alive and threw everything that came to hand. I fear that it is an experiment that we shall never be able to repeat and I am content in that knowledge. It was a series of fortunate coincidences that brought Keme to his tribe and then to us and a series of unfortunate coincidences that brought Jack to us. Tonight, we shall send Jack into whatever there is after this life and if it meets with Keme there, then it will need the luck of the devil."

Anton removed the sheet from the body and stood facing the audience. Many had not seen the creature for decades but some had been frequent visitors.

Red was one of those that had been frequent in her visits to the house but not always to see the experiments. She had last been to witness an experiment ten years before and yet she was still surprised at how Jack had aged. Red was used to her 'family' – which comprised Anton, Victoria, Oscar, Steve, Elizabeth and a few others – remaining the same visual age as they had always appeared to her, never aging nor becoming affected by disease, but this creature before them was an ancient man. Even Mingan was jolted into making an exclamation of surprise.

Jack was a much older man than he should ever have survived to; he appeared to be at least a century and a half in age. His skin almost pooled under his body, there seemed to be far too much of it and it reminded Red a little of people who had lost vast amounts of weight and whose skin had not shrunk back to fit their new body shape. The ears were large and pendulous and the lobes drooped down almost to the table top. When he opened his eyes, she could see that they were age-spotted in the whites (more beige) and though the pupils were clear of cataracts, their depths held within them

296

an entire universe of insanity. If Jack had been insane before he was captured, then the century of experimentation had taken him further than any lunatic had ever travelled. If he had been this far gone at the time of the 'Ripper Murders' then half of London would have been slaughtered, the River Thames would have run red and been impassable to shipping – she could see that much in those depths.

The eyes cleared of the psychosis as he focussed on her face and she was unable to suppress a shudder as he smiled. It was not a smile that she could ever be comfortable in knowing that it was directed at her.

The brows were drawn down so that his eyes were only half showing – if he wore spectacles, it would be as though he were peering over the top of them. The smile itself was insidious and sly as though he knew a terrible secret about her and he chose to keep that confidence until it suited him and for no other reason but that. Then his eyebrows twitched in a parody of partnership – kind of 'watch this' and she was chilled to her marrow. Then he tried to speak and it took a few attempts before he managed to form words.

"I know what you are," he whispered "I know what you do and how you do it." He managed to get to the end of his little speech with difficulty and Red thought that he had finished but he hadn't.

"You are a Werewolf!" he yelled at the top of his ancient lungs. "You slaughter people and eat their flesh! I killed Keme because he stole my love but you eat people!" The outburst dissolved into a maniacal laughter, cracked and high-pitched and it saddened Red.

The tirade sent a shockwave through the audience; none had ever heard him speak before, he seemed to have saved his conversations for when he and Anton were alone.

Victoria and Oscar were bemused at the show but remained

silent as they watched, glancing at each other in mutual wonder.

Anton placed a hand on Jack's shoulder to let him know that he was there. "Yes, Jack, Red is a werewolf, so am I and so are you, remember?"

"Red? That is not her name!" he became agitated and began to strain against the straps which held him. "Her name is Hazel; she is a friend of Keme. I killed him, I killed them all, dirty, filthy streetwalkers. I killed them and I ate their juicy bits!" and saliva drooled from his slack lips and in another instant, his tone became maudlin and he whined like a kicked dog. "Why can't I be a Wolf, Anton? I ate them, I did, and it's not fair you know. I did everything that I was taught." He seemed to become calm again until he had given himself a moment to think and he unleashed a fury that such an old and decrepit body should not have been able to contain, let alone set free. "I did everything that I was taught! I did as I was told! I ATE THEIR GLANDS!" he raged through his insanity and Anton was at a loss.

"He has never behaved this way. I shall have to sedate him if he does not calm down."

Jack was thrashing so hard on the gurney that it was bouncing and if hands were not holding it, it would have overturned. He was repeating the phrase "I ate their glands!" over and over in a mantra.

And as sudden as it started, it finished. Red was not alone in the thought that Jack had suffered a heart attack but it could not be possible, his Wolfen heart was too strong, even though it was old and had never been given the proper sustenance to maintain it in peak condition as other Wolves had.

Jack turned his head for the first time and acknowledged the crowd. He smiled then, a more normal and sane smile and he said in a voice that was old but clear: "I am sorry that I killed Keme. He was strong and young and so very brave. I should have liked to have been his friend. I should have liked to wear his pelt and have run with you, Hazel. I used to dream that I ran alongside you and your pack. Anton was there, I recognised him. Keme and Almyra and Marcellus were all there. I did so want to be a Wolf, my mother would have been so happy. Do it, Anton, I deserve the punishment. I skinned Keme and it hurt him but he didn't make a sound but I heard him howl in his mind, I felt it all through him. I know secrets, Hazel, I know your secrets. I know that you killed Marcellus's brother and his father, I know because Anton knows. I know many, many things about you that you don't know yet. Anton keeps secrets from you." And Jack turned his head away from her and began another mantra in a sing-song voice; "I know a secret, I know a secret."

"Let's finish this." Red nodded to Anton that he should begin.

Perhaps it would have been easier on Mingan if the operation had been upon a wolf form but he held up to the demonstration of utter and ultimate revenge. He had never met his grandfather Keme, neither had his father met him but he was proud to be descended from such a legend and he understood the symbolism of the punishment that was being meted out before his eyes. He did not quite understand why there were so many witnessing the punishment but he realised that with the right questions, he would know all that he wanted to know – and perhaps a little more than he should.

When he returned to his tribe, he would be better able to decide which part of the story he would retell in exact detail and which part would be glossed over, for to embellish this would take a better imagination than even he possessed.

As the old one was skinned, he did not move, nor make a sound for he had been paralysed by a concoction of drugs – Anton knew his craft and worked it to perfection. Unlike when Jack had flayed Keme, Jack was still alive at the end of the operation, due to Anton's skill and patience over Jack's excitement and eagerness to possess a pelt that could transform him into a magnificent beast.

Mingan had been asked prior to the ceremony if he would be able to perform the death blow and he knew that he could.

At the appointed moment, Mingan stood and walked to the head of the flayed body of the one that had slaughtered his ancestor. It was not with hate that Mingan lifted the large ceremonial dagger that he had brought with him across the ocean, but with pride in his heritage and the legend which was Keme. With both hands, Mingan lifted the dagger above his head and he looked into the eyes of the man that had killed his grandfather.

"Keme manidog!" Mingan said as he brought down the dagger to slice through the raw flesh and brittle bones into the still strong heart of the Throwback-turned-Wolf.

Mingan left the dagger in Jack's chest and it sizzled and smoked for a moment as the silver blade did its job.

"You brought a silver dagger? Who told you?" Anton asked.

Mingan looked into Anton's eyes for a moment, taking in the aeons of knowing that Anton possessed. "It has always been known that silver kills Wolf spirits, Anton. My grandfather's spear was silver and we have known since before you came to us that we can protect ourselves from evil manidog – or spirits – with this metal and only this metal. You are wise, Anton-Pahana but we also have wisdom and with all respect to you, I was not about to come into the company of werewolves without a little of my own wisdom."

Anton seemed to be astounded at first and asked "Have your tribe always been wary of me? Have you always known what I am?"

Mingan gave him a look which told Anton that he was being ridiculous without a word from Mingan's mouth. Red laughed and Anton scowled.

Victoria approached then to greet the old Obijawe Shaman and she was respectful and courteous, as was Oscar.

Red decided that perhaps she would extend her stay in order that she could hear some of Mingan's stories and indeed, some of Anton's. There was also one other story that she thought she may like to hear about, one that concerned her because it involved her directly and she would have never have known about it if Jack the Ripper had not told her of it.

The End...

The next book in the Werewolf series by D Michelle Gent, released Oct 31st 2011

ISBN: 978-1-907939-10-5

BLOOD... on the Moon

Chapter 1

The dishevelled teenage girl stood waiting in the shadows; she was watching the comings and goings of the dregs of society, observing thugs and thieves, muggers and murderers perhaps. And though she should have been nervous of her surroundings and of the people who passed by her, she wasn't; she was fascinated.

To a casual observer, she could have been anywhere between fifteen and twenty years old but she didn't seem streetwise or cocky; she was quiet and stayed out of sight if she could.

The drunks, either habitual or occasional, swayed past and barely noticed her. The muggers and thieves ignored her; they could tell that she wasn't worth the effort, from the clothes she wore and the almost neglected air she had about her. Her hair was damp and straggled around her face. It clung to her cheek and the rest hung in lank strands and it was either dirty and greasy or just wet from the constant drizzle, but either way, it was plain that she didn't care.

The girl knew what she was looking for, even though she could probably not have described it. She was looking for someone with a certain attitude, a supreme confidence or even just the merest hint of a gleam in an eye. The girl spent most of her evenings in places such as this one. Dark places, secluded, yet in the middle of a bustling town. She waited and watched for a glimpse of the object of her obsession.

The girl played a very dangerous game, it was a very hazardous pastime and it was beyond insanity. She was a hunter but her prey was not vulnerable. The prey she sought was the type that was very capable, both in terms of strength and purpose, of killing her without a moment's hesitation. If she was discovered and caught, there would most likely be one conclusion and that would involve neither guilt nor compassion; she would be killed, disposed of and thought no more about.

For the past two years she had been actively seeking them out, these people who were different in ways that she couldn't begin to describe, ways that she saw and recognised but could neither explain nor understand. The girl was methodical in her observations but committed her discoveries strictly to memory: for some reason, perhaps self-preservation, she wouldn't write any of her findings down, not even in a secret diary.

Over the months, she was proud to say that she had positively identified a good number of their kind, possibly twenty or more. She had also witnessed their kills, not many, but enough to make her yet more wary of them noticing her.

The first one that she had been in a position to observe the way he moved and operated up close and personal, so to speak, and therefore her favourite one, was Paul; he had been a bouncer at a local nightclub at that time. She was with her friends, drinking and dancing and she noticed the fight erupt and she pulled Ellie, her best friend, to one side out of the way of the feet and fists. The other girls followed Ellie off the dance floor and they stood in relative safety by the bar and watched how the doormen dealt with the trouble.

She remembered all the details, she savoured them and as she stood in the cold and damp, waiting for something or

304

someone to make it worth the night's discomfort, she mulled over the details of that night. She could recall every aspect as though she was there again; the smell of moist heat from dancers as they passed her, and the stink of stale sweat from those who only cared what they looked like and not whether they were clean under the veneer of their designer clothing. She could smell the odour of cannabis and sometimes a sharp chemical stench that was gone swiftly but would make her eyes prickle and her nose twitch. If she concentrated hard enough before she started drinking for the evening, and if the conditions were just right and it was dark enough, she could sometimes see a difference in people's faces. On occasion, she wondered if she was perhaps psychic but decided that she was being stupid and idealistic.

Paul was one that rushed into the fray first, he had gone in to stop the fight and her group had watched him with the curiosity of those close enough to see the fists and blood flying but far enough removed to feel safe. He was young, strong and good looking in a 'bit of rough' type of way.

At six feet tall, he was able to heft the fighters around with ease, preventing them from getting into the fray once more. His colleagues jumped in with equal certainty, yet she noticed him above the others. As he turned at last to hoist a struggling fighter out of the mêlée, it was his blue eyes that entirely captivated her. They were so blue as to be startling even in the subdued light of the darkened nightclub. But there was something else, an animalistic quality about him, a raw wildness that screamed 'danger,' and her body recognised the call and she wanted nothing more than to bolt. It was something that only she seemed to have noticed. She felt her own eyes widen and her jaw drop. Her hands became clammy and she moved to stand behind Ellie and peered out from the side of her friend. She quickly recovered and glanced around

305

to see if her friends had noticed the effect that he'd had on her, but no one seemed to have, no one watched her, little Jessica 'Rabbit'.

It was maybe half an hour later before he returned in a more peaceful manner. He was still watching the crowd as he walked and he went directly to the bar to flirt with the barmaids. Jessica's friends had all but forgotten about him and the fight until he came to stand right next to them.

Ellie was the most daring in their group, she was the prettiest, most outspoken and if truth be told, the biggest slut, and she leaned forward in as casual a manner as she could manage, given her advanced drunkenness and she said to him, "So when do you get off?" The comment drew giggles from her equally drunken entourage.

He looked at her for a moment and his eyes travelled from her pretty face, lingered on her cleavage and moved down to linger again on her long legs. "Usually about five minutes after I start, love," he quipped back to her, his attention diverted from the busy barmaids for the moment.

Undeterred, even encouraged by the way he had looked at her, Ellie carried continued: "Only five minutes? It's not worth getting undressed for that," she said and the comment drew more giggles from her friends.

"Who needs to get undressed? You've got a skirt on, and if you want to know if it's worth it or not, come with me, you can judge for yourself." He winked at her and held out his hand. Ellie was never one to back down in front of her friends and she put her glass on the bar and took his hand and went along with him. She looked back to the friends that she'd left and she gave a cheeky grin and put the tips of her fingers to her mouth as though she was miming that she sometimes shocked herself. The group laughed again and then went back to drinking and chattering about how daring Ellie was. Jessica just listened.

Ellie had been gone for less than a quarter of an hour before she was back sporting a huge grin on her face.

The friends crowded around her to get the details straight from the horse's mouth and Jessica found herself at the back of the crush as usual but she didn't mind, she didn't really want to know all the details anyway. She wasn't as impressed with Ellie's bravado as the others were, she knew Ellie better than they did and she also knew that a deep seated desire to be liked by everyone was what drove Ellie to make the kind of assignation that she had just returned from. Instead of feeling a bit sorry for Ellie though, Jessica found that she was a little bit angry. Was it jealousy that had sparked the annoyance? Jessica was puzzled and tried to work it out in her head, she didn't fancy Paul, he was fascinating but in a far different way to how Ellie found him attractive. As Jessica tried to work out her mood, she could hear Ellie as she regaled the group with her account of what had happened upstairs in the outer office.

"He wasn't kidding! He did only take five minutes, but God, it was worth it! He went like a steam train. He was like an animal! It may have been one of the shortest fucks I've ever had, but it has to be one of the best, my legs are still wobbly. Has he torn my dress?" She finished her tale and looked around as far as she could to see if there was any damage to her clothing.

They were still talking about Ellie's escapade when the lights went up and the last track of the night was played.

If Ellie had any ideas about going home with him, she was sorely disappointed. Even though it would have meant that Jessica had to make her way home alone, it wouldn't have been the first time that Ellie had dropped Jessica to go home with a bloke she fancied. Ellie tried to talk to Paul as they left, but he didn't acknowledge her as she said goodnight to him; he didn't even seem to recognise her. Ellie covered the insult well though and no one saw the hurt in her eyes, or so she thought.

Two years later, cold and damp in the early morning drizzle of a particularly wet January, the memory of her friend's pain returned in a flood as Jessica saw him again. They were the same startling blue eyes, the same cheeky smile and the same self-assured walk as she remembered. She saw him and took advantage of the fact that he wasn't looking in her direction, and she moved deeper into the shadows inch by inch so that he wouldn't notice her movement. Jessica knew that no one could see her there in the darkness - well, no one human.

Her heart thudded painfully in her chest and her stomach did flip-flops as he stopped, turned and looked directly at her. She didn't move and neither did he. She didn't dare to and he was studying the shadow-swathed area. He looked into the depths of the shadows which hid her and she knew that he had seen her.

Then he was gone and she managed to breathe easy again but her relief was cut short by a tickling whisper close to her ear.

"You've been told to stay away from us, Rabbit," Paul said.

"Don't call me that, Paul."

"Why not? It suits you, especially right now. You're shaking like a scared rabbit."

"I know, I can't help it, you made me jump."

"Can't help what, being scared or watching us?"

"Both. It's more than curiosity even though I'm scared out of my wits when I'm close to you."

"Just me or any of us?"

"Any of you, all of you."

"I know you're scared - Rabbit." He emphasised her nickname, the one that she had outgrown with everyone except for him. He waited for a few moments, tickling her ear with his breath and he made sure that she was past worried and well into frightened before he spoke again. "Well, the last time was your final caution. We don't want you snooping around anymore. You've been warned off nicely too many times now. Come with me." He took her by the arm and all but dragged her behind him. Her feet didn't want to go and she tried to talk, to tell him that she would leave and never come back. That she would even leave the country if he'd give her one last chance, but even before the words formed on her lips, she knew that she wouldn't mean it even if she could say it. She also knew that he wouldn't believe her anyway. The truth was that Jessica Warren - hence the nickname of Rabbit - wanted their attention and had yearned for it ever since she had realised that living amongst humans in her town was a pack of werewolves.

About the author
D Michelle Gent

Michelle was born in Wirksworth, Derbyshire at the beginning of December 1964. As the first-born of three children, and the fifth living generation in a local mining family, she hit the news early, appearing in the Derbyshire Times for her mother's efforts.

In recent times a more stable lifestyle has allowed her to follow jobs better in line with her character. She spent a number of years working as a Door Supervisor at public houses and night clubs, trying out different ways of keeping fit – such as kick boxing and gym work - she likes to do things girls don't normally do and she loves a challenge.

In the last few years she has been writing down ideas for this and other books and after a nine-month spell working at a school decided to take a year off work to finally produce her first book Deadlier... than the Male.

A number of years later, a few rejection slips under her belt and as much determination as ever, Deadlier... is about to be joined by Cruel... and Unusual in the Werewolf series. These will be followed by Blood... on the Moon later this year.

She lives in the heart of Sherwood Forest.

Links

Blog - http://deadlier-than-the-male.blogspot.com
Website - www.gingernutbooks.co.uk/authors/dmichellegent
Facebook - Michelle Gent
Twitter - Shell Gent
Email - michelle.gent@gingernutbooks.co.uk